PRAISE FOR THESE AUTHORS

JASMINE CRESSWELL

"Cresswell's superb story matches her best work, stretching nerves to the breaking point."
—*Publishers Weekly* on *The Disappearance*

"Cresswell delivers a sexy, romantic suspense story with a subtle sense of humor, a pace that doesn't let up, and characters who make you care."
—*Library Journal* on *No Sin Too Great*

COLLEEN COLLINS

"Warning: Colleen's books contain large quantities of giggles, warm fuzzies and sizzle. This combo is highly addictive. So stock up!"
—*New York Times* bestselling author
Vicki Lewis Thompson

"Colleen Collins' *Building a Bad Boy* is funny and tender."
—*Romantic Times BOOKreviews*

KATHLEEN LONG

"Long's *Reluctant Witness* shakes deception, passion, environmentalism and murder with a deft hand."
—*Romantic Times BOOKreviews*

"Another excellent story full of excitement, tension, danger and passionate love. *A Necessary Risk* is sure to be a hit for Kathleen Long."
—*CataRomance*

ABOUT THE AUTHORS

Jasmine Cresswell is a *USA TODAY* bestselling author of more than sixty novels, including suspense and historical fiction as well as many contemporary romances. Born in Wales and educated in England, Jasmine met her husband while working at the British Embassy in Rio de Janeiro. She and her family have lived in a dozen different cities in the United States, as well as Australia and Canada. Jasmine and her husband are lucky enough to have homes in both Florida and Colorado, a perfect combination of sea, mountains and sun.

Like the heroine in "Miracle on Bannock Street," **Colleen Collins** is also a private investigator who spends a lot of time at the Denver courthouse on Bannock Street. In 1996 she sold her first book, a romantic comedy, to Harlequin Books. Since then, she's written twenty more novels/anthologies for Harlequin. Her books have placed first in the Colorado Gold, Romancing the Rockies and Top of the Peak contests, and placed in the finals for the Holt Medallion, Award of Excellence and Romance Writers of America RITA® Award. To read about Colleen's upcoming books, go to www.colleencollins.net.

After a career spent spinning words for clients ranging from corporate CEOs to talking fruits and vegetables, **Kathleen Long** now enjoys creating worlds of fictional characters, places and plots. An award-winning author of both romantic suspense and romantic comedy, she divides her time between suburban Philadelphia and the New Jersey seashore. There she can often be found hands on keyboard, bare toes in sand. After all, life doesn't get much better than that. Please visit her at www.kathleenlong.com, or drop her a line at P.O. Box 3864, Cherry Hill, NJ 08034.

JASMINE CRESSWELL

COLLEEN COLLINS

KATHLEEN LONG

It's a *Wonderful* Christmas

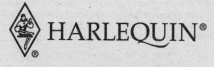

HARLEQUIN®

TORONTO • NEW YORK • LONDON
AMSTERDAM • PARIS • SYDNEY • HAMBURG
STOCKHOLM • ATHENS • TOKYO • MILAN • MADRID
PRAGUE • WARSAW • BUDAPEST • AUCKLAND

ISBN-13: 978-0-373-83720-5
ISBN-10: 0-373-83720-8

IT'S A WONDERFUL CHRISTMAS

Copyright © 2007 by Harlequin Books S.A.

The publisher acknowledges the copyright holders of the individual works as follows:

AN AMERICAN CAROL
Copyright © 2007 by Jasmine Cresswell

MIRACLE ON BANNOCK STREET
Copyright © 2007 by Colleen Collins

IT'S A WONDERFUL NIGHT
Copyright © 2007 by Kathleen Long

This edition published by arrangement with Harlequin Books S.A.

® and ™ are trademarks of the publisher. Trademarks indicated with ® are registered in the United States Patent and Trademark Office, the Canadian Trade Marks Office and in other countries.

www.eHarlequin.com

Printed in U.S.A.

CONTENTS

AN AMERICAN CAROL

Jasmine Cresswell

CHAPTER ONE

THE CAVERNOUS INTERIOR OF Brentwood Industries was unnaturally quiet—the staff had all gone home, phones and computers silenced by the arrival of Christmas Eve. Gloria Alvarez checked one last time to make sure no memo was left uncirculated on her desk and no folder poked out of its appointed file drawer. Satisfied that nobody, not even the notoriously difficult and demanding Charles Brentwood, would be able to complain that she'd left important work unfinished, she shut down her computer and got up from her desk.

Instead of immediately walking into Mr. Brentwood's office, she stood by her chair for a full minute, summoning the nerve to confront her bad-tempered employer. Finally, as ready as she was ever likely to be, she crossed the deserted outer office and tapped softly on the door of his lair.

"Come in." Her boss delivered the words in his usual snarl.

So much for the joys of the Christmas season,

Gloria thought, rolling her eyes. Still intimidated by his grouchy attitude after almost a year working for him, she dug deep to find some courage. Then she squared her shoulders, opened the door and walked in.

The president's office was quite small and hadn't been refurbished since the death of Mr. Brentwood senior a dozen years earlier. Given that Brentwood Industries was among the most successful plumbing supply companies in the country, the current CEO could probably have sprung for a new rug and a comfortable chair without breaking the bank. However, Charles D. Brentwood was notorious for never spending a dollar if he could squeak by on a dime, so it was only to be expected that his office would be as cold, cheerless and shabby as the man himself.

Astonishingly, Mr. Brentwood wasn't seated at his desk, barricaded behind his laptop, poring over the latest logistics chart or whatever the heck it was he spent so much time scrutinizing. Instead, he was standing by the grimy window, looking out at the view of Trenton, New Jersey, and the warehouses that ringed Brentwood's headquarters.

Gloria so rarely saw her boss standing up that she was shocked to realize he was both tall and well built, with thick brown hair that he had allowed to grow unfashionably long. Probably because he was too cheap to pay for a haircut, she reflected with a cynicism that was alien to her usually sunny nature. In profile, when you couldn't see his expression, he was good-looking in a boring sort of way. Old, of course, but since she had celebrated her nineteenth birthday only a month ago, Gloria had to admit that anybody over the age of thirty looked old to her.

She followed her boss's gaze out the window. For once, the view was worth looking at. It was snowing: the sort of crisp, powdery snow that hushed the noisy clamor of the city and laid a thick coat of glistening white on the ugliness of decrepit and abandoned buildings. Gloria felt her spirits lift. Even inside the bleak headquarters of Brentwood Industries it seemed that Christmas could impart a touch of magic, a shimmer of hope in a wintry world.

She seized the hope and clung to it, allowing optimism to bloom. So what if it sometimes felt as if she carried the weight of the world on her inadequate shoulders? Tomorrow was Christmas Day, and she would sit down with her family to eat delicious roast turkey and *pan dulce* and forget for a few hours that her father still didn't have his green card and that there was never enough money to pay Timoteo's medical bills. When her mama's *pan dulce* was on the table, she thought with a silent laugh, the world couldn't be all bad.

Besides, there was always a chance that Mr. Brentwood would reward her hard work with a Christmas bonus. Well, it *could* happen, Gloria told herself. It was possible. Even twenty dollars would mean that she could stop at the drugstore on the way home to buy chocolate candies for the family and some of the special diabetic lollipops her little brother loved. She'd worked hours of unpaid overtime in the six months since she had been promoted to the job of Charles Brentwood's personal assistant. Maybe it wasn't silly to hope for a small holiday bonus.

"Mr. Brentwood, it's four o'clock and it's Christmas Eve. If it's okay with you, I'd like to leave now."

"Of course it's not okay with me." Charles Brentwood slowly turned to face her, his eyebrows drawn together in a heavy, disapproving line. "The workday finishes here at five-thirty. Why would today be any different?"

Because it's Christmas Eve, you mean old grouch, and every other person in the building has gone home. Gloria drew in a deep breath. "I'm sorry, sir, but I still must leave early. There is a special service at our church tonight and it starts at six. There will be a nativity play and songs from our Mexican tradition. I promised my little brother I would take him, and I won't be home in time unless I leave now. There are not so many buses tonight because of the holiday."

Charles Brentwood's frown grew darker. Gloria felt sweat trickle down her spine. This was not a man who appreciated employees with the backbone to stand up to his harsh demands. The fact that everyone else had already left wouldn't protect her if he decided to fire her. Mr. Brentwood had made it clear when he promoted her that she wouldn't keep her new job and fractionally increased salary unless she worked harder and longer than the rest of his underpaid, overworked staff.

"The holidays and buses aren't my problem," Charles Brentwood said. "They're your problem. *My* problem is that the agenda for the January sales meeting hasn't been prepared—"

"Yes, sir, it has. I e-mailed it to you an hour ago."

Far from looking pleased by her efficiency, her boss frowned so ferociously that Gloria thought for sure he would fire her on the spot. She contemplated the possibility of losing her pay for however many weeks it took to find a new job and shivered with fear at the prospect. At this time of year, in a manufacturing town that had lost most of its factories, people weren't exactly rushing to take on new hires, and her family lived too close to the edge to have any wiggle room for grand gestures.

Then she thought about Teo and the rest of her family, waiting for her at home, eager for the festivities to start, and she decided not to give in. If there had been a genuine emergency, she would have been willing to sacrifice family time, even on Christmas Eve. But there was no crisis, and if Mr. Brentwood wanted to play the Grinch, he could do it by himself. She wasn't going to hang around on such a special night with a man who was making work for no real reason except that he was mean all the way through to his shriveled black heart.

"And now, I must go," she said, her resolution firm even if her voice was shaking. "My brother is still very young and he won't understand if I'm not there when my family leaves for church. Good night, Mr. Brentwood. I wish you a merry Christmas."

Gloria turned and walked out of the room. A holiday bonus had obviously been a crazy fantasy, but she crossed her fingers tightly and prayed that she wouldn't lose her job. Not today. Not at Christmas. But whatever happened, she wasn't going to disappoint Teo.

"Gloria!" Charles Brentwood's voice thundered behind her.

She stopped, but didn't turn around. "Yes, sir?"

"I'll…see you on Thursday morning. Make sure you're not late."

She had a feeling he'd been going to say something else, but Gloria didn't care what it might have been. She sent up a quick prayer of thanks to the Baby Jesus because at least she hadn't been fired. That was the main thing. Her salary kept the Alvarez household afloat at this time of year when her father found it so much more difficult to pick up work as a day laborer, and of late her mother's meager wages from the motel had all been eaten up by Teo's diabetic supplies. Gloria had been born in the United States and could work legally, thank goodness, but her parents were condemned to the hazards and insecure paychecks of the underground economy.

She escaped Mr. Brentwood's bleak, depressing

office, grabbed her thick parka, and hurried to the bus stop. She was already smiling by the time she reached the sidewalk. She turned her face up to feel the feathery caress of snowflakes falling on her cheek, and her cares dropped away, dissolved by thought of the pleasures waiting to greet her in the next few hours. It was Christmas Eve, the church would be warm and glowing with the light of a hundred candles. Teo was doing better than usual, a huge cause for celebration. And tonight her friends would be at the church, and all her family, as well, including her favorite cousins from the other side of town. Her sister was playing the role of an angel in the nativity play, and Teo was singing a solo. Afterward, when the play was done, they would all drink hot apple cider and eat Christmas cookies and everyone would laugh and hug as they wished each other a merry Christmas. How could anyone be sad on such a wonderful, magical night?

Poor Mr. Brentwood, who had no idea that although his bank account might be overflowing, his life was a dark, dank cave, lacking almost everything that made life worth living. Gloria ran to catch her bus, her feet made nimble by hope and joyful anticipation.

CHAPTER TWO

CHARLES LISTENED TO the sound of Gloria's footsteps running across the linoleum and heading out of the building. The huge, iron-barred front door slammed, leaving him alone. Entirely alone on Christmas Eve, just as he had been for every holiday over the past dozen years. Ever since Rachel had left him. He felt a clenching in the pit of his stomach and told himself that in future he'd better stop eating dill pickles with his lunchtime sandwich. Clearly, they didn't agree with him. Besides, they cost a dollar a pickle, which was money he didn't need to spend.

He walked over to the window, angling himself so that he could see Gloria running to catch her bus, her bright scarlet knitted cap a beacon of color in the gathering winter darkness. She looked so young. So…happy.

With an impatient click of his tongue, Charles turned away from the sparkling snow to the familiar dingy grays and beiges of his office. That was the trouble with immigrants, he thought sourly. They had no work ethic. Everything was fiesta and mañana. If good help weren't so hard to come by, he'd have fired Gloria for quitting before the end of the workday. He'd come damn close. At the last minute, though, something had held him back—something less rational than the difficulty of finding a replacement.

In retrospect, he couldn't understand what had precipitated that foolish, sentimental lapse of judgment. He was just as willing to cut nonperforming employees on December 24 as he was on any other date. You couldn't keep a business profitable for long if you ran it on sentiment instead of economic reality. China and India had plenty of manufacturers willing to step in and grab your market, and their workers considered themselves lucky if they earned enough to eat three square meals a day. Here they all complained because he didn't provide health insurance for dependants and three weeks' paid vacation, for heaven's sake! These ungrateful immigrants needed to wake up and smell the competition.

Charles glanced at his watch. Four-fifteen. In England it would already be after nine at night. His mother, Annelise Brentwood, née Annelise Dickens, would no doubt be entertaining her friends with wine and literary conversation. If the guests were really unlucky, he thought cynically, she would treat them to a recital of whatever poem she'd just finished writing—probably something about the joys of the holiday season, since his mother tended to embrace the banal. She certainly wouldn't welcome a phone call from her boring, inarticulate son, he could be quite sure of that. In fact, he had no idea why the possibility of calling her had even crossed his mind. His mother wanted only one thing from him—money. He wanted nothing at all from her.

Charles pulled himself out of a rare few moments of reflection. Brooding about failed family relationships was a waste of good thinking time and he had more productive ways to spend the evening. He returned to his desk and sat down at the computer, opening up the design program he'd been working on when he'd been overcome by a crazy impulse to stare at the snow. Brentwood Industries needed to have a totally revamped product line by the end of January and the specifications ought to have been finalized by now. Unfortunately, he'd been wrestling with one particular design for kitchen hardware for over a week now. He'd told himself repeatedly that time was money and he couldn't afford to waste any more hours fiddling with details that were aesthetic, not functional. Still, he couldn't quite convince himself that the design was ready to go into production.

"This is your last chance to do it right," he muttered, settling back into the rhythm of work. "Get to it, Charles."

His fingers curved over his mouse, the smooth plastic comforting in its familiarity. He was soon absorbed in reconfiguring the design for the faucets, along with the accompanying manufacturing specifications. As usually happened when he was working on a new design, he focused so intently that he lost all awareness of his surroundings. He stopped only when he realized his fingers had stiffened to the point that he could barely grip the mouse. He was freezing cold, he finally noticed. The heat in the building was timed to automatically turn down to fifty degrees at five-thirty, and since it was now past nine o'clock, his office was as chilly as the abandoned warehouse across the street.

Stretching cramped muscles, Charles reluctantly pushed back from his desk. He packed up for the night, but slowly. There was no reason to hurry home. He wondered if Gloria had enjoyed her church service. When he had been in high school, his younger sister had already begun to sing with the church choir and Christmas Eve had been a special time. Shortly before midnight she would perform one version or another of *Ave Maria*, and he could still get chills remembering the crystal purity of her voice reaching out into the darkened church, right before a blaze of lights greeted the stroke of midnight and the arrival of Christmas morning.

"Load of sentimental claptrap," Charles muttered, wrapping his scarf around his neck. That was the trouble with the holiday season: there were too damn many reasons to look back.

"Going to church and singing like an angel didn't save Lizzie," he muttered angrily. "A lot of good all her talent did her. And her kindness wasn't much use, either."

He'd noticed recently that he'd developed an alarming habit of talking to himself. Probably because the rest of the world was made up of fools and rascals, he thought acidly. At least when he talked to himself, he knew he was conversing with an honest, hardworking man.

"More than you can say about ninety percent of the people you meet," he told himself, tucking the ends of his scarf into his overcoat.

He drove home along roads made slick by the accumulation of snow and slush, letting himself into the house he'd lived in since childhood. His parents had bought the house in the late sixties, and it had last been refurbished by his mother in the eighties, but he no longer noticed the faded wallpaper and drab woodwork. Time had long since transformed all the original patterns and colors into varying nondescript shades of beige, but tonight for some reason Charles found himself wondering why he had never hired a painting crew to add color to the walls and breathe new life into his dingy surroundings.

"Because painters cost money," he said, setting his briefcase on the hall table. "You keep the place spotlessly clean. What's the point of wasting money on fripperies?"

Purposely not looking at the shabby wallpaper, he went into the kitchen and opened the freezer door, suppressing a sigh when he saw the neat rows of T.V dinners. With a distinct lack of enthusiasm, he scanned his choices, finally selecting a chicken patty with mixed vegetables and pasta shells, all for four-hundred-and-fifty calories. Only weak-willed fools and gluttons overate just because it was Christmas, and he was neither.

While the meal heated, he loosened his tie, washed his hands and arranged cutlery and a thin paper napkin on a tray. When the food was hot, he carried it into the family room so that he could watch a TV program while he ate. He clicked from channel to channel, but there was nothing to be seen except people singing Christmas carols, and movies where kindly old men brought snowbound families bountiful gifts, usually while a young woman went through labor in the upstairs bedroom, or the horse barn, or some other equally unlikely place for a twenty-first-century birth.

"If people didn't keep having children they can't afford, the world would be a better place." Charles nodded in agreement with his own wise comment, but somehow he couldn't work up any satisfying outrage at all those irresponsible women delivering babies on the TV screen, encouraging asinine viewers to do the same. The movies implied all those Christmas babies would grow up feeling loved and welcomed, even if the rest of the holiday magic faded within a few hours. Charles knew the promise was false: the world was a cruel place and there were few happy endings.

"Christmas movies are all a big lie. They're delivering nothing but a load of sentimental hooey," he muttered, getting up to take his tray back to the kitchen. "They shouldn't be allowed to broadcast so much drivel over the public airwaves. Babies don't automatically receive love. Lots of them get rejected. Ever hear about the crisis in foster care because of all the neglected and abandoned kids? Besides, love doesn't keep you warm when it's freezing. For that you need money to buy a parka and snow boots."

So how many foster kids have you bought snow boots for this Christmas?

The question seemed to come from somewhere outside his own head. Disconcerted, Charles snapped an impatient response. "None. Looking after other people's unwanted kids isn't my responsibility. Absolutely not."

Then whose responsibility is it?

Charles decided to ignore that question. Usually he went to bed as soon as he'd finished eating dinner, but tonight he felt strangely restless. He poured himself a glass of whiskey and carried it back into the living room. "Happy holidays," he said mockingly, raising his glass in a toast to the local news anchor. "Here's to you and your smart new toupee, Mr. Anchor Man."

The anchor happened to choose that moment to sign off, wishing all his viewers a very merry Christmas. "However you choose to spend the day tomorrow, I hope you are able to celebrate in the company of those you love."

Charles snorted. "Yeah, great idea. So that everyone can be yelling at everyone else by the time the turkey gets on the table. Face reality, Mr. Anchor Man—tomorrow is just another cold, miserable December day. And in case you haven't noticed, in New Jersey, December ain't pretty. What do you have to say to that, huh?"

The newscaster had already been replaced by advertisements, so he didn't answer. He was probably glad to escape into a commercial break, Charles thought. That way he didn't have to justify his ridiculous holiday wishes.

.Charles blinked and set his whiskey to one side, sitting up a little straighter. *Whoa!* Time to get his head back on straight. It was one thing to talk to the TV screen, but it was scary when you expected it to talk back. He clicked off the latest Santa-Claus-brings-happiness movie and carefully set the remote in its special box next to his chair. Disorder led to waste, and he despised waste.

Leaning back against the lumpy cushion, he glanced broodingly around the room, his thoughts tumbling so fast that he couldn't be sure what he was actually thinking. He was searching for something, but he couldn't identify precisely what that something might be. He was much too careful ever to lose anything, and he couldn't imagine what was provoking the strange sensation of being desperate to recapture a lost item of immense value.

"If you're looking for your grandfather's pocket watch, you know your mother took that with her to London," he reminded himself.

Charles nodded, hoping he'd found an explanation for his restless mood. His grandfather had given that pocket watch to him one Christmas, and Charles had been furious when he realized his mother had taken it to England with her—stealing it from him, to be bluntly accurate. She'd always coveted the watch, not because it had been her father's, but because it was rumored in the family to have belonged to their famous ancestor, the great Charles Dickens himself. Charles didn't care two cents about his famous ancestor, but he wished he had his grandfather's pocket watch. He'd really loved his grandfather, and his grandma, too.

Thinking about his grandparents made him uneasy. "Enough already with this pointless nostalgia. Either get to bed, Charles, or settle down to doing something useful."

He did neither. Instead, he tossed off the last of his whiskey and poured himself another shot. It had been a long time since he'd drunk any alcoholic beverages, and he already felt light-headed. Sinking deeper into the chair, he glared at the blank TV screen.

"You're in a strange mood tonight, Charles. What's up with that?"

"You've felt my presence ever since you walked into the house. That's what's up, Charles, my boy."

The once-familiar voice seemed to come from the television, and it sounded incredibly, frighteningly real. Charles turned toward the source of the sound and his body froze in shock. Only his eyes moved, widening in horror at the tiny image in the center of the TV screen. Good God, it really was Jacob Marley! Hadn't he turned off the television just a few moments ago? He could have sworn he had.

As soon as his muscles unfroze enough to allow him to lift his hand, Charles reached for the remote control, spilling his whiskey in his haste to press the off button. He barely noticed the wasted whiskey because the image on the TV screen didn't go away, however many times he clicked the remote. Worse, it grew larger, filling the entire screen as it took on the unmistakable shape and form of Jacob Marley, the former chief financial officer for Brentwood Industries.

How in the world had images of Jacob Marley's head ended up on his TV screen? The man had died alone in his apartment on Christmas Eve, collapsed across his desk, where he had apparently spent the holiday preparing tax returns for Brentwood Industries. Given that his death had occurred seven years ago, his sudden reincarnation on the TV screen was several stages beyond unsettling.

Charles considered himself the least superstitious person in the world, but he had to admit that chills were running up and down his spine as he stared at the disturbing image. The fictional Jacob Marley, created by Charles Dickens, had been business partner to the infamous Mr. Scrooge, surely one of the literary world's most famous misers. For a wild moment, Charles wondered if the real Jacob Marley could be imitating his namesake—not just by dying on Christmas Eve, but also by returning seven years later in the form of a ghost. Then he realized how crazy such an idea was, and he gave an impatient shake of his head, sending superstitious thoughts flying.

"You're drunk and you're confusing fiction with real life," Charles admonished himself, struggling to stay calm. "A couple of minutes ago you were thinking about Dickens and his pocket watch, so it's not totally surprising that you started to fantasize about his famous Christmas story. Get a grip, Charles, before your imagination runs away with you."

"You're not confusing fiction and reality," the talking head on the TV announced. *"You're not imagining things, either. I'm a ghost and this is where I hang out these days."*

Jacob Marley lived in his TV set? Charles might actually have laughed if he hadn't been busy fighting the urge to yell at the image on his screen. He was afraid he might not be able to stop shrieking if he ever once got started.

"You're dead," he told the vision, or the nightmare, or whatever the hell it was invading his viewing space. By a miracle of self-control, he managed to sound quite polite as he gave the order. "Go away, Jacob. You're not here."

"It would be hard to go away if I weren't here." Jacob Marley sounded as dyspeptic now that he was dead as he had when he was alive. *"But as it happens, I am really here and I have no intention of going away. I've been following you around all night, waiting for you to get in the mood for a chat."*

Charles gave a small, dry laugh. Laughter was so alien to him these days that the laugh immediately turned to a cough. "I'm definitely not in the mood to chat with a ghost! Go away, Jacob."

"Sure you want to chat with me, otherwise I wouldn't be here. Trust me, my boy, conversing with me is a lot more interesting than talking to yourself."

"Last warning, Jacob—go away. I'm not in the mood to talk to a figment of my imagination."

"You wish. You know very well I'm no such thing."

"Right," Charles replied, with heavy sarcasm. "You're not a figment of my imagination. Of course you're not. You're a ghost living inside my TV. I hope the accommodations are to your liking?" He gave another dry laugh. "Lucky for you I didn't buy one of the new flat panel sets. That would have left you without much room to flex your ghostly muscles."

"Fortunately, I'm not confined to the television." Jacob Marley stepped out from the screen, expanding instantly to the five feet ten inches he'd been during his life. He perched on the edge of the coffee table, looking dapper in his familiar three-piece business suit and favorite striped maroon and gold tie. Jacob's hands, however, hung awkwardly at his sides, and from the way he kept shuffling his feet, it seemed as if he might be having trouble settling his legs into a comfortable position.

This time Charles couldn't help it—he yelped in horror. *I must be a lot drunker than I'd realized,* he thought feverishly. He tried to pull up his scant store of folklore concerning ghosts. Didn't a ghostly visit usual precede disaster? Did that mean something terrible was about to happen to him? And why did his former business mentor look so awkward when he moved? Charles couldn't remember hearing that ghosts had trouble controlling their body parts. How could you have trouble with something that wasn't actually there? Presumably Jacob Marley's legs were rotting inside the memorial plot where they had been safely buried seven years ago, which pretty much guaranteed that they couldn't be planted awkwardly— or any other way—in front of the coffee table.

"You're right, my body is in the grave," Jacob Marley said, squirming around a bit as if he still hadn't found a comfortable spot for his ghostly haunches to rest. *"Actually, I don't have any visible*

form these days. What you're seeing is nothing more than your own remembered image of me. I'm guessing you see a sixty-year-old man wearing a three-piece suit and a striped tie?"

How in *hell* had Jacob Marley known what he was thinking, Charles wondered? The answer to his question was immediately apparent. Jacob's ability to read his thoughts was proof that the apparition wasn't a ghost at all. As he'd guessed in the first place, this spectral Jacob Marley was simply a figment of Charles's own imagination. The semi-transparent figure hovering on the periphery of his vision wasn't really there, except as a by-product of accumulated fatigue and too much whiskey.

Unfortunately, the ghost didn't seem to know he was an illusion. He continued to sit on the coffee table, looking alarmingly at home. It was time to get rid of this disturbing hallucination, Charles decided. Something in his brain was obviously misfiring, and he needed to block the neural paths creating the illusion. He could probably change his brain chemistry by walking out of the room. Movement—the simple act of walking—would disconnect whatever mental wires were scrambled, obliterating the annoying images of Jacob Marley.

He would get up and go to bed, Charles decided, leaving the nonexistent Jacob Marley in possession of the TV screen and the coffee table. A simple solution, but in life, as in the world of plumbing design, simple was often best.

Never one to shilly-shally once he'd reached a decision, Charles immediately tried to stand up. His muscles seemed to respond just as they should, but somehow at the end of it all, instead of finding himself out in the hallway and climbing the stairs, he discovered he was still sitting in the chair in front of the television. And Jacob was still perched on the coffee table, exhibiting a ghostly patience that he had certainly never demonstrated in life.

This is ridiculous, Charles thought, his fear not quite buried under a surge of anger. He tried not to look in Jacob's direction, but he couldn't help noticing that his former financial officer was watching him with an expression that alternated between sorrow and pity. And that was even more ridiculous than the rest of it, Charles reflected. He was fairly sure that Jacob had never wasted ten seconds of his entire life feeling pity for another human being.

Maybe the reason he couldn't go upstairs to bed was because he was already asleep, Charles thought. Of course! He must have dozed off in front of the TV. There was no other rational explanation for what he seemed to be experiencing, he concluded.

If he was dreaming, that would explain why he had confused his real life with the Christmas story written by his famous ancestor. When his father was still alive, they'd often shared a quiet laugh that the chief financial officer for Brentwood Industries had the same name as the ghost in Charles Dickens's famous novel. Somehow, Charles realized, because it was Christmas Eve and he was already in a strange mood, his mind was taking a mildly amusing coincidence and reshaping it into a holiday nightmare.

The fact that he was dreaming would also explain quite logically why he couldn't move. Charles was sure he'd read somewhere that the body was paralyzed during dreams so that people wouldn't hurt themselves by acting out their fantasies. Satisfied he understood what was going on, he gave himself a stern order to wake up.

"You're not asleep," Jacob said. *"And, as I'm getting tired of repeating, I'm really here. I've been here for most of the past seven years, in fact. Watching you make a complete mess of your life is part of my punishment for having been such a miserable human being while I was alive."*

"I'm not making a mess of my life," Charles was stung into retorting. "On the contrary, Brentwood Industries is more profitable now than it's ever been. In fact, profits have increased every year since you died, so if watching me is supposed to be a punishment, it doesn't seem a very terrible fate. The fact is, Jacob, you're watching your student outshine his mentor."

"I guess watching you at work wouldn't be a pun-

*ishment if I cared about the profitability of Brent-
wood Industries. But I don't."*

"You don't care about profitability at Brentwood
Industries?" Charles stared at his former mentor in
utter disbelief. Could ghosts be crazy? Did they bear
no resemblance to the people they'd been when they
were alive?

"I'm not a person anymore," Jacob said, and his
voice was almost gentle. *"I'm a ghost. And although
this fact seems so far to have escaped your notice,
money and profits aren't much use to a ghost."*

Charles simply couldn't wrap his mind around a
Jacob Marley who didn't care about money and
profits even if he was dead. During his lifetime, Jacob
had made it quite clear that there was nothing in the
world he prized more than squeezing every last drop
of profit out of every single transaction. It was dis-
concerting, to say the least, to learn that Jacob Marley,
of all people, no longer had even a passing interest in
the accounting sheets for Brentwood Industries.

Uneasy, not wanting to pursue the causes of such
a bizarre character transformation, Charles changed
the subject. "If you've been here for seven years,
why haven't I seen you before? Why tonight and not
any of the other few thousand nights you've been
hanging around?"

Jacob gave what might have passed for a shrug in
the world of ghosts. *"You weren't ready to see me. I
wasn't hiding, that's for sure. Believe me, it's a relief*

that you've finally noticed me. Makes me think there may be some small ray of hope for you yet, and perhaps even for me. I sure hope so. I need you to shape up if I'm ever going to have any chance of moving on to somewhere a bit closer to heaven."

"Why do I have to shape up, whatever that might mean, in order for you to get into heaven? Aren't we all responsible for our own choices? How can *your* fate depend on the way *I* behave?"

"Because, to my shame, I helped make you the sorry excuse for a man that you've become. You said it just a moment ago. I was your mentor, and you were my student."

"I appreciated your advice. You have nothing to reproach yourself over, Jacob. When my father died, the firm would have gone under without your experience to guide me."

"Maybe, but probably not. Your instincts were sound. You're a brilliant designer, Charles, with excellent engineering skills, and you have enough common sense that you'd probably have taken most of the steps necessary to keep the company afloat without me standing over you, making sure that you extracted every wretched nickel of profit out of our business—and to hell with any other consideration."

"Business is all about the bottom line. Commerce isn't another name for social welfare."

"I taught you that, didn't I? Your father knew better. Business...commerce...is about a lot more

than profits. It's about dedication to quality, and providing the chance for employees to utilize their talents to the fullest possible extent. It's about honesty and integrity when we negotiate deals. How we behave when we conduct a business deal is likely to affect how we behave in every other aspect of our lives."

That sounded like a load of horse dung to Charles, so he ignored it. Besides, he had no life outside business. "Brentwood Industries never indulges in dishonest practices, so your advice is irrelevant. Besides, the company never realized its full potential when my father was in charge—"

"Full potential for what? Inflicting hardship on the employees?"

"No! For making an honest dollar through hard work and attention to the bottom line!"

Jacob didn't answer. Instead, he stood up and moved slowly from the coffee table to the couch that Charles no longer sat on because of the broken springs. *"When your father suffered his heart attack, and your sister died in that terrible accident, you were still a very young man, hardly more than a boy, with a heavy burden of responsibility suddenly thrust onto your shoulders. Two people you loved died and then your mother rejected you—abandoned you without a word of kindness or love. Remember what she said to you at the airport, when you went to say goodbye to her?"*

"No, I don't remember."

"Yes, you do," Jacob said softly. *"But that's her burden to carry, and it's a heavy one. My burden is that instead of bolstering your confidence and helping you to understand just how much you were capable of achieving, I did everything in my power to make you believe that friendship and love and all the other positive human emotions were unimportant—that only efficiency, money and profit were goals worth pursuing."*

"Those goals have served me well enough," Charles said. "I have no issues with the advice you gave me."

"Don't you? I think you've begun to understand that a life filled only with money and deals is empty of almost everything that matters. Otherwise you wouldn't have seen me tonight." Jacob lifted his hand and slowly, painfully, moved it so that it rested in his insubstantial lap.

"A life without money is empty, too," Charles snapped. "Without money, you can't buy an education or health care, not to mention food or clothing. It's easy for you to despise money—you never had to live without it. Ask Gloria how she feels about never having enough money to meet essential household expenses. Ask her how she'd feel if I offered her another fifty bucks a week, then you'd realize how important money is!" He was so caught up in the argument that he forgot Jacob had never met Gloria, who would only have been a child in school when Jacob died.

But the ghost seemed to have no difficulty understanding who Charles was talking about. *"So you do realize that Gloria is working her fingers to the bone in an effort to satisfy your unreasonable demands,"* Jacob said sadly. *"And it seems you even realize that she deserves a raise. Since you know all this, why are you still taking advantage of her?"*

"I'm not taking advantage of her." Charles was infuriated by the accusation. "She's only nineteen. She has no work experience. She doesn't deserve more money, of course she doesn't!"

"Try to hire anybody half as competent as she is for the same wage—"

"There are a dozen illegal immigrants who'd be thrilled to have her job and her salary, too!"

Jacob raised a ghostly eyebrow. *"Illegal immigrants, Charles? Is that what you're reduced to? Making your profits by exploiting people who are defenseless against you? And, by the way, I thought you said Brentwood doesn't indulge in dishonest business practices?"*

"Immigrants aren't defenseless," Charles said angrily. "If they don't like the wages I pay, they can go back to Mexico, or wherever else they came from!"

"Gloria was born right here in New Jersey. Is she to go back to Mexico, too?"

"No! Yes! I don't know." Charles knew he sounded petulant. "I didn't fire her this afternoon." He couldn't believe he was citing that failure to act as if it were cause for praise. Good grief, he ought to be ashamed of himself for not having made a necessary business decision. "She left an hour and a half early—an hour and a half!—just because it's Christmas Eve, but I didn't fire her, although I thought about it, that's for damn sure!"

Jacob sighed. *"And the fact that you didn't fire her gave me my first real twinge of hope in several years."* Slowly, painfully, he pulled himself out of the armchair. *"I thought there was a chance you were ready to hear my message. It seems I was mistaken, and I'm sorry for both of us. I doubt if you'll be given another chance now that you've blown this one."*

"Wait! You're getting fainter and we haven't finished talking!" Charles rubbed his eyes. "Where are you going?"

"That I'm not permitted to tell you. Goodbye, Charles. I'm sorry this didn't work out, and I'm truly sorry for my part in making you the man you've become. I wish my regrets didn't come too late." Jacob Marley walked slowly and heavily toward the TV set.

"What's that noise? My God, what is it? I hear a terrible jangling noise." Charles put his hands over his ears, the sound loud enough to be painful.

Jacob swung around, his expression suddenly eager. *"You hear something jangling?"*

"Yes, yes. It's horrible. Like chains rattling on concrete as prisoners are marched to execution.

Worse, it's as if I can feel all the sadness of the people imprisoned by the chains."

With huge effort, Jacob lifted his arm. *"You still don't see them?"*

"See what? Your arms?"

Marley shook his head, looking depressed again. *"I suppose it's something at least that you can finally hear them."*

"Stop talking in riddles! Hear what, for heaven's sake?"

"The chains wrapped around my body, choking me with their weight, dragging on the ground behind me. I carry them with me into eternity. They are the reward for my misspent life. Every unkind act I committed, every moment of avarice, every disdainful thought...hundreds upon hundreds of cruelties, forging hundreds and hundreds of links in a chain that binds me to earth instead of allowing me to fly free into eternity."

Jacob lifted his foot and took another painful step. *"That you couldn't see the chains was discouraging. It provided me with yet more proof that you are forging the same cruel links I forged for myself. And, just like me, if you don't change, one day you will carry similar heavy chains into the afterlife. But the fact that you* can *hear the chains that weigh me down with the misery of a thousand wrong choices gives me a faint gleam of hope. Perhaps there is a chance that you can be saved from yourself, Charles. If it's permitted, I will try to arrange for you to have other visitors tonight—"*

"What sort of visitors?" Charles was in no mood for a lecture about invisible chains, and even less in the mood for any more ghostly hallucinations.

Jacob Marley was now so faint, and his voice so low that Charles had to strain to hear him. *"I sometimes have the power to dispatch visions, but only you have the power to decide whether or not you will see them. If they come, if you are fortunate enough to sense their presence, I beg you to open your heart to them. Your life depends upon it, Charles. Don't send them away."*

CHAPTER THREE

BY THE TIME THE LAST vestiges of Jacob Marley disappeared from sight, Charles discovered he could walk again. The staircase, which a few minutes earlier had seemed impossibly distant, was once again within easy reach.

He bounded up the stairs two at a time, eager to get away from the living room and its ghostly visions. If he could get the blood flowing into his brain with sufficient force, he figured that the increased blood supply ought to dispel the aftereffects of his silly, drunken hallucination.

Unfortunately, even when he reached the top of the stairs, he couldn't quite shake the conviction that he really had seen the ghost of Jacob Marley, so he ran down again at double speed and then swung around and ran up for good measure, determined to get his heart pumping and his adrenaline flowing.

A dozen runs up and down the stairs got rid of all trace of the whiskey but did nothing to block out his memory of what Jacob Marley had supposedly told him. Charles took himself off to the shower and stood under the hot water, scrubbing every inch of his body in a determined effort to wipe away his crazy conviction that he'd just finished a conversation with a ghost—a ghost who claimed to live inside his television set!

"There are places designed to take care of people who chat with visitors popping out from the inside of a television," Charles warned himself. "And you have no desire to find yourself in any such institution. So shape up, old man. Get with the program."

He wasn't quite sure what "the program" was. Perhaps he needed to renew his dedication to keeping Brentwood Industries successful. The New Year was about to begin, and his New Year's resolution would be to take the company to even more impressive heights of profitability. One thing was for sure: he had no intention of spending any part of the next twelve months discussing his problems with men dressed in starched white coats.

Contemplating a year of improved profits didn't inspire its usual warm and fuzzy glow but, instead, it induced a sensation alarmingly close to panic. Fighting for calm, Charles carefully hung up his bath towel and tugged on the T-shirt and boxers he used as sleepwear. So what if Jacob Marley didn't seem too happy with the consequences of a life devoted exclusively to financial success? That was Jacob's problem. Charles sure as heck couldn't think of a better goal.

"Besides, you didn't really see Jacob Marley! Repeat after me until you get it through your thick skull—Jacob Marley is dead, therefore you didn't see him. Now can we agree to stop talking about Jacob Marley?"

It occurred to Charles with sudden unwelcome force that his habit of talking to himself had passed well beyond mild eccentricity and moved on to something much less healthy. How in the world had he ended up at the ripe old age of thirty-eight with nobody to talk to but himself? Was he so scared of being hurt again that he was unable to develop normal friendships? He didn't need to form deep, life-altering relationships, just acquaintances he could call now and again to have a conversation with…to chat about something that wasn't related to plumbing or freight delays out of Shanghai. How threatening could it be to have two or three friends he could join for a quick beer on a Friday night, or a movie over the weekend?

"You don't like beer. And since when do you have time for movies on the weekend?" he demanded, and then realized he was talking to himself yet again. Still, he couldn't quite quell a stirring of regret for the fact that he'd once again turned down the invitation from his cousin, Jeff, to spend the holidays with him and his family. But Jeff lived in Princeton and had once been a good friend of Rachel's….

Will you quit with the maudlin memories, Charlie-boy? And, for the last time, stop talking to yourself!

His mouth tightening, Charles marched over to his bed just as the grandfather clock in the upstairs hallway struck midnight. He halted in his tracks, his heart pounding, and then was furious with himself for allowing superstition to get the better of him. There was nothing significant about midnight, except the ignorance of past generations. If you'd never traveled more than twenty miles from the village where you were born, the idea of midnight and the witching hour might seem magically significant. But Charles had all the advantages of a modern college education, and he knew better. What with daylight savings and varying time zones, midnight was no more than an arbitrary number, voted in by Congress. And he knew exactly how much confidence to place in that bunch of liars and spendthrifts.

He marched into his bedroom, suppressing all thoughts of ghosts, ghoulies and things that go bump in the night. His bed with its clean but threadbare sheets and blankets seemed less than inviting, despite the fact that he was bone tired. He stood at the side for several minutes, so reluctant to lie down that he gritted his teeth with the effort of lifting his foot from the floor and setting his hips on the mattress. He finally managed to dive between the sheets, pulling the covers up to his chin—*like a child hiding from the bogeyman,* he thought with bitter self-mockery.

After a few moments, he turned quickly from his back to his side. Nothing happened, except that the bed creaked in protest against his moving so vigorously on the fifteen-year-old mattress. Relief sent blissful warmth and relaxation coursing through his veins.

He wriggled lower on the pillows, grateful to be out of the dank chill that seemed to permeate the whole house tonight. He asked himself what he'd expected to happen when he got into bed, and this time he remembered to make the question a silent one. Had he been waiting for Jacob Marley to pop out of the bedroom closet and start another conversation? Snug in his bed, Charles could almost laugh at the stupidity of such a delusion. Almost.

CHAPTER FOUR

CHARLES WASN'T AWARE OF falling asleep. One moment he was tossing and turning in fidgety pursuit of rest. The next moment he smelled the spicy, pungent scent of pine needles, as though there was a fresh-cut Christmas tree in his bedroom.

Excitement surged through him, as powerful as when he'd been a little boy getting ready to drive to his Grandma Brentwood's house on Christmas morning. He bolted upright in the bed, the mingled smell of evergreen and cinnamon so strong that he glanced around the room, searching for the source. As if he truly expected to find a Christmas tree sitting in the corner waiting to be decorated—with a plate of cookies set out for Santa on the nearby table, Charles thought derisively.

There was no tree, of course, and no cookies. As soon as he realized that his room was its usual empty shell, the wonderful smell began to fade and his stomach rumbled with regret. He felt bereft, as if he were indeed a young boy again and a promised treat had been whisked away at the last moment.

Growing up, he'd been well accustomed to promises that never materialized. Dangling the prospect of a wonderful treat and then snatching it away at the last moment had been a favorite trick of his mother's. He'd been a slow learner, Charles reflected cynically, but he'd eventually figured out how to cope with Annelise Brentwood's subtle cruelty: he had simply stopped believing her. If he never expected promises to be kept or treats to materialize, then he couldn't be disappointed when he was proven right and the treats were never delivered.

The wonderful, evocative smell of Christmas evergreens had almost completely faded now. Charles cast one last, sad glance around the dark room—and saw the wall in the corner blur and a figure walk through the plaster, the wall reforming behind him.

It was Santa Claus, Charles saw, unable to smother a crack of laughter, despite his underlying fear. Of course it was Santa! On this crazy night, who else would it be? But it wasn't the fat and jolly Santa Claus of department-store merchandising efforts. Instead, the figure was tall and rather lean, wearing a jeweled miter and a floor-length, fur-trimmed cape the color of a rich burgundy wine. He looked, in fact, exactly like one of the old Victorian engravings depicting Saint Nicholas, the third-century bishop of Myra. Saint Nicholas was the man whose generosity to the poor provided the basis for the legend of Santa Claus.

Charles gave another self-mocking laugh as he took in the full details of his latest vision. If he was going to have delusions, it was nice to know that he was capable of fabricating such fancy ones. Strangely enough, now that he'd actually conjured up a second ghostly visitor, he wasn't as scared as he had been earlier when he'd feared what his sick brain might fantasize about next.

Watching St. Nicholas stroll with a measured and stately tread toward his bed, Charles accepted not only that he was sliding into madness but that he could do nothing to halt the slide. One ghost per night could be excused as an aberration. Two within the space of a couple of hours could only be considered proof positive of his deteriorating mental health.

Oddly, acknowledging his impending madness didn't depress him. He might be racing inexorably toward full-blown psychosis, but his id, or his ego, or his something-or-other had apparently decided that he might as well enjoy the ride. In fact, if he'd been forced to identify his mood right at this moment, honesty would compel him to admit that he felt more alive—closer to happiness—than at any other time during the past decade.

He leaned back against his thin pillow, arms crossed to ward off the chill. There seemed no point in going through ten minutes of fruitlessly pretending he couldn't see what was plainly in front of his eyes, even if he recognized that his eyes couldn't be trusted. This time, Charles decided, he might as well cut straight to the chase.

"Well, hello, Saint Nicholas." He actually directed a tired smile at the phantom. "I'm honored that you decided to come calling on your busiest night of the year. How are you, old man?"

"Hello, Charles. I'm well, thank you for asking. But I'm not Saint Nicholas, you know. Is that how you see me? How interesting!"

"You're wearing a fur-trimmed robe and you're holding a bishop's crook, so if you're not actually good ole Saint Nick, I'd have to say you're doing a fine impersonation."

"I deliberately came to you without assuming any specific shape or form. It is you who supplied images of Saint Nicholas to give visual substance to my presence."

"Is that so? Well, let's play this your way." Charles gave a sarcastic laugh and realized that, sarcastically or not, he'd laughed more tonight than in the entire previous year. Madness, it seemed, had its compensations. "Okay, Mr. I'm-Not-Saint-Nicholas: Who are you, then? Are you about to tell me that you're really Jacob Marley playing dress-up? Or are we going to play Name This Specter for the rest of the night?"

"Not at all. We have much more useful ways to spend the next hour. As it happens, I am the Ghost of Christmas Past, and although I have nothing directly to do with Jacob Marley, I've been dispatched at his request. He seems to feel that reminding you of some important events in your earlier life will bring you to a realization of how badly you've lost your way."

"You're the Ghost of Christmas Past?" Charles rolled his eyes. "Damn! How uninspiring, not to mention clichéd."

"Why do you say that? I can imagine many reactions to my sudden appearance in your bedroom. Accusing me of being a cliché would not have been one of them, however."

"That's because you're not the several times great-grandson of Charles Dickens! You didn't spend the first twenty-two years of your life having the wonders of your ancestor's literary genius thrust down your throat on every possible and impossible occasion. Apart from cooking roast goose because she thought that sounded more Dickensian than roast turkey, my mother's only contribution to holiday merriment was to insist on reading *A Christmas Carol* out loud the week before Christmas."

"Did you enjoy the story?" the ghost asked politely.

Charles snorted. "The first half-dozen times I heard it, maybe. In case you aren't aware, you have a starring role in that novel."

The ghost nodded. "I haven't read the book, but I've seen some of the movies. On the whole, I wasn't impressed. They're a bit too sentimental for my taste. That Tiny Tim character just doesn't do it for me. Dickens has a deplorable tendency toward schmaltz."

If he'd needed further proof of his rapid progress toward madness, it would only have required this conversation, Charles decided. Discussing movie versions of *A Christmas Carol* with a vision claiming to be the Ghost of Christmas Past would have to be about as close to a definition of insanity as you could get.

The odd thing was how real this vision felt and looked. But that, perhaps, was the point of madness: the delusional state felt normal to the person suffering from it. Charles gave a mental shrug, feeling too exhausted to fight the inevitable.

"I suppose you're going to show me carefully selected scenes from my past life so that I'll look at myself when I was young and wonder how in the world I ended up in the place I'm at now. That's the usual pattern in the book and in the movies." Charles didn't bother to conceal his impatience. "If that's the plan, would you please get on with it? I'm wasting good sleeping time, and I have a busy day tomorrow."

"What are you going to be so busy with tomorrow?"

"Work."

"I hope not, Charles. I really hope not." The Ghost of Christmas Past sat on the end of the bed, and once again the wonderful smell of fresh evergreens was suddenly strong.

Closing his eyes, Charles drew in a deep, hungry

breath. Evergreens with a hint of rosemary, he thought. Rachel's apartment had been full of them on that long-ago Christmas Eve. Mad delusion or not, he wanted to capture that smell and imprint it on his mind forever....

CHAPTER FIVE

CHARLES OPENED HIS EYES again and glanced toward the end of the bed, about to ask the supposed Ghost of Christmas Past about the evergreens, but Saint Nicholas was gone. A second later Charles realized that he himself was no longer in his bedroom. Instead, he was walking across the elementary school playground on a crisp, September morning, the sun shining out of a high, blue sky and the sound of a red-winged blackbird calling from a nearby tree.

He wasn't alone. His little sister, Elizabeth, was holding his hand, her fingers twined tightly in his. "Is Mrs. Hasham really nice, Charles?" she asked anxiously.

Charles squeezed her hand. "She's great, Lizzie. She's the best teacher in the whole school and she plays the piano really well. I know you'll like her."

"If you like her, I'll like her, too." Elizabeth looked up at him, her childishly perfect features framed by a cloud of soft, light brown curls tucked behind a velvet headband. "I'm glad you're my bruvver,

Charles. You're nice. Not like Debbie's big bruvver. Peter is *mean*."

Charles smiled at his little sister. Even though she was only five and he was nine and going into fourth grade with the other big kids, he realized he was glad his mom had ordered him to take Lizzie to school on her very first day ever. It was good to know that because of him, she wouldn't have to walk into the building alone, the way he had done four years ago. When you were just a little kid, that big brick building looked a bit scary.

He ruffled his sister's hair, an odd lump in his throat. "I'm only nice sometimes. I'll turn into double-mean Oscar the Grouch if you take my colored pencils again."

She smiled at him, untroubled by his threats—probably because experience had already taught her that he never lived up to them. "Oscar the Grouch isn't real and *Sesame Street* is for babies. I'm going to big kids' school like you, and I'm going to watch cartoons on Saturday morning. Cartoons is fun."

"Okay, but you still can't take my pencils."

Elizabeth thought for a moment and then tried to explain why she'd needed them. "I wanted to draw a picture like you draw for me, Charles, but I can't. My people don't come out right. I drew Daddy a kitty cat and he said it was a horse!"

"Your pictures will turn out just right one day, Lizzie. You're still learning."

She shook her head, her fine hair already escaping from its headband. "Daddy says you have magic drawing fingers. My fingers aren't magic."

"You have a magic voice instead. Nobody gets a magic voice *and* magic fingers." They had arrived at the door to the kindergarten classroom, and Charles gestured to indicate she should walk inside. "There's Mrs. Hasham, Lizzie. Look, she's waiting for you, I can see her."

His sister gave an audible gulp. "I think I'm scared. Maybe we should go home."

Charles wasn't about to hug a girl in full view of anyone passing by, even if she was his sister and a pretty cool person, as far as girls and five-year-olds and sisters could be.

"No, you're not scared. You'll be fine." His heart seemed to constrict when she looked at him out of huge, stormy eyes. "I'll see you at lunchtime, okay? And you can tell me if you learned a new song."

Her face broke into a giant grin and she stood on tiptoe to kiss his cheek before he could stop her. "Yes, I will. Bye, Charles! I love you!" She turned and ran into the kindergarten classroom, her new book bag bouncing on her skinny shoulders.

He scrubbed his cheek, scowling, but then he laughed. "Bye, Lizzie. Enjoy your first day of school! I love you, too."

The classroom door slammed shut behind his sister, and Charles was immediately seized by an overwhelming sensation of loss. He wanted to see her smile one more time, and the need was so powerful that he banged on the panels of the door, not caring if Mrs. Hasham told him to move on as soon as she opened it.

The door was tugged open so fast that Charles was left with his hand hovering in midair. But the door wasn't opened by the kindergarten teacher or even by his five-year-old sister. Instead, he was greeted by a grown-up Elizabeth, laughing as she stood on tiptoe to kiss his cheek. He was in his sister's room at college, Charles realized, and he'd just arrived to pick her up at the end of her freshman year.

"Charles! You're early."

"No, I'm on time." He grinned. "But you're late, as usual."

"There were so many people I wanted to see before they left for the summer that I've been running around all morning like a headless chicken." Lizzie seemed momentarily contrite, but she soon cheered up again. "Don't worry, Charles, I'm almost done packing. I won't be a minute, I promise."

It was inevitable that Lizzie would be late, Charles thought, resigned rather than irritated. Where she was concerned, friendship expanded to fill the time available, and then spilled over in giant waves. She'd undoubtedly spent the morning helping everyone else get their stuff together and bubbling with plans for the fall, when they would be together again. If there were fifty students living in this building, it was a safe bet that Lizzie had made fifty new friends over the course of the past year.

His sister was as outgoing as he was introverted, Charles reflected with rueful amusement, which must show something about how wrong stereotypes could be. Creative artists were supposed to suffer in lonely garrets, wrestling with their muse, but Lizzie accepted her gifts with an easy, openhearted pleasure, and her love of music didn't seem to cut her off from an active social life. She had no problem at all relating to other people even though she had a singing voice so melodic and powerful that all her rivals ought to have been green with envy. And, to crown her musical gifts, she was attractive enough to turn heads anywhere she went.

For some reason, though, the other students weren't jealous of her looks or her talent. Instead of plotting and scheming to sabotage her success, they all seemed to take pride in her amazing gifts, as if Lizzie's generosity of spirit convinced them that they all shared in her achievements.

Charles, on the other hand, was introverted to a fault, even though he didn't share his sister's creative talents. Right up through high school, he'd dreamed of forging a career in commercial design, but his art teacher had rewarded his best efforts with no more than a B grade, and he'd soon realized that his mother was right to warn him against pursuing a career for which he was so unsuited. His technical drawing skills were excellent, everyone agreed on that, but gradually he realized his mother must be correct: he'd learned those techniques by constant practice rather than through inborn talent. Clearly, he had no innate talent, otherwise his art teacher would have encouraged him instead of advising him never to enter any of his work in local contests. With a real sense of sadness, Charles accepted the fact that he lacked creative vision, and so would never succeed in the competitive world of commercial art.

Following his mother's urgings, he'd abandoned his dreams and enrolled in engineering school, slogging through courses that often bored him. He'd graduated last year, and when he'd started to look for a job, his father had begged him to come home and share the burden of running Brentwood Industries.

His engineering degree had proved extremely useful in helping his father update the factory and renovate the assembly lines, although Charles had argued strongly against the modernization. He could already see the writing on the wall, and it was written in Chinese. If Brentwood Industries was going to survive, Charles recognized that production would have to move overseas. Still, his father didn't want to close the plant, which had been operating in the same location for three generations, and Charles had no desire to worry his father, whose health was precarious. Bob Brentwood already faced a barrage of criticism from his wife for not making enough money to satisfy her social ambitions. Charles had no desire to add father-son disputes to the burdens his dad already carried.

The result was that ever since he'd left college, Charles had been working in ways that he knew to be inefficient, on products he knew he could design better if only his father would trust him. He was young and impatient but he loved his father, so he bit his tongue and tried to smooth the bumpy path he knew the family firm was facing.

Sometimes he felt as if he might explode from all the good ideas he had squashed down inside, with no place to go. He had no supporters inside the company, since the other employees were men in their fifties and early sixties, and they had zero interest in listening to a whippersnapper's ideas about fresh designs, innovative marketing campaigns and the urgent need to identify new retail outlets. The sales manager and the production manager, old pals of Bob, had been with the firm for thirty years, and they simply laughed when Charles suggested sales would increase if they could find ways to make buying bathroom fixtures and laundry room faucets more appealing to women. Only Jacob Marley, the chief financial officer, agreed with Charles that continuing production in the United States would put Brentwood Industries out of business sooner rather than later.

To compound his woes, his social life wasn't exactly flourishing. Charles wasn't good at casual conversation, and it was tough to make friends when you tended to stumble over your own tongue every time you found yourself in a group of strangers.

"Lots of people like you, Charles," his sister had told him more than once. "You're a very likeable man once people get to know you. Your problem isn't that you're tongue-tied, or even that you're naturally a bit shy. Your problem is that Mom has worked a total number on your self-confidence. Don't let her get away with it. Remember, living well is the best revenge." She grinned as she said it, a firm believer in her own statement.

A quick knock on the door snapped him out of his reverie. "Get that, will you, Charles?" Lizzie poked her head out of the closet, her arms overflowing with shirts and jeans. Her definition of "nearly finished packing" was clearly more flexible than his, Charles thought laughingly.

He opened the door—and felt as if somebody had just taken a fist and driven it hard into his rib cage. While he struggled to catch his breath, the woman standing in the entrance called out a greeting to Lizzie and then turned to him with a smile that transformed her from stunningly beautiful into the sexiest woman he'd ever set eyes on.

"Hi, I'm Liz's friend, Rachel Chandahr. You must be her famous big brother." Rachel's smile warmed her whole face. "Liz has told me so much about you, I'm really glad to meet you at last."

"Er...hi." It wasn't exactly the conversational gambit of his dreams, but at least he'd managed to speak, which amounted to a minor miracle given the way that his heart was pounding and his mouth had turned dry.

He was usually attracted to blue-eyed blondes, but not on this occasion. Rachel had long, straight black hair that hung down her back almost to her waist, along with huge brown eyes and smooth light brown skin that he already yearned to touch. Her last name suggested she might have at least one parent who was from India or Pakistan; there was definitely a touch of the exotic about her looks.

"I'm Charles. Charles Brentwood." He managed to get his systems to function with sufficient coordination to hold out his hand. He meant to say that he was pleased to meet her. Instead, he blurted out, "You're so beautiful."

Rachel didn't laugh at him. Her cheeks momentarily glowed with an enticing flush of pink. "Thank you." She smiled again, her eyes gleaming with mischief. "You're rather handsome yourself."

She shook his hand and, at the touch of her fingers, Charles felt sensation shoot all the way up his arm and then shoot down again before lodging in the pit of his stomach. He had never before felt such an immediate and intense sexual attraction, and he was grateful Rachel couldn't read his thoughts. Each time he looked at her, he saw some new and erotic variation on the theme of how she would look lying in his bed without a stitch of clothing, her hair spread in a magnificent cloud across his pillow. The sexy visions were delightful; they also fried the speech center of his brain.

"It's great to meet you, Rachel." Charles swallowed, searching desperately for something clever to say. Clever turned out to be beyond his current capabilities, but he did manage to dredge up a reasonable question. "Are you a freshman, too?"

She shook her head. "No, I just finished my junior year."

"Are you a music major like Lizzie?" Hey, two coherent questions in a row. There was a faint chance she wouldn't conclude he was a complete and total dumb-ass.

"Yes, I am. My main instrument is the clarinet, but I play the guitar, as well, just for fun, and I've accompanied Liz quite a lot when she sings. That's how we first got to know each other."

"I can't carry a tune," Charles confessed. "I like to listen to music, though, and I'm envious of people who can sing. Or play."

"But Charles is a wonderful artist," Lizzie piped up, zipping her bulging duffel bag. "When I was a little kid he used to draw these incredible pictures for me and make up stories about the people he drew.

Even in those days, I realized the pictures were special, but I didn't appreciate just how terrific they were. Now I wish I'd kept some of them, they were so fabulous."

Rachel started to fold the T-shirts heaped on Lizzie's bed. "If you ask him really nicely, I bet he'd draw you some new ones."

Lizzie pulled a face. "I wish. These days Charles is so busy keeping the family business afloat that he never draws or paints just for the fun of it."

"That's a shame. When you have a talent, you need to use it. Still, I know real life has an annoying habit of getting in the way of our dreams."

"Especially when real life means running a family business for a father who wants to retire," Charles said wryly.

"The family business is important, of course, but you have to remember your own dreams." Rachel gave him another of the friendly smiles that caused his heart to gyrate like a demented centrifuge. "Liz has talked a lot about how conscientious you are and how everybody piles all their responsibilities onto you. That's great, I guess, but sometimes you have to take a stand and make space for your own talents, you know? From everything Liz ever told me, you're way too gifted to let your art get pushed permanently onto the back burner."

"You can't take everything Lizzie says about me as gospel truth." Charles spoke casually, but he felt a warm glow of pride that his sister appreciated his artistic talent, limited as it was. Most of all, he was grateful that he didn't look like a completely boring dork in front of the most beautiful woman in the world.

He gave his sister a quick, affectionate hug. "Ever since I saved her from Pete Orin, the fourth grade bully, she's felt this obligation to say nice things about me."

Lizzie returned the hug. "I'm grateful that you rescued me from Putrid Pete, but that's not why I say nice things about you. I say them because they're true." With her usual lightning speed, Lizzie darted to another topic of conversation. "Rachel lives in New Jersey, too. Isn't that an amazing coincidence?"

Rachel lived in New Jersey. *Thank you, Jesus.* He'd been afraid she might be an exchange student from somewhere far, far away, although he would willingly have flown to the most distant corner of the globe if that was what it took to see her over the summer. "Whereabouts in New Jersey?" he asked.

"In Princeton. My parents work for the university. They're both statisticians and I'm a complete mystery to them. They can't believe they've produced a daughter who doesn't quite grasp the earthshaking significance of sample size. Or even, truth be told, the difference between average and median." She laughed at her own inadequacy, seemingly confident that her parents still loved her despite her failure to become a statistician like them.

"Princeton isn't very far from Trenton, where Lizzie and I live."

"I know." Rachel looked at him, her gaze intent. "You should come and visit one weekend. The campus is beautiful all year, but I love it in summer when everything is lavishly green and there aren't as many undergrads around as usual."

"I'd like that," Charles said. God, would he ever like that! "How can I get in touch with you?"

"Liz knows how to reach me. She has my address and phone number. I'm teaching at a summer camp during the day, but I'm free on the weekends, and most evenings, too."

It sounded as if Rachel really wanted him to come. The most beautiful woman in the world, who also seemed a kind and talented person, wanted him to visit her over the summer! The age of miracles had returned, Charles thought with only a slight touch of self-mockery.

A loud knocking on the door of his sister's room drew his attention once again. "Do you want me to get that?" he asked Lizzie.

"Please." This time she emerged from the closet with an armful of shoes. "I'll be done with my packing in a couple of minutes, Charles, I swear."

"I'll believe that when we're in the car, with twenty miles of Interstate behind us and the dorm."

Lizzie blew him a sarcastic kiss and then grinned. She knew that where she was concerned, his patience was almost endless.

"Speaking of packing, I should go," Rachel said. "My cousin is driving me to Washington, D.C., for a week. He'll be arriving any minute and I still have all my sheet music in a locker on the other side of the campus."

Charles opened the door so that Rachel could walk through. He was about to introduce himself to the young man waiting outside, but the moment Rachel passed him, darkness fell, as if somebody had thrown a heavy cloth over his head. When the darkness lifted, he was no longer in his sister's college dorm.

This time he found himself in the living room of Rachel's tiny apartment in Atlantic City, New Jersey. She'd rented the apartment six months earlier when she graduated from college and landed a job playing clarinet in the band at one of the casinos. She was making a decent salary, although her hours were a little crazy, and she could never be sure when she would be called in for a wedding or some other celebration requiring music.

She loved living near the ocean, and Charles loved coming to visit her. From her bedroom window you could actually see a thin sliver of shoreline if you got the angle just right, and although Rachel joked about the real estate ad that had hyped *magnificent apartment with ocean views and working gas fireplace,*

Charles recognized the happiness behind the laughter. Rachel was a born homemaker, and it had taken her only a few days to turn the barren apartment with its boxlike interior into a place that offered a relaxed, understated welcome to everyone lucky enough to cross the threshold.

Charles surveyed the living room, relishing the now-familiar sense of contentment that enveloped him when he was with Rachel. The time he spent with her each weekend was what kept him going through the long, arduous hours he worked at the family business. His father had been struggling to overcome one health setback after another since suffering a mild heart attack the year before, and Charles sometimes felt that at the ripe old age of twenty-four, the world was closing in on him. If he wasn't careful, his horizons would soon be limited to his father's bedside and the offices of Brentwood Industries.

By contrast, his sister's singing career seemed to be taking off in all sorts of exciting ways. Right now she was working on a movie that was being filmed in Africa.

Since she couldn't be home for the holidays, he'd decided that this year he would break loose from the constraints of his family's dismal Christmas Eve traditions. Instead of gritting his teeth through the forced, chill perfection of his mother's holiday dinner, he would share this special day with the woman he loved. His parents had each other, after all, and perhaps his mother would rediscover her store of Christmas spirit if she was alone with the husband she'd presumably loved once upon a time.

Everything about his day with Rachel had been wonderful. In the morning they had finished decorating the tree the two of them had bought the previous weekend. An angel with transparent silver wings and a gleaming halo perched on the top branch, keeping a benevolent eye on her surroundings. Lights girded the tree in a twinkling garland, and shone on the little collection of gift-wrapped packages underneath. Two fat red candles on the coffee table in front of the fire offered the only other illumination, and the finishing touch was provided by a tape of his sister singing Christmas music. The view of gray skies and icy rain outside the windows seemed almost pleasurable because it contrasted so vividly with the cozy interior of the apartment.

That afternoon they had nothing on the schedule beyond enjoying each other's company. Rachel had piled cushions on the rug in front of the fireplace. The logs in the gas fire were artificial, but in the subdued light from the candles they looked real, the flames leaping and flickering with hypnotic beauty. She handed Charles a mug of steaming hot chocolate, topped with whipped cream and a sprinkle of cinnamon. The wonderful smell of fresh evergreens tickled his nostrils, spiced by the cinnamon in the hot chocolate and by the delicious richness of the ham baking in the oven.

"Merry Christmas, Charles," she whispered.

"Merry Christmas, my love." He set his mug on the hearth and pulled her close, breathing in the smell of her shampoo, running his hands through the long, silky perfection of her hair.

She leaned away from him, her expression serious. "You are my love, you know that, don't you, Charles? Forever and always. I can't even imagine what my life would be like without you in it."

He was so happy, he felt as if he might burst from the sheer excess of it. He had planned to wait until dinnertime to ask her to marry him, but he couldn't contain himself any longer. He reached into the pocket of his jacket and pulled out the small, dark blue jeweler's box he'd been carrying around for three days now. He opened the lid with hands that shook and turned it around so that Rachel could see the ring inside. Not a traditional diamond solitaire, but a square-cut topaz, entirely surrounded by diamonds. He'd saved for months to afford it, and he hoped that she would realize he'd chosen a topaz because the rich honey-brown of the stone was almost as beautiful as her eyes.

"Marry me, Rachel." He'd worked for days on what he would say when he asked her to be his wife, but as usual, there was a disconnect between the overflowing emotions in his heart and the meager words that emerged from his mouth.

He handed the box to her, watching her expression

change from excitement to joy to love and then back again in rapid succession. Rachel, thank God, seemed to understand everything that he hadn't found the words to tell her.

"It's the most beautiful ring in the world, Charles. Thank you."

"Does that mean you're saying yes?"

She laughed. "Of course I'll marry you. I can't wait to start our life together. To have children and a home of our own. Oh, it's going to be so much fun! You're such a good, kind man, Charles."

When he was with Rachel, he could almost believe that. "I love you," he said, and drew her close so that he could kiss her, the ring box squashed between their bodies.

When they broke apart, she held out her left hand. "Put it on, Charles. You do it, please."

He carefully slid the ring onto her finger, then turned her hand over and kissed the shiny gold band. "Merry Christmas, my darling."

She wrapped her arms around his neck and nestled her head against his chest. "Merry Christmas, Charles."

The candles flickered, extinguished by a sudden draft of cold wind. Charles got up to switch on a light, but when he walked across the room he felt thin, worn-out carpet beneath his feet and he realized he was back in his own bedroom.

CHAPTER SIX

"No!" HE LET OUT an anguished cry. He didn't want to be back in the real world. He wanted to lose himself inside one of his mad dreams, where Rachel still loved him and his future shone with the promise of future happiness. He stumbled toward his bed—his cold, solitary, lonely bed—and saw that the Ghost of Christmas Past had returned.

"Take me back," he pleaded. "Let me go back to Rachel."

The Ghost raised an inquiring eyebrow. "Why are you so anxious to see her again? You were the one who broke off the engagement and ordered her to leave. Why do you want to go back?"

"Because I was happy then." The confession was torn from him. "Because I loved Rachel with all my heart."

"Loving someone doesn't necessarily bring happiness. In fact, love often hurts. You know that."

"Even hurting is better than not being able to feel anything at all." Charles couldn't believe he'd said something so crazy. Then he remembered that he was mad, and therefore extremely likely to say crazy things. But there was a little part of him pushing the rebellious thought that what he'd said was true. It would be better to hurt again than to live out the rest of his life in this terrible state of nonfeeling.

"You don't sound happy." The Ghost leaned on his crook, looking puzzled. "What have you got to be miserable about, Charles? You live alone and do exactly what you want to do, at the moment you want to do it. You accept no responsibility for the welfare of other people, so you are untroubled by the cares of the world. Perhaps you're feeling sentimental because you've just relived the night you asked Rachel to be your wife? Consider rationally—was that really such a great time in your life? These days you have money beyond anything you ever dreamed of. Your career is a brilliant success. In your father's day, Brentwood Industries was a small, family business. Now it's one of the biggest and most important plumbing supply companies in the entire United States. You've done that, Charles. You've caused that spectacular growth in profitability, and it's quite an achievement."

"The success of Brentwood Industries is worth nothing in comparison to losing Rachel and everything else that made my life worthwhile." Charles wasn't sure if he spoke out loud or merely thought the terrible, depressing truth. "Take me back," he pleaded again. "Let me go back to Rachel."

The Ghost stood up. "I can send you back," he said and rapped his bishop's crook on the ground. "But which point of time you end up in is out of my control. Your own heart dictates the destination."

"Just send me there," Charles said, impatient to be gone from his chilly bedroom and into the warmth of Rachel's apartment. He slipped off the end of the bed, and reached out imploringly to the Ghost, but it was Rachel who took his hand.

She caught up with him, out of breath because she'd been running, her cheeks glowing from the nip of the February wind, and her hair ready to spill out at any moment from the heavy tortoiseshell clasp that kept it somewhat haphazardly contained. Charles never tired of the magnificence of her hair, and his fingers itched to twist the little latch and set her hair tumbling around her shoulders.

She slipped her hand through his arm and matched her stride to his. "What happened at the interview? Did you get the job?"

Charles grinned. "I got the job, and they want me to move to Atlantic City by the first of March—"

Rachel high-fived him, then flung her arms around his neck in an exuberant hug. "That's terrific! But I already knew they'd love your portfolio because it's totally awesome. That means we can get married—"

"As soon as you set the date." Charles laughed, still having a hard time believing that he'd been accepted as an account executive at the agency that handled advertising for two of the biggest casinos in Atlantic City. "They said they loved my ideas. That they were fresh and innovative and showed exceptional creative talent." For once his words flowed freely, tumbling over each other as he reported the incredible things the interview committee had said as they reviewed his portfolio, seemingly more impressed with each page they examined.

"I'm so happy for you." Rachel squeezed his arm. "Now maybe you'll be able to put aside all those terrible lies about your lack of creativity that your mother drummed into you for years." She drew in an audible breath. "You know she only said that stuff because she was terrified you'd branch out on your own, don't you? She knew you were Brentwood Industries' last, best hope."

Charles still couldn't quite accept that his mother would be that cruel. "I expect she just honestly misjudged my abilities. After all, the art teacher when I was in high school flat out told me I didn't have what it takes, so my mother was in good company."

"Yeah, she sure was. Your mom and the art teacher, working in perfect, two-part harmony."

"What do you mean, Rach? I'm hearing the sarcasm, but I'm not getting the message."

She hesitated for a moment, then shrugged. "Charles, no honest art teacher with eyes in his head could possibly say that you have no talent—your creativity bursts out of everything you do. It's not just what you draw, it's apparent in all the design work you do for Brentwood Industries, and even little things like decorating the Christmas tree. We had the best-decorated tree in the state of New Jersey last year! You just instinctively knew what colors to mix, and how to make everything perfectly balanced."

"But why would my high-school art teacher lie about my abilities? What reason could he have?"

"Because he was jealous of your talent? Because your mother bribed him to lie? Because your mother was having an affair with him?" Rachel gave an impatient shake of her head. "I don't know exactly why, Charles, but I know he wasn't telling the truth—and everything that happened at your job interview this morning proves I'm right."

Rachel had shone a brilliant light in a dark corner and Charles was stunned by the new perspective that light provided. When he looked back, he could see now that the signs of an affair between his mother and the art teacher had all been there. As a high-school kid, he'd simply been too naive—too trusting—to interpret them.

He drew in a deep, angry breath, furious on behalf of the shy, confused teen that he'd been, and sad for the years spent getting a degree in engineering that he didn't want, when he could have been doing something he loved so much more.

He put his arm around Rachel's waist, drawing strength from the feel of her leaning against his body.

"If you're right about my mother being so manipulative, at least I can feel less guilty about leaving Brentwood Industries in the lurch to take this new job."

"You shouldn't feel in the least guilty, Charles. From what you've told me, your father has an entire team of managers who've spent the past eighteen months ignoring every suggestion you make. Leave them to do things their way and discover for themselves how invaluable you are. Ever since we first met, I've watched you run in circles, trying to plug the gaps and keep the roof from falling in because your father and his management team have their heads buried six feet deep in the sands of wishful thinking."

"Jacob Marley listens to me. He likes my suggestions, but even with Jacob's support, my dad won't consider most of them." He knew that his father was feeling tired and old, with climbing blood pressure and arthritis that left him fighting pain on a daily basis. Still, that wasn't an excuse for sticking blindly to the methods that had worked thirty years ago. Surely that was a reason for his father to listen to somebody who had plenty of energy and fresh ideas about how to reinvigorate the company.

Rachel spoke, echoing his thoughts. "Until your father is willing to take a stand against the old-line management, there's nothing you can do except leave them to fight it out among themselves. It's not your fight, Charles, because they've deliberately shut you out. That means you're not responsible even if Brentwood Industries goes under after you leave. Besides, you're entitled to lead your own life. You have no obligation to spend the next twenty years rescuing your parents from their mistakes."

Charles wasn't entirely convinced of that, but he was almost too happy to have room for worrying about his parents. The creative director at one of the country's most prestigious ad agencies had called him "seriously talented," and Charles was floating high in the stratosphere, supported by clouds of euphoria.

"Race you back to the apartment," he said, tugging on Rachel's hand. "Come on, slowpoke. We need to pick a date for our wedding!"

They arrived at the apartment panting and puffing. "Jeez, I must be out of shape," Charles complained. "I need to haul out the treadmill and put in some serious time."

"It was the cold catching your breath. I can still feel some pretty good abs in there." Rachel gave a light punch to his ribs, then tossed her scarf onto the sofa. "Oops, there's the phone. I'd better get it. Mitch said something about maybe needing to call me in to work tonight." She picked up the phone. "Hello."

As she listened, her expression became first puzzled, then alarmed and finally ravaged by grief. All she said was, "I'm so sorry. I'm so, so sorry. Yes, I'll get him for you." Then she held out the phone to Charles, her eyes brimming with tears. The color had drained from her cheeks, he noticed, leaving her complexion a sickly yellow.

"It's your dad, Charles." She drew in a shuddering breath. "He needs to speak to you. There's been an…accident on the set where your sister is filming."

"But Lizzie is okay, right?"

Rachel didn't answer and Charles snatched the phone. "Dad? What happened? Rachel says there's been an accident on the set—"

"Charlie-boy, I have terrible news." His father's voice broke and when he finally managed to speak again it quavered like a man in his nineties. "They just called us now from the hospital in Nairobi. Part of the set collapsed and Lizzie…Lizzie was hit by a falling beam. She's dead, Charles. Your sister is dead."

"No, she can't be." Charles spoke feverishly. "They've made a mistake. They must have made a mistake. I just got a letter from her yesterday!" A few minutes ago he'd been happier than at almost any other moment in his life. It wasn't possible that Lizzie could already have been dead when he was so happy. He and his sister had been best friends; he would surely have felt some deep foreboding if Lizzie were really gone forever from this world.

"I'm sorry, Charles. There's no mistake. Your sister is dead. They've made arrangements… They're flying her body home tomorrow."

"No!" The cry of anguish ripped from his throat, but when he turned to Rachel in a desperate search for comfort, she was gone, and Charles was alone in his bedroom once again. Alone, that is, except for his stupid delusional image of the Ghost of Christmas Past.

Saint Nicholas walked out from the dark corner of the room where he had been lurking. "Why did you send me back to that terrible time?" Charles demanded, his voice thick with rage and bitterness. "How could you have been so cruel? If you're the spirit of Christmas, aren't you supposed to bring people joy?"

"I told you I'm not in control of which visions you enter. Besides, I can't bring joy, as if it were a package to be handed over," Saint Nicholas said quietly. "I can only show you how to find it for yourself. The fact that you relived your sister's death tells me that before you can be happy again, Charles, you need to heal the wounds that the acid of regret has etched into your soul."

"Then bring back my sister," Charles said. "Bring her back to life and I'll have no regrets."

"You know I lack the power to rewrite the past, much less return a soul to earth when it's moved on to the next plane of existence. But your sister lives in your memories. You saw for yourself how vivid those memories are, and how happy until the very end. You had a great relationship with Lizzie. You cared about each other, you made each other laugh, you tolerated each other's little human flaws. You loved each other. There are millions of people who stand around at a funeral and wish they could look back on their dealings with the person who's just died with as much innocent pleasure as you can look back on your relationship with your sister."

"I want her here. I want her to be part of my life *today*."

"Since you know you can't have that, why don't you try allowing yourself to remember all that was good? In the long run, trust me, that's a lot less hurtful than trying to blank your mind of every image of Lizzie so that you can pretend she never existed."

"I can't bear to remember her—I just can't do that," Charles protested, rubbing his hand across his eyes.

He felt a momentary disconnect and then he realized that the person taking his hand and gently lifting it away from his face was Rachel.

"Why can't you do that?" she asked. "Charles, look at me. Speak to me. I'm sorry your sister died. I'm sorry that we've just buried your dad. It's tragic that you lost them both within two weeks of each other. But that isn't a reason to throw away your future. You have a job waiting for you at the ad agency. We have a marriage to arrange and a life to start building together, here in Atlantic City. How can you even consider going back to Trenton to live with your mother?"

"She has no money. If I don't pull Brentwood Industries out of the ditch and get it on a successful footing, she'll have no income—"

"Is that the garbage she's feeding you now, Charles? Because it is garbage, and at some level you know that. I heard the terms of your father's will, remember? She owns a house free and clear, with no mortgage, that's valued in the top ten percent of real estate in Trenton. Your father had a life insurance policy that's going to pay her fifteen thousand dollars a year for the rest of her life. On top of that, she's not even fifty years old! She could get a job, for heaven's sake!"

"She's never worked—"

"Then now would be a great time to start."

"I never realized you could be so harsh, Rach."

"And I never realized you could be so easily manipulated! Your mother is using you, Charles. You have too much of a conscience and she has way too little. You're not obligated to put your life—our lives—on hold because your mother is selfish. She'll never set you free, so if you want a life other than endlessly meeting her demands, you'll have to grab it with both hands."

"I will break free, Rach—after I get Brentwood Industries on its feet. I promise."

Rachel looked at him, her brown eyes dark with tears. "And who is going to decide when the company is—quote—on its feet? Your mother?"

His sense of loss was so profound that Charles could scarcely tell where one hurt ended and another began. "I can't abandon my mother—"

"I'm not asking you to abandon her. Atlantic City

is seventy miles from where she lives. You can visit her every week. She can visit us every week, if she'd prefer." Rachel put her hands on his arms, her expression despairing. "Charles, I love you. Give us the chance to make a life together. Don't throw away everything that we've built together."

"I won't. Of course I won't." He wanted to kiss her, to take her to bed and find solace in the power of their lovemaking, but somehow it seemed almost indecent to take pleasure in human contact when his sister and father were lying next to each other in graves so new they had no headstones. "Just give me time, Rach. Okay?"

"Okay." She tried to smile, but the tears overflowed and she grabbed a tissue, turning away and scrubbing fiercely at her eyes.

Her tears were like drops of acid scalding his soul. Charles longed to reassure her that everything would be all right, but in his heart of hearts he knew that nothing could be all right in a world where he'd lost his sister and his father within two weeks of each other, and his wonderful new job had to be sacrificed on the altar of his mother's financial security. The world wasn't a place designed for happiness, he realized, and he'd been a naive fool to believe that his love for Rachel provided the magic bullet that would carry him through life unscarred by the malevolence of fate.

Rachel dried her tears and wrapped her hands

around his, forming a protective cone. "Charles, don't shut your grief inside. You don't have to play macho man, especially with me. It's okay to cry for your dad, and for Liz, too. They were wonderful people. Of course you're sad."

He couldn't cry because the place inside him that produced tears seemed to have dried up, leaving behind nothing except a thin trickle of desert dust. He felt brittle, insubstantial, as if only an outer shell remained, wrapped around a core hollowed out by grief.

He searched for words to explain how he felt, but when he looked down to see if he could make Rachel understand, she wasn't there, and his hands were held out in front of him, in a pleading gesture that was made not to Rachel, but to his mother.

He was at the airport in Pittsburgh with Annelise, he realized, waiting in the first-class lounge for her to board her flight to London.

"You can always come back if you don't enjoy life in London as much as you expect." Charles sat down across from his mother, but she wasn't looking at him and his movement didn't attract her attention. Her gaze darted impatiently from one to the other of the occupants of the lounge.

"You have to wonder how half the people in here managed to afford the first-class fare," Annelise said. "They're not exactly a prepossessing bunch, that's for sure. Look at that woman by the window. She must be at least forty pounds overweight and there's a run in her stocking. I hope she won't be sitting next to me." She took another sip of Scotch and crossed one slender, elegantly shod foot over the other, examining her own trim ankle with visible satisfaction.

"There will always be a room in the house for you, Mom." Charles spoke doggedly, not convinced that his mother would find contentment in London, despite the optimism with which she'd made all the arrangements. She seemed to feel that a circle of distant cousins and Dickens aficionados were only waiting for her plane to land in order to welcome her into their literary bosom with cries of joy and pleasure. He wasn't so sure.

Annelise gave an airy wave of her hand. "If you marry that wretched little Rachel person I'm quite sure she'll see to it that I'm never invited into your home. I suppose, since I'm leaving, I may as well speak my mind and here it is—can't you do better than Rachel? She's an immigrant, for goodness sake, not even a real American, much less a woman who lives up to the prestige of your heritage. You're a descendant of the immortal Charles Dickens! That's something worth boasting about."

"Mom, Charles Dickens died over a hundred and thirty years ago! And I'm incredibly lucky that an amazing woman like Rachel is willing to marry me."

Annelise raised a supercilious eyebrow. "Her parents come from Pakistan, for God's sake. I guess we should be grateful she's not a Muslim."

Charles was stung by his mother's words. "Rachel is a warm, loving person with an extremely interesting cultural heritage. As it happens, she was born here, so she's as American as you are. But so what if she were an immigrant? Your great-great-grandparents were immigrants. Dad's parents were immigrants after World War II. Does that make Dad less of an American?"

"My ancestor who came here was Charles Dickens's own son! Even your father's parents came from England. That's entirely different."

How was it different? Charles wondered. What in the world did it matter which country you came from as long as you led an upright, honorable life once you arrived here? "Rachel's parents are fascinating people with brilliant minds and successful careers. As for not welcoming you into our home after we're married, of course she'll welcome you—"

"It's irrelevant anyway, because I don't plan to come back, ever." Annelise set her glass on the table with a vicious thump. "I endured almost thirty years of living in Trenton while I was married to your father and, trust me, that was twenty-nine-and-a-half years too many. I kept telling him we needed to move but he wouldn't listen. But then, he never did listen to me. Beneath that quiet exterior, your father was a stubborn, opinionated man."

The mystery, Charles thought, was why Annelise had remained married to him. When his mother spoke again, it was as if she was answering her son's unasked question.

"At least when we were first married, your father made a respectable income and provided a comfortable living for us all. These past eight or nine years, he wasn't even doing that. Now it's your turn to pick up the slack, Charles, and I hope you remember just how much you owe me."

"Brentwood Industries has always operated in the black—"

"And make sure you keep it that way." Annelise yawned. "I've given you the house, Charles, which was extraordinarily generous of me. In exchange, I expect you to provide me with enough income to support the lifestyle I deserve. I've earned my retirement after sticking with your father through thirty years of unspeakably boring marriage. Keep Brentwood Industries running at a profit, that's all I ask. You're only dealing with plumbing fixtures, for God's sake, so that shouldn't be too difficult, even for you."

"I'll do my best—"

"Listen to Jacob Marley. He's the only smart man in the place. Get rid of all the old managers, move production overseas, and vamp up the product line. That way, the company can become a money-making machine." She gave a tiny shrug. "At least redesigning the product line should be right up your alley."

"Why would you trust me to redesign our products? According to you, I have no creative talent."

"Oh, for God's sake, Charles, buy a clue."

"What does that mean? Are you suggesting I have more artistic talent than you were willing to admit when I was in high school? That maybe you had no right to pressure me to attend engineering school?"

"That was the Scotch talking. Forget I said anything. Besides, your choice of career is water under the bridge, however you came to it. Now that Bob is dead, you have no choice other than to run Brentwood Industries. Unless you want to see everything your father spent his entire life working for swept away in bankruptcy court. Is that what Rachel is persuading you to do?"

"Leave Rachel out of this. I've promised you that I'll return the business to profitability before I quit—"

"Don't forget your promise, that's all I expect from you." The flight to London was announced and Annelise rose to her feet, looking unusually flustered. "There's no need to wait any longer, Charles." The effort to show affection seemed to strain her resources to the limit, but she grudgingly turned her cheek so that he could kiss her. "Thank you for driving me here today and for waiting with me to say goodbye. You're softhearted, Charles, but you mean well. If you toughen up, you might become a more than adequate president for Brentwood Industries."

"You know that isn't where my ambitions lie long-term, don't you?"

"I know when I hear Rachel talking through you.

Don't let that woman delude you into thinking you can be more than a plumber, Charles. You're your father's own son, all right."

"In my book, that's a pretty good thing to be."

Annelise sighed, turning away for a moment, and when she looked at him again he saw sadness and anger fighting for dominance in her expression. "I loved Elizabeth," she said. "Your sister took after me in the way she looked and in her amazing singing voice. She inherited her musical abilities directly from me. You're the one who took after your father."

"Is that so bad? Dad was a good man."

Annelise sighed. "It wouldn't be so bad if only Elizabeth had lived."

Charles drew in a sharp, painful breath. "I miss my sister every day, Mom. Nobody could wish she was alive more than I do."

His mother made a small, anguished sound, quickly silenced. "You don't know what you're talking about, Charles. You've no idea what torment it is for a mother to lose a beautiful, talented child and be left with…"

Annelise's voice tailed off. Then her gaze hardened and she looked at Charles with an emotion that seemed frighteningly close to hatred. "It's a cruel world, Charles, and it's time you recognized that. The truth is, when I look at you, all I can think of is that you're alive, and my talented, gorgeous daughter is dead. There, I've said it. It needed to be said." She didn't wait for him to respond, just swung on her heel and disappeared down the Jetway into the plane.

Charles stared after his mother, not quite able to absorb the fact that his own mother had told him that she couldn't bear to look at him. The shocking cruelty of her comment didn't seem to have left him especially upset, and he wondered why not. And then he realized to his great relief that some time during the past few weeks he'd lost the capacity to feel. Battered by too many disappointments and too much sorrow, his emotional register had ceased to function.

He could only be grateful for the reprieve. He hoped the numbness would last for a long, long time, preferably forever. Because if he ever did find himself feeling again, he was afraid the pain might kill him.

CHAPTER SEVEN

IT WAS A HUGE RELIEF FOR Charles to open his eyes and discover that he was once more tucked safely in his own bed. A little while ago, he'd begged the specter of Saint Nicholas to send him back into the past. Now that he'd made the trip, he remembered exactly why he had spent the past decade determined to avoid excursions down the bramble-strewn paths of Memory Lane. He'd worked so hard to forget the brutal cruelty of his mother's words at the airport. Now they were like fresh wounds, gushing blood and pulsing with pain.

Shivering, he pulled the covers up to his chin and slid down in the bed. Next time he smelled evergreen or cinnamon he would ignore it. Saint Nicholas…the Ghost of Christmas Past…or whatever he was calling himself…had nothing more to show him that he wanted to see.

Despite his resolution to forget, Charles found it hard to put what he'd just experienced out of his mind, and even harder to convince himself that it had never really happened. With a few carefully selected visions, the Ghost of Christmas Past—or his own troubled psyche?—had forced him to face the unpleasant reality of his past mistakes. For the first time, Charles accepted that the true disasters in his life had been of his own making. He'd lacked the power to prevent his sister's death or his father's. He couldn't even prevent his mother from being a cruel, self-absorbed woman. But he could certainly have reacted differently to those tragedies. Above all, instead of retreating deep into himself, where Rachel couldn't reach him, he could have turned outward and shared her strength as they rebuilt their lives. At some level, he had always known Rachel would stand by him through thick and thin. When their relationship ended, it was because he had pushed her away; otherwise she would never have left him.

The Ghost of Christmas Past had brought him to the point of recognizing where he'd gone wrong and the terrible errors in judgment he'd made, but Charles wasn't grateful for the gift. Surely it would have been better to remain in ignorance of his own stupidity? How had he let Rachel slip through his grasp while continuing in his frantic, fruitless attempts to please his mother? Why had he sought so desperately for Annelise's good opinion when she not only deserved nothing from him, but didn't want anything from him except money? In retrospect, that was a mystery beyond comprehension. It was crystal clear to

Charles that if he had to make the same decisions again today he would choose very differently. Sadly, life didn't provide the chance to retake the test. What was past couldn't be changed, as Saint Nicholas himself had acknowledged.

Charles resolved to forget about his ghostly visitors. There was no point in tormenting himself about decisions that could never be changed and losses that could never be reversed, so it was best if he put tonight's visions behind him and tried to climb out of the madness that had temporarily seized hold of him.

He closed his eyes, determined to sleep without dreams for the rest of the night. Sleep, however, proved elusive and he was wide awake when the grandfather clock in the hall struck two. Charles was astonished that the night was still so young, relatively speaking. Was it possible that he'd experienced so much and only an hour had elapsed?

"Time is an elastic concept," Santa Claus said, adjusting his position on the edge of Charles's bed. "You know that, my boy. An hour waiting on the airport runway for your flight to take off isn't the same as an hour spent walking on the beach with the woman you love."

Charles bolted upright in bed and stared at the corpulent, ruddy-cheeked visitor who was now comfortably ensconced six inches from his feet. "Who are you?" he demanded, putting out his hand to ward off the vision. As soon as he'd spoken, he regretted the question. "No, don't tell me! I don't want to know. Go away! I don't want any more ghostly insights into my past mistakes."

The specter—a fat and jolly Santa Claus with a snow-white beard and twinkling blue eyes—looked disappointed at his dismissal. "Well, if you don't want me, I have to go. That's a pity. I had some interesting stuff to show you." He started to fade, his scarlet suit and shiny black boots losing color until they were semitransparent pinks and grays.

"Stop! Stay here, Santa! I've changed my mind!" Painful as it was to review the past, Charles discovered he wasn't quite ready to clamp down on his mad fantasies. For the past decade he'd been content to live in a cocoon of miserable isolation, questioning nothing and feeling nothing. Now his feelings had woken up with a vengeance and his curiosity pricked at him, along with all the other newly awakened nerve endings. Much as the cowardly part of him wanted to send this Santa Claus specter away, a braver part suspected that he would discover important truths about himself if he could only bear to subject himself to whatever visions waited to confront him.

He gulped, stomach churning, but forced himself to set the process of self-discovery in motion. "First, tell me who you are," he said. "Are you really Santa Claus?"

"No, indeed I am not. There is no Santa Claus,

you know, he's just a myth, albeit a powerful one. I, however, am very real. I am the Ghost of Christmas Present."

Charles gave a little snort of laughter, his fear replaced by wry humor. "Ah, I see we're still in the *Christmas Carol* groove. God bless dear old many times Great-Grandpa and his corny novel."

"I wouldn't call it corny." Santa Claus sounded huffy. "I consider it a fine tale. One of my personal favorites, I have to admit."

"Sure it is. And let me guess, you don't really look like Tim Allen, hot off the set for *The Santa Clause IV.* You came to me without any specific form, and the scarlet pants and fluffy white beard are all in my imagination, right?"

"Right." Santa Claus gave a ho-ho-ho kind of a chuckle. "You're learning, my boy, you're learning. Well, come along, take my hand. We have a lot to get through in the next hour."

"Where are we going?" Charles asked.

"To visit some acquaintances of yours, so that we can see how they'll be celebrating Christmas this year."

Thank goodness they weren't going to be taking another trip back into the horrors of his past. Charles extended his hand, wondering how it would feel to touch a ghost. It felt like nothing, he discovered. There was the slightest sensation of airy warmth around his wrist, followed by a sharp tug. The next thing he knew he was sitting in the crowded family room of a house he was quite sure he'd never seen before. A table had been set up in the center of the room and covered in a cheap white plastic cloth with holly leaves printed in bands down the sides. In the center of the plastic cloth, childish handmade ornaments had been arranged as a centerpiece, circled by oranges and little plastic bowls of nuts.

The eight mismatched chairs crowded around the table were occupied by a middle-aged man, three children and one wrinkled, toothless old woman wrapped in a black shawl. All five of them were laughing and talking more or less at once. Three of the chairs were empty, but Charles could smell turkey roasting and he could hear pots clanging in the kitchen. He supposed the three missing people were putting the final touches to Christmas dinner.

"Where are we?" he whispered.

"No need to whisper," Santa Claus said. "They can't see us or hear us. And we're in the home of the Alvarez family."

"You mean Gloria's family? My assistant?"

"Yes. At the table you see her father and her grandmother, and those three children are her sister and two brothers. Gloria is the eldest and Timoteo—the little boy seated next to his grandmother—is the youngest. Grandma happens to have been born on Christmas Eve, so she's just celebrated her sixtieth birthday."

"Her *sixtieth* birthday?" Charles exclaimed.

Good grief, the poor woman looked every day of eighty—and more.

Santa Claus shrugged. "She worked in the fields for forty-five years as a migrant farm laborer. She started when she was fifteen and ended last year, when her arthritis became almost crippling."

At that moment, Gloria walked into the family room, carrying a tray piled with steaming serving dishes. "We're in luck today, people! Mama's tamalitos are the best ever!"

"And I expect you've been tasting them just to be sure," her father said, chuckling.

"You're right!" Gloria set the platter down on the table and pointed back toward the kitchen. "Get ready for our feast. Here comes Mama."

An older woman carried in a golden-brown turkey, surrounded by cornbread stuffing. The aroma was heavenly and Charles felt his stomach rumble in hungry anticipation.

"Maria Alvarez is a great cook," Santa Claus informed him. "Gloria is getting to be pretty good, too. It's amazing how tasty you can make tortillas and a bit of ground beef if you have the knack. The Alvarez family can't afford to eat this way every day, that's for sure."

"Turkey isn't expensive," Charles protested.

Santa Claus looked at him. "No, it isn't, is it? You'd think with Gloria and her parents working so hard they'd be living comfortably. You'd certainly expect them to be able to afford roast turkey and a few tamales whenever the fancy struck them."

"Why can't they?"

"Well, partly because Gloria is underpaid—"

"I pay more than the minimum wage," Charles snapped.

"Yes, you're right. You do. You pay enough that Gloria makes a couple of hundred bucks a year above the poverty level for one person. She deserves a lot more, and you know it."

"She can find another job if she doesn't like my—" Charles bit off the tired excuse. "She deserves a raise, doesn't she?"

"Of course, and I'm glad you recognize that, my boy. Are you going to do something about it when she comes back to work tomorrow?"

"Yes." Charles was astonished that he'd taken so long to do something so right and necessary. "Yes, I'll give her a raise." He found himself smiling, and there was an odd stirring sensation in the pit of his stomach, as if something long-forgotten was waking to new life.

"If both her parents are working, as well, why is money so short?" he asked.

"They're working as hard and as long as they can. Unfortunately, they don't have their green cards, so they're here illegally. That means they routinely get paid less than they would if they were part of the legal workforce, and of course they get no benefits.

Gloria's mother is one of the cleaning crew at the local motel, but the owner often underpays her and she really has no recourse if she comes home and finds her wage packet has been shorted. Who's she going to complain to? Not the police, that's for sure. Not even her boss at the motel. If she loses her job, there's no guarantee the next one would be any better, and she'd be sacrificing the bit of seniority and security she's managed to establish."

"What about Gloria's father?"

"He works as a day laborer. He's a skilled carpenter, and he's learned a lot of English over the years, but the truth is he can barely read in Spanish, let alone in English. At this time of year, with construction jobs scarce, it's even more difficult for him to pick up work. Gloria pays her own way, of course, but there are three other children and grandma to support. The old lady has no pension, no income of any sort, so that's a heavy outlay."

"They should have stayed in Mexico," Charles said, but this time it wasn't an angry comment. He just wanted to find some way to explain why life was so hard for the Alvarez family. "If they'd stayed in Mexico, they could have worked legally."

"I agree it would be great if they could all have stayed in Mexico. Unfortunately, they were born in Guerrero, one of the poorest regions of the country. The plots of land are so small farmers can't feed their families and there's no other work there except for a very fortunate few. Official government statistics claim there's less than six percent unemployment in Mexico, but the true estimate is that half the men in a state like Guerrero can't find enough work to support their families. In those circumstances, it's not much of a surprise if they choose to come north. Besides, in the case of the Alvarez family, the grandfather died and his widow—the old lady you see here—was kicked off the little plot of land that had previously sustained them—"

Santa Claus broke off. "Listen, there's someone knocking at the door. Do you see how scared they all look? They think it might be someone from Immigration."

"It can't be Immigration, not on Christmas Day," Gloria said. "It must be Tia Marisa." Everybody laughed and relaxed, agreeing that it must indeed be their aunt, Marisa.

"I'll let her in." One of the children at the table, a girl of about thirteen, jumped up and ran out into the hallway. She came back hanging on to the arm of a good-looking woman in her midforties. A chorus of welcome greeted the newcomer, along with many wishes for a merry Christmas.

"Stay and eat with us, Marisa." Gloria's mother pointed to the empty chair. "You see, we set a place for you. We were hoping you would find the time to stop by."

"I can't stay. I only have three hours before my

shift at the hospital, and I want to drive over to see Jorge and his family before that." She smiled and walked around the table until she reached the smallest child, the one Santa Claus had identified as Timoteo. He was a thin boy, probably no more than seven years old, with a thatch of thick, dead-straight black hair. Marisa rumpled his hair with evident affection.

"How are you, Teo? Have you been keeping well? I couldn't let Christmas Day pass without coming to give a hug and a kiss to my favorite seven-year-old nephew."

"I'm great. Gloria says I'm getting new muscles every day." Teo made a fist and flexed his biceps. Then he pointed to his thin arm, where he apparently could see a muscle that was certainly invisible to Charles.

"Why is he so skinny and pale?" Charles asked Santa Claus. "The other kids all look healthy, but he looks as if nobody ever feeds him!"

"The Alvarez family takes wonderful care of him and he's loved a lot. But he has Type I diabetes, the most serious sort. He needs insulin to stay alive and the cost of his drugs and the syringes are a constant drain on the family income."

"Why don't they get the drugs through Medicaid? Timoteo's entitled to enroll if he was born here."

"Yes, he's entitled, but the family is afraid to bring themselves to the attention of the authorities in any way. Gloria has tried to persuade them to claim benefits for her brother, but so far her parents are too scared to risk filling out all the forms. Fortunately for them, Marisa is a nurse, so she helps monitor Teo's health. Sometimes she gets him an appointment with a sympathetic doctor who slips them a supply of needles and a few free doses of medication. It all helps, but not enough."

Charles frowned. He watched as Marisa pretended to squeeze her nephew's muscles, and then bent down and enveloped him in a giant hug. "My goodness! I think you've been working out, Teo. Soon you'll be running marathons. What else have you been up to since last week?"

He laughed. "Lots of mischief, Tia Marisa. But I've been good about my diet, I promise. Santa Claus knows I've been good. He brought me thirty-six colored pencils for my drawing. Thirty-six! And he brought a jigsaw puzzle and a book about famous artists of the world, too. There are so many different colors in my new pencils, Tia, I'll be able to draw you a great picture."

"Thank you. I'm sure I'll love it. And since you've been so good, if you look inside this bag, you might find a present that goes very well with those colored pencils."

"For me? Another present?" Eyes shining with anticipation, Timoteo opened the bright red plastic bag and drew out an artist's sketch pad. He squealed with delight and hugged his aunt, pouring out thanks. Marisa smiled, obviously pleased with the success of her gift, and moved on to hand out her remaining gifts, ending up with a pale blue sweater for Gloria.

Charles watched his assistant as she instantly put on the sweater and fastened the buttons. "Ta-da!" Gloria twirled, twisting her wrists to display the little bands of glitter around the sleeves. "Marisa, it's perfect. Thank you so much." She hugged her aunt, and Charles could see that there were tears of gratitude in her eyes.

"That sweater is the only gift Gloria will receive this holiday season," Santa Claus told him. "There's no money for the Alvarez family to provide gifts for the adults. You might expect Gloria to receive gifts from friends or even from her coworkers, but she moves in a circle where nobody has money to spare. In many offices the employees arrange for a party and give each other small gifts. At Brentwood Industries, of course, there's no office party and the employees have no money to spare for exchanging gifts, however small. Their salaries are too meager to stretch that far."

For a couple of thousand tax-deductible dollars he could have arranged a party for all twelve office employees and their families, Charles thought. He could have provided a giant baked ham with all the holiday trimmings, along with chocolate brownies and ice cream and hot cider and a really fancy Christmas tree ornament for each child to take home and hang on the tree. He would really have enjoyed watching the kids' faces as they opened their gift boxes and saw a sparkling golden angel, an overstuffed Santa Claus or perhaps a fluffy white snowman with a cheerful striped scarf. Such a party wouldn't have put even a small dent in the profits of the firm, and it would have meant a lot to people living close to the financial edge. He could even have added a five-hundred-dollar holiday bonus for each employee, which would have been barely a hiccup in the year's accounts.

"Just because you messed up at Christmas, there's no reason why you can't give your employees a New Year's bonus," Santa Claus said. "Trust me, they'd all appreciate it."

Charles turned to look at him. "How can you read my thoughts?"

"It's a little bit of Christmas magic," Santa replied.

"Yeah, either that or I'm just imagining you."

"Of course you're not imagining me." Santa sounded irritated. "Until I brought you here, you had no idea that Gloria had a brother with diabetes or an aunt who is a nurse, much less a grandma who worked in the fields. How could you produce such detailed visions of a family you know almost nothing about?"

It sounded reasonable, but Charles suddenly remembered that he'd once overheard Gloria talking to the office accountant. At the time he'd paid no real attention, but now he seemed to recall that his assistant *had* mentioned her little brother's poor health and the struggle her family was having to find the money to pay for his insulin shots. Perhaps his subconscious had raked up long-buried information and was now presenting it in this vivid form so that he would be compelled to deal with it.

"Even if your subconscious holds a few scraps of memory about Gloria's family, it doesn't know a thing about Rachel," Santa Claus said.

"What's Rachel got to do with this? You're supposedly the Ghost of Christmas Present and Rachel is in my past—"

The rest of what Charles had planned to say was snatched away by the rush of wind that wrapped around him, blowing him out of the Alvarez home and into a long, dark tunnel. When the sensation of being hurtled through a tunnel ended and he could finally catch his breath, he found himself inside the Princeton home of the Chandahrs, Rachel's parents. He and Santa Claus were seated in a pair of armchairs placed next to a lacquered game table, where chess pieces were positioned in the middle of a game.

The Chandahrs were seated together on the sofa on one side of the fireplace, while Rachel was seated opposite them, playing her guitar. Two young children, a boy and a girl, sat at Rachel's feet. The little girl's head rested against Rachel's knees. The boy was more aloof, his arms clasped tightly around his knees, but he was listening intently, his whole body seeming to soak up the music.

Charles wanted to ask about the children, but

Rachel was singing "O Holy Night," and her voice was so beautiful he couldn't speak. Rachel had played this for him the night he'd asked her to marry him. That night, as she sang and plucked the strings of the guitar, the light had struck fire from the depths of her topaz engagement ring. Charles had thought then that life couldn't possibly be happier than at that moment. Tonight, looking back, he realized he'd been right. That night had represented a pinnacle of joy for him.

He also realized that despite the two children seated at her feet, Rachel's hands were bare of rings. He wasn't sure why that produced a crazy surge of hope. After so many years, he wasn't arrogant enough to believe that Rachel would still care for him. He'd be lucky if she remembered his name except as an annoying, youthful mistake, Charles reflected wryly.

Rachel finished the song; her parents applauded briefly and the children joined in. "That was just lovely, sweetheart. Thank you." Her father stood up. "I'm going to make a pot of tea. Anyone care to join me?"

"Me, please," Rachel said, setting her guitar back in its case. She bent down and tilted the chins of both children upward, so that she could look straight into their eyes. "Do you want some of Grandpa Amal's special tea?"

"Is he going to make chai?" the boy asked.

"Yes." Rachel smiled. "How clever of you to remember the name, Kevin."

"It's sweet," he said. "I like it." He turned to Rachel's father and gave him a shy, tentative smile. "Would you like me to help?"

Mr. Chandahr gave a friendly nod. "I can always use an extra pair of hands. Thanks, Kevin." He turned to the little girl. "What about you, honey?"

The little girl looked worried. "I didn't never have chai before."

"No," Rachel agreed. "You never did. But Kevin likes it, so you'll probably like it, too."

The little girl's face lost its worried look and she smiled. "Yes, I 'spect so." She turned back to Mr. Chandahr. "I want chai." She sounded faintly aggressive, and Charles wondered if she knew the routine of promised treats that never materialized.

"Please, Grandpa Amal, may I have some chai?" Rachel corrected gently. "Let me hear you say it using nice words. Okay, Daisy?"

The girl frowned again and then shrugged, parroting Rachel's words.

"The children don't look alike," Charles commented. "And where's their father? I noticed that Rachel isn't wearing a wedding ring."

"She's never been married," Santa informed him. "She's had a couple of fairly serious relationships. She even lived with a music professor for a couple of years, but the relationship never quite worked out."

"Are the children his?" Charles asked. "The music professor's, I mean."

Santa shook his head. "They're both foster kids. Rachel has been licensed as a foster mom for eight years now. That's partly why her relationship with the musician fell apart. He wasn't into kids, and she wasn't willing to give up being a foster parent. She's taken care of six different children over the past eight years. It's almost impossible to measure how much good she's done, but I can promise you it's a lot. Especially in this state, where foster care has been such a mess."

Charles watched Kevin make his way into the kitchen. "He's limping."

"Yes," Santa acknowledged. "Although he walks a lot better than he used to. Kevin's been living with Rachel for over two years and there's a really special bond between the two of them. She'd like to adopt him, but so far his mother refuses to sign the papers. The Department of Children and Family Services is gradually getting its act together to arrange for a court-ordered termination of the mother's rights, but you wouldn't believe how long these things can take."

"Why would the court terminate his mother's rights? If Kevin's mother wants him back, wouldn't it be better if he was returned to his birth family?"

"Probably not," Santa said drily. "You noticed that Kevin limps. That's because the last time Kevin lived at home, one of his many 'stepfathers' tried to burn off the soles of his feet. He's had skin grafts, but he still can't walk quite right."

"Oh, my God! The poor kid." Charles gulped. "What about the little girl? Did Rachel call her Daisy?"

Santa nodded. "That's right. Daisy's mother loves her a lot and was the best mother she could manage to be. Unfortunately, she had a drug problem so her best wasn't very good for Daisy. She's in prison now, serving three years for selling meth. Three years isn't all that long when you're an adult, I guess, even if you're behind bars. To Daisy, it's half her lifetime. Still, Rachel hopes that eventually Daisy and her mom will be reunited."

"So Rachel knows she'll have to give Daisy up after three years of caring for her?"

"Yes, that's exactly what she'll have to do. As you can imagine, it requires a very strong woman to take a child into her home and offer unconditional love for three years and then turn around and hand the child back to her birth family. Rachel is one of the special and remarkable few."

"Is Rachel happy?" Charles asked. "She looks happy."

"Do you want her to be happy?"

Charles stared at Santa. "What kind of a crazy question is that? Of course I want her to be happy!"

Santa shrugged. "You're not happy," he pointed out. "You're miserable, and you must have heard the saying 'misery loves company.' In my line of work, I find that to be sadly true. Most unhappy people want the rest of the world to be unhappy, too."

"Not me," Charles said. "Rachel deserves to be happy after the lousy way I treated her."

"My, my. You are making some surprising statements tonight, Charles. I thought you blamed her for the breakup of your relationship? I'm quite sure you informed her that if she wasn't so pushy and unreasonable in her demands, you'd eventually get around to marrying her."

He'd used almost those precise words, Charles reflected, his stomach constricting with the sickness of regret. Good lord, what a total and complete *idiot* he'd been. "Since you're so smart, you must know I didn't mean what I said."

Santa Claus nodded. "Yes, I know. Unfortunately, Rachel didn't."

Charles watched Daisy climb onto Rachel's lap and settle down to listen to a story. "She's still the most beautiful woman I've ever seen in my life," he murmured. "She's not just beautiful on the outside, but all the way through. I knew I missed her. I just hadn't allowed myself to remember how much."

"Astonishingly, I believe she misses you, too."

Charles laughed, but wistfully. "Why would she miss me?"

"Believe it or not, once upon a time, you were a fun person to be with. Even more extraordinary, you had a conscience and a burning desire to make the world a better place. You were the person who first mentioned the possibility of becoming a foster parent to Rachel.

You had neighbors who fostered several children while you were growing up, and you saw what a huge difference it made in the lives of those children."

He'd considered becoming a foster parent, Charles thought, because he'd wanted to have the chance to love an unwanted child. Somehow, he'd known when he was younger that showering love on somebody else was the best way he would ever find to make up for the pain of his mother's emotional abuse. He wondered why he'd been so wise when he was young, yet lost his wisdom as he'd piled on the years.

"Say goodbye to Rachel," Santa murmured. "Our time is up, Charles."

"Let me stay with her. I'll just watch—I won't try to talk to her."

Charles discovered he was talking to the air. He was back in his own bed, and the Ghost of Christmas Present was nowhere to be seen.

CHAPTER EIGHT

WHEN THE CLOCK in the hall struck three, Charles resigned himself to the unavoidable. He'd grown up listening to the *Christmas Carol* story and he'd seen at least three different movie versions, so he knew what was coming next. From a logical perspective it was ridiculous—insane—to accept that he was living out the plot line of a novella written by his famous ancestor. But ridiculous or not, insane or not, that seemed to be what was happening.

Bowing to the inevitable, Charles sat up in the bed and waited for his next visitor. Sure enough, a blurring of the darkness at the foot of the bed was followed seconds later by the arrival of a young woman dressed in a dazzling, rainbow-hued gown. Her hair was so fair it was almost transparent and the sparkling edges of her robe kept dissolving into a cloud that drifted and folded back into the darkness.

Charles cut straight to the chase. "Well, hello, nice to see you." He hoped there wasn't too much sarcasm in his greeting. "I assume you're the Ghost of Christmas Yet to Come?"

"Exactly." The specter inclined her head in gracious acknowledgment, wisps of light scattering and floating off into the dark corners of the room as she moved.

"You're a lot better looking than your namesake in the movies," Charles commented. "They usually depict you as the most horrific of all the spirits who come to haunt Mr. Scrooge."

"Well, you can't expect movie producers to get everything right." The Ghost of Christmas Yet to Come gave an airy wave of her hand, leaving a trail of glittering silver vapor. "Besides, you've heard this explanation several times already, from the other ghosts. I came to you without form and you interpret my appearance according to your own inner vision. Other people would see me very differently. Just as a matter of interest, what do you see when you look at me?"

"Nothing very substantial," Charles said. "You're wearing something rainbow colored and glowing, as if light is being broken into its component hues, but your body is so…formless…that each time you move, you seem to shape-shift."

"Hmm…interesting. I expect my form is insubstantial because the future hasn't happened yet. There's always the possibility of change, right up to the last second, but if you see me as shape-shifting and almost transparent, I guess that means your future is even less certain than most people's. And if I were you, I'd count myself as mighty fortunate that you see me clothed in the colors of the rainbow. Personally, I'm not much for metaphors, but I'd have to say that sounds as if your future currently shines with the potential for good things to come."

Charles felt almost cheerful as he heard that bit of good news. Perhaps he was going to break with the tradition of his grandfather's story and not be subjected to terrible images of a bleak, lonely future. "Okay then, Ghost, let's get started. Where are you going to take me?"

"Here," the Ghost said, and Charles saw that he was back once again in the Alvarez family room. He knew instinctively that it was Christmas, but this time there were no homemade decorations or heaping platters of Mrs. Alvarez's *pan dulce* on the table. There was no elderly grandma beaming with toothless pleasure at her family, and no Mr. Alvarez in his chair by the window. There was also no Timoteo, Charles realized with a flash of panic. Where was Teo? What had happened to him? Were these visions of his future to be filled with gloom and doom after all?

Gloria came into the room, a bundle of jackets and scarves clasped in her arms. Charles had never before realized how much life and hope there always was in his assistant's expression until he saw her now, her eyes dark with grief and her cheeks hollowed out from suffering.

"Here, Mama," Gloria said quietly. "It's time for us to leave or it will be dark before we get home."

Mrs. Alvarez rose to her feet. In his previous vision, she had been plump and rosy cheeked, brimming with happiness as she had served her family Christmas dinner. Now she was gaunt and lifeless, every movement a visible effort.

"Come, Elsa. Come, Javier." She tried to inject a note of encouragement into her voice as she spoke to the children. "Put on your jackets. It's time for us to go to the cemetery."

"Who is dead?" Charles asked with deep foreboding. "Is it Grandma?"

"Yes, Grandma is dead," the Ghost informed him. "She just seemed to give up hope and in a couple of months, she was gone."

"And…Timoteo?"

"Yes, he's dead, too."

Charles sucked in a horrified breath, although it was exactly what he'd dreaded hearing. "How did that happen? This is the twenty-first century, for heaven's sake. Kids don't die of diabetes. Not here. Not in America."

"The Alvarez family ran out of insulin and Teo ended up in a diabetic coma. They rushed him to the hospital, but it was too late. Despite heroic efforts by the E.R. doctors, they never managed to bring him back."

Charles felt sick. "What about Mr. Alvarez? Is he dead, too?"

"No, but he's in prison. Immigration officials

came to check out his papers soon after Teo died, and Mr. Alvarez was so distraught that he punched the official trying to arrest him. He's in county jail, serving a ninety-day sentence."

"Only ninety days?" Charles perked up a little. In comparison to the news about Grandma, and especially about Timoteo, ninety days in county jail didn't sound so terrible. "Well, he'll be out soon, right? And then he can help his family get back on its feet again."

"Of course he won't be coming back home again," the Ghost replied, sounding impatient at Charles's naiveté. "He's an illegal immigrant. As soon as he's served his sentence, he'll be deported to Mexico. If he's lucky, they'll provide transportation back to Guerrero, which is where he came from years ago. If he's really lucky, he may find a cousin still living there who'll put a roof over his head while he looks for work. If he's unlucky, Immigration will drop him off across the border and he'll most likely starve. Or not, as fate decrees. And, of course, since he will be a foreigner with a criminal record, he will have lost all chance of ever obtaining legal entry into the United States."

"But he isn't really a criminal," Charles protested.

The Ghost raised a delicate, almost invisible eyebrow. "He's been convicted of a crime and served time in jail. If he isn't a criminal, what is he?"

"Well, I meant that he's not a bad person."

"The Immigration Service isn't in the business of

making moral judgments. It's in the business of administering the law. Which is as it should be, of course. Besides, there are millions of people without criminal records who are hoping and praying to get permission to enter the States. It makes no sense to let in a criminal and keep out somebody else."

The Alvarezes had left the house and were trudging toward the bus stop along messy, slush-covered sidewalks. Charles walked behind them, the Ghost floating in and out of sight beside him. "This doesn't have to happen," Charles said. "Teo doesn't have to die. Mr. Alvarez doesn't have to punch a law enforcement official."

"True. It doesn't have to happen. I am simply showing you the most likely future, given everything that's happened up to this moment."

"I can change what happens," Charles said feverishly. "You said yourself that you look so insubstantial to me because the future hasn't happened yet. I can increase Gloria's pay. I can introduce a group health insurance policy for my employees, and Gloria can sign up. Then Teo won't die because he has no insulin, and Mr. Alvarez won't be so distraught that he does something really stupid. It's quite likely the incident with the immigration people will never happen. Maybe I could even find him an immigration lawyer, so that he could start the process to get a green card."

"You could do those things and they would have

an enormous impact on the Alvarez family," the Ghost agreed. "Gloria is a very smart woman. With a little help from you, and with some of the burden taken from her shoulders, she could go on to become one of the country's most successful entrepreneurs. But will you raise her pay? Tomorrow morning, when you wake up, will you tell yourself that changes need to be made in *your* life? Or will you tell yourself that you have just endured a night of bad dreams and you don't have to think about any of this again?"

"I can change," Charles said. "I want to change." He realized they were still following the Alvarezes, who were now on the bus en route to the cemetery. He frowned, puzzled. "Why are we still trapped inside this vision? I want to get out! I'm not going to let these terrible things happen to the Alvarez family, so it's not relevant."

"There is one more thing you need to see. And for that, we must go to the cemetery."

"No! I don't want to go there."

The Ghost didn't bother to answer. She drifted up through the roof of the bus, pulling Charles behind her. "Come, it is taking too long to follow the Alvarez family here."

"You've brought me to the cemetery after all," Charles said, looking around with a marked lack of enthusiasm. The late afternoon was bitterly cold, the ice-covered paths between the rows of graves sprinkled with gravel that turned the pristine snow into a dirty slush, and the sky already transforming from glowering dusk to full winter darkness.

"Why are we here?" He asked the question with dread, because he remembered the Dickens story all too well, and he could make a pretty good guess as to why the Ghost had brought him here.

As he feared, the Ghost pointed to a patch of brown earth. "This is the site of your grave. The headstone will be installed this afternoon."

"You sound very casual about my death," Charles said. "I hope it takes place many years in the future."

The Ghost didn't respond. She pointed instead to the gate, where a woman had just entered, accompanied by a boy of about nine.

"It's Rachel," Charles said, his voice husky. "And…is that Kevin?"

"Yes, Rachel has finally managed to adopt him. They're very happy together. She's come today because she knows nobody else has bothered to visit your grave and her kindness won't allow anyone, even you, to go entirely unmourned."

Charles had to swallow before he could speak. "When am I going to die? How did I die?"

The Ghost floated above the grave, scattering beams of light. "Remember, this is only one possible future, Charles. The truth is that nothing is certain in this world, not even the exact time and manner of our death. All I can tell you is that in this, the most likely of all your possible futures, you died alone."

"No!" Charles gave a cry of despair. "No, I don't want to be alone anymore."

The Ghost of Christmas Yet to Come was floating higher, out of his reach. Desperate for a peek into a happier future, Charles grabbed for a corner of her billowing, multicolored robe. Just as his fingers touched the sparkling, shimmering hem, he woke up, clutching the sheet in his own bed, his cheeks wet with tears.

"It was just a dream," he said feverishly. "It was all fantasy. None of it happened." He repeated the mantra of reassurance over and over, but it provided no solace. Charles finally faced the fact that even if the phantoms haunting his sleep had been nothing more than figments of his tormented imagination, their warnings remained valid: he was heading fast down the wrong road. Even worse, he was making himself miserable in the process.

So why on earth was he wasting precious time pretending that nothing of significance had happened? Impatient with his own cowardice, Charles threw off the covers and jumped out of bed, running downstairs to the kitchen. He grabbed the carton of orange juice from the fridge and, ignoring the neat row of glasses, chugged back a hefty few swallows directly from the carton before running back upstairs again to brush his teeth. He searched through his closet, picking out jeans, a much-washed chambray shirt and the brightest sweater he could find—if gray with navy-blue trim could be considered anything other than dreary, he reflected ruefully.

It was only 7:00 a.m., not the best time to be shopping on Christmas morning. He ran downstairs and got in the car, driving to the first supermarket he could find that was open. He pushed the biggest shopping cart available through the aisles, picking out boxes of chocolates for Grandma and Mrs. Alvarez, red wine for Mr. Alvarez, cookies for the children, some ridiculously expensive imported strawberries for Teo and a giant scarlet poinsettia for Gloria.

"You left your Christmas shopping a bit late," the woman at the checkout commented with a chuckle.

Yesterday Charles would have withered her with a cold stare. This morning he returned her smile. "I'm hopeless. But next year I swear I'm going to do better."

"Have a happy holiday," the clerk said, handing him his change.

"You, too." Humming along to Bing Crosby's classic rendition of "White Christmas," which was blaring out through the supermarket speakers, Charles pushed the cart to his car and loaded his purchases into the trunk. It was eight o'clock, probably not too early to call on the Alvarez family. He was pretty sure the children would have been up for a while, eager to discover what Santa Claus might have left for them. Then he remembered that he'd have to swing by the office to discover Gloria's home address: pity the ghosts hadn't provided him with a zip code and street address, he thought with a grin.

It was a few minutes after nine when he knocked on the door of the Alvarez home, which looked, he had to admit, startlingly like the house he'd dreamed about last night. Still, he'd decided he wasn't going to obsess about whether or not he'd "really" been visited by the ghost of Jacob Marley and the Spirits of Christmas. Whatever had happened, it was pretty damn close to a miracle, and he'd take his miracles any way they came.

The door to the Alvarez home was opened by a boy of about fourteen or so, and Charles recognized him as Gloria's brother.

"Hello, Javier. Merry Christmas to you!"

"Hey, you, too. Have a great one." Javier frowned. "Do I know you, dude?"

"I'm your sister's boss—"

Javier scowled. "She can't come into work today! It's Christmas."

"I don't want her to come into work," Charles explained hurriedly. "I've brought some gifts for the family." He gestured to the trunk of his car. "Could you help me carry them inside?"

Javier's frown deepened. "Wait a moment, okay?" He shut the door with something close to a bang.

This was not going quite the way he'd planned, Charles thought wryly, wrapping his scarf a bit tighter to protect against the cutting blasts of wind. A few moments later, the door opened a crack and Gloria poked her head around the opening.

"Oh, it really is you, Mr. Brentwood." She opened the door wider. "Sorry, Javier thought you must be from Immi—" She cut off her statement. "What can I do for you, Mr. Brentwood? Would you care to come inside and have some hot chocolate? We just made a jug and it's very good."

"Thank you, some hot chocolate would be terrific. But first, I need some help carrying in the gifts I've brought for your family."

"Gifts?" Gloria stared at him as if he'd spoken a word from some alien language lost to civilization for a thousand years or so. "Gifts? For us? From you?"

"Sure. They're not much, but perhaps the Christmas bonus I've tucked into this envelope will help make them seem more exciting." Charles smiled as he handed over the holiday card he'd bought in the supermarket, along with the enclosed check for a thousand dollars.

"A bonus?" Gloria's voice sounded breathless with shock and anticipation.

"Yes. It is Christmas, after all. Go ahead. Open it."

Fingers shaking, Gloria tore open the envelope, but instead of laughing when she saw the amount, she turned dead-white and stared at him with eyes swimming in tears.

"What is it? What's wrong?" Charles was appalled

that his holiday surprise hadn't worked out better. First Javier suspected him of being from Immigration; now Gloria was crying over his check.

Gloria's tears overflowed almost as fast as she wiped them away, but to his overwhelming relief, Charles saw that she was smiling through her tears. "Thank you, Mr. Brentwood. This check is so generous, I can hardly believe it's real. You have no idea what this money means to me and my family."

"Well, I know about Timoteo's diabetes. I hope this will keep him in medical supplies until we can find a better, long-term solution. I don't know any immigration lawyers myself, but I bet we can find somebody good once we start looking. It seems to me, everything for your family would be easier if we could just find a way to get your parents established here with legal status."

"Oh, it would! It would be heaven if they could get green cards." Gloria looked at him, her forehead wrinkled in puzzlement. "What's happened to you, Mr. Brentwood? You don't even look the same. You look…" Her voice died away, the changes in him too great for her to find words.

"Happy?" He laughed. "I guess I am. I just realized that I'm a truly fortunate man. I'm healthy, I run a profitable company, I enjoy using my creative skills to keep the design of our product line elegant, as well as cutting-edge. I have great, hardworking employees, and on top of that there are dozens of opportunities every day for me to make a difference in people's lives. That's quite a lot to make anyone happy."

"Yes, I guess so." Gloria still looked wary.

Charles smiled. "That hot chocolate will soon be cold! Can you help me bring in the packages from the trunk of my car? I'd enjoy spending a few minutes chatting with your family." Almost to himself he added, "After that, I may even have enough courage to visit the next family on my list."

CHAPTER NINE

CHARLES REALIZED he'd been sitting in the car outside the Chandahrs' home for almost fifteen minutes. He was going to get arrested for loitering if he didn't soon pluck up his courage and knock on the front door, he reflected wryly. Still, in view of the terrible way he'd treated Rachel at the end of their relationship, he had no right to expect even a tepid welcome.

Gathering every dreg of resolve he could summon, he got out of the car and marched determinedly up the snow-bordered path to the front door, carrying the oversized platter of Christmas cookies he'd brought as his peace offering. Somehow, he suspected it was going to take more than two dozen store-bought, nutmeg-and-brown-sugar-sprinkled cookies to reinstate him in the good graces of Rachel and her parents.

He rang the doorbell and waited no more than thirty seconds before it was swung open by a smiling Rachel. "Come in. We hoped..." Her words of welcome died away, and she stared at Charles in silent disbelief.

"Hello, Rachel. How are you?"

"Charles… *Charles?*"

Her voice was musical despite her surprise, and she looked as breathtakingly beautiful as ever, but there was a strength and maturity in her gaze that hadn't been there when they'd parted. His heart started to beat so hard and fast that it seemed as if he could feel the pounding throughout his body. He gulped and it was several second before he found his voice.

"Merry Christmas, Rachel." He held out his offering of cookies and prayed that she wouldn't shut the door in his face.

Her welcoming smile faded and she drew in a long, deep breath. "What are you doing here? Why have you come?" She sounded puzzled rather than angry, but he wasn't reassured. Her low-key reaction might be a sign of her generous nature and a willingness to suspend judgment. It could also mean she had so little feeling left for him that it wasn't even worth wasting the energy to yell.

"I missed you so much I couldn't stay away any longer."

For a moment, the soft contours of her face tightened and her voice took on a note of sarcasm. "You managed to stay away for the past dozen years, Charles. What's changed?"

"Me," he said. "I finally took a long hard look at myself and realized that my life had no meaning without you in it. Is it too late to apologize? Is it too late to tell you I'm deeply sorry that I was such a total and complete moron when we broke up?"

"It's never too late to say you're sorry," she said quietly. "But sometimes, being sorry isn't enough to change the consequences of what you've done. And, for the record, we didn't exactly break up. You pushed me away so hard and so often that there was no way I could keep coming back."

"You're right. If it's any excuse, I think the death of my dad following less than two weeks after Lizzie's death made me a bit crazy. It wouldn't have been so bad if there'd been time for me to grieve, but there didn't seem to be a minute to come to terms with what I'd lost. The company my father and grandfather had worked all their lives to build was tumbling into ruins. Creditors were threatening foreclosure. My mother was starting to drink a little earlier each day. You accused me of throwing myself into my work to avoid the pain of mourning for my sister, but that's only partly true. I felt an obligation to my dad and to all the people who relied on Brentwood Industries for their jobs. I couldn't just let the company go under when I knew exactly what steps had to be taken to save it."

Rachel gave a wintry smile. "I've heard how successful you've been. Congratulations, Charles."

There was barely a trace of irony in her words, but Charles picked up on it. "The *company* has been successful," he said. "*I* haven't been successful. In fact, on a personal level, I've totally messed up. First I pushed you away, and then I wasted years of my life acting as if the most important thing in the world was how many kitchen faucets Brentwood Industries shipped to various retail outlets, and whether my high-end bathroom fixtures were competing well against the Linea Aqua line. I want to change that. I *really* want to change that."

"I'm glad." This time her smile was warmer. "I always knew you would do something more rewarding with your life than simply finding more ways to make money."

Her smile gave him his first twinge of hope. "I'm going to make changes in my life whatever happens with you today. But whatever changes I make, unless you're in my life, I'll always have regrets."

"We were young when we got engaged, Charles. Perhaps you're idealizing our relationship—"

"No! I agree that we were young and inexperienced when we fell in love, but that doesn't mean our relationship wouldn't have worked out if circumstances had been different. Looking back, I'm more certain than ever that what we had was something unique, something very special that could have lasted us a lifetime."

"I agree. I loved you, Charles." She looked sad for a moment. "That's why it hurt so much when you threw our relationship away."

He winced, because her assessment of what had

happened was so painfully accurate. He had taken something of immense value and thrown it away.

"Believe me, Rachel, I understand there's no reason in the world for you to consider renewing your friendship with me, and a thousand reasons why you would be justified if you closed the door in my face. I guess I'm asking for you to show compassion I don't deserve. I'm asking you for the chance to show how much I care about you, and how much I regret the decisions I made right after my father and sister died."

Rachel hesitated, but she looked up and held his gaze. Charles discovered that her dark brown eyes had lost none of their hypnotic, sensual appeal. "I have children now," she said. "There are other lives at stake here, not just mine. I can't afford to take any risks that might harm them. They've both had more than enough to cope with in their lives already. I'm not going to introduce them to somebody who'll walk into their lives and then waltz out again the moment things get busy at work."

"That's not going to happen," he said. "I know about Daisy and about Kevin. I understand a little bit of what Kevin has been through with his so-called stepfathers, and how sad Daisy must be, coping with the fact that her mother is in prison. Let me help. Let me be a friend to all three of you. You don't have to let me very far into your life, Rachel. Just open the door a little way, and I swear I'll prove that I'm worthy of having you open it wide a few months down the road."

"I don't know, Charles. Trust doesn't come as easily for me these days as it once did…"

"It's Christmas," he urged. "Remember how special the holidays always were for both of us? This is the season of forgiveness—the season of goodwill and new beginnings. It's the time of year when we celebrate the birth of a baby who grew up to sacrifice his life for the good of humanity. Let me show you that I can be a worthy partner for you, Rachel. It's what I want more than anything else in the world."

She looked at him for a long, assessing moment. And then she opened the door, although she still didn't smile.

"Come inside, Charles. Merry Christmas."

"Merry Christmas, Rachel." He handed over the cookies. "I'm not sure if these are much of a peace offering, but knowing you, I guess a platter of diamonds wouldn't have worked any better."

"Oh, I don't know." She laughed, and the sound reached all the way inside him, to the deepest part of his heart. "An entire platter of diamonds might have been a bit hard to resist."

"Rachel, your smile…the way you laugh…" He drew in a long shaky breath. "I've spent the past twelve years trying not to remember how much I love you. For what it's worth, I failed miserably."

She shook her head. "Charles, it's been a long

time, a lot of things have happened. We can't just wipe away all those years of experience and pick up where we left off. For now, let's just work on being friends."

It was enough—for now. "Okay, friends it is. I'm really looking forward to meeting Kevin and Daisy."

"How do you know about them?"

"An acquaintance told me. He said that you've helped a lot of abandoned and hurting kids over the past few years."

"It was an easy decision to get involved with the local foster care program. I've discovered that if you give a teaspoon of affection to most kids, you get a quart-sized package of love in return. That's a pretty good deal, don't you think?"

"It sure is." Charles walked into the Chandahrs' home, saying a silent thank-you to his ancestor, Charles Dickens, and the ghosts who had made him realize the barren horror his life had become. Then he added a prayer of gratitude that Christmas had once again worked its transforming miracle. If the Ghost of Christmas Yet to Come paid him another visit, Charles thought, that future would glitter with hope and happiness.

"My parents are in the family room with Kevin and Daisy. Come and say hi."

The Chandahrs were exquisitely polite hosts even though it was clear that they would take a long time to forgive Charles for his miserable treatment of their daughter. As for Kevin and Daisy, he could see how much Rachel had already achieved when both children accepted him as a potential friend simply because that was how Rachel introduced him.

Friendship was a pretty amazing gift, Charles thought. It wasn't quite as good as being a lover and nowhere near as good as becoming a husband. But he would dedicate the next year to proving his worth to Rachel, and by next Christmas he'd have earned his place in the Chandahr family circle.

Rachel brought him a mug of steaming apple cider, and as he thanked her, he raised the mug in an unspoken toast. "Here's to you, Rachel, my love and my life."

Charles was almost sure that if he looked over his shoulder he would see that Jacob Marley and the spirits of Christmas were all smiling.

* * * * *

MIRACLE ON BANNOCK STREET

Colleen Collins

To Shaun Kaufman

CHAPTER ONE

Morning After Thanksgiving, 1955
Denver City and County Court, Bannock Street

"DAMN STILETTOS," muttered Stella as she precariously navigated her way up the seemingly endless steps of the Denver City and County Court. She'd laughed when she'd first seen women wearing them, had sworn she'd never be caught dead in a pair, but if she'd learned anything in her twenty-six years it was that if you wanted something bad enough, you did whatever it took to get it.

Today, she wanted free publicity for her business, Gray's Investigations, and she knew it'd serve her better to ditch the down-and-dirty P.I. look and dress the part of a lady. So long dungarees and flats, hello skirt and stilettos.

"Hey, Stella, have a good Thanksgiving?" Jimmy Leonard, the *Denver Post* reporter covering the court beat, leaned against a marble column at the top of the stairs, his paunch straining his red-and-black plaid wool jacket. He took a last drag of his cigarette before flicking it into the air.

"Yes." She'd had dinner with her landlady, Mrs. Marshall, who'd been widowed around the time Stella's father had died two years ago.

When Jimmy leaned over to rummage for something in a beat-up leather briefcase, she noticed that his flat-top was shorn so close to his head, she could see his scalp. With Denver temperatures dipping into the thirties, his head had to be hurting. Probably forgot to grab his hat while making a mad dash to get to the courthouse by nine, the prime time to meet Denver's movers and shakers on their way to court.

She knew because she'd made that mad dash plenty of times herself. By positioning herself on the court steps around 8:00 a.m., she had opportunities to say hello to attorneys heading into court, join them on their cigarette breaks, slip in a word about Gray's Investigations. She'd nailed a few jobs that way. Would've been more if she'd been a man, but that's the way it was when you're were the only female P.I. in a city full of male private dicks.

Jimmy straightened, a steno notepad in his hand. "I had a great Thanksgiving, too. Turkey, stuffing, the whole works." He dug a pen out of his jacket pocket. "So," he said, flipping open the notepad, "ready to shoot down Santa?"

"You've been waiting out in the cold just to ask me that?"

"Hey, the day after Thanksgiving is one of the busiest days at court, so I've been waiting to ask a lot of people questions." He scribbled something down. "Let's chat about this 'crazy Santa' case, which readers are eating up. You're the D.A.'s key witness, right?"

"Right."

"Which means a lot hinges on what you say on the stand."

He'd answered his own question, if it was one, so she didn't respond.

He glanced up, his pen poised on the paper. "Let me guess—you're gonna say he's out-and-out crazy, a guy who's a danger to society, even if all he's doing is spreading Christmas cheer."

Her dad, well-known P.I. Pete Gray, would have known how to handle this reporter. Pete had been everyone's pal, thanks to years of bending his elbow at local bars with cops, politicians, even reporters, all of whom slipped Pete insider tidbits and gave him room if he needed to protect a case he was working.

It wasn't that Stella couldn't hold her own in a conversation, it was just that she had more of her mother's sensible, Midwestern genes than her father's wild Irish ones.

A gust of chilly wind blew past, sweeping strands of her hair across her face. "He's an elderly man who needs proper care." She brushed back her hair with a gloved hand. "I'm here in the hopes of his getting the help he needs so he doesn't endanger himself or others again."

Jimmy wrote as he talked. "Let's see…Stella Gray, the only lady P.I. in Mile High, is determined to put the kibosh on Santa."

"I never said I wanted to put the kibosh on Santa."

"But it's what you meant."

"No—"

"Okay, not what you meant, but definitely what you're doing."

"This is starting to feel like the trick question on *Truth or Consequences*," she muttered.

He barked a laugh. "But unlike that TV show, if I don't get the truth, you don't have to do one of those zany stunts."

She blew out an exasperated breath. "Look, Jimmy, I'm trying to give you an interview, but if you're going to—"

He held up his hands in mock protest. "Hey, hasn't the *Post* been good to you? Why, right after you stopped that robbery and saved Santa and the others, didn't we put your pretty face, and a hot story, on page one?"

True, the paper had been good to her. Two weeks ago, an elderly man named Kris Kringle, who claimed to be Santa Claus, had risked his life and others by interrupting a robbery in progress. Stella, one of the bystanders, had saved the day by holding the robber at gunpoint until police arrived. The story had made page one in the *Post* and netted her several new clients, a boost for her business.

But she'd barely had a chance to bask in the limelight before a second story had run that played up the poor, victimized Kris Kringle, who, despite his claims he was returning to the North Pole the day after Christmas, was actually a hobo. This had gotten the attention of the D.A.'s office, which wanted to deem Mr. Kringle mentally incompetent so he could be permanently placed in a state mental hospital rather than forced to survive on the streets.

She glanced at her watch. "Court starts in fifteen. I gotta go."

"Is Santa's beard real?"

"What?"

"You saw it up close—maybe touched it—is it real?"

"I don't make it a habit to touch men's beards."

Jimmy gave her a sly smile. "Except the deputy D.A.'s, I guess."

"Oh, good grief." She rolled her eyes. "And I thought you wanted to play nice."

"C'mon, Stella, you two were engaged."

"We *dated*. Six years ago." She'd been twenty, trying to play mother to her kid brother in a house her dad avoided. Pete Gray had preferred to crash at his office and drink than face memories of his dead wife. When Stella met Oscar Tomich, a first-year law student, he had seemed like everything her life wasn't—namely, stable and uncomplicated. Six months later, those traits felt more like boring and simple. Not that she was Oscar's dream come true, either—more and more, he'd complained she was too unpredictable and adventurous. They'd both been relieved to go their separate ways.

They didn't speak again until shortly after her father's death when Oscar, married and working as a deputy D.A, called to offer his condolences. Learning she'd taken over Gray's Investigations, he'd pulled strings and landed her a few investigative gigs.

"Look, Jimmy, I know you want an angle, but let's stick to the important issue. Kris Kringle needs a residence where he'll be cared for, not left on the streets interrupting more crimes in progress. This isn't some schmaltzy story about a real-life Santa spreading joy to the world. This is about an old man who needs help."

A slow grin spread across Jimmy's face. "You just gave me my hook, baby!"

She frowned.

He scribbled on the notepad as he talked. "Joy, or no joy? Will Santa get the shaft, or will the world let him release the true spirit of Christmas?"

"Jimmy, that's nonsense—"

He cut her off with a wave as he headed inside. "See you in court, Stella! Thanks for the lead-in to my story!"

She glumly followed him inside, chiding herself for yammering to a reporter. Next time she wanted to wax poetic, she'd save it for the witness stand.

A FEW MINUTES LATER, Stella navigated her way across the courthouse marble floor toward Oscar, who was busily flipping through a stack of papers. The metal tips of her heels clicked loudly on the polished marble, drawing his attention.

He glanced at her feet as she stopped next to him.

"I wanted to look sophisticated for court," she murmured, teetering slightly on her heels.

"So I see."

She glanced around the room at the congregation of suited-up attorneys and their frightened-looking clients, a disgruntled-looking cop who'd probably been called to testify on his day off and the usual mix of associates, family and hangers-on like Jimmy— everyone waiting for the courtroom doors to open.

She turned back to Oscar. "Where are we on the docket?"

"Second. Now, listen up." He gave her a look over the thick black rim of his glasses. "As we discussed, when you take the stand, emphasize that Kris Kringle is a risk taker. Don't let them veer the questioning to *you* being a risk taker."

"I wouldn't be a good P.I. if I *wasn't* a risk taker."

Oscar waved that aside. "If the questioning focuses on *your* risk taking, that'll sink our case. Got it?"

"Got it."

"In fact, if the questioning even begins to go into that area—'Why were you in the store that day, Miss Gray? Were you, perhaps, following a felon? A dangerous criminal your father had never been able to nail?'—say you were shopping."

"But I was following a felon."

He gave her a look.

She sighed. "I'll say I was shopping, although I hate to. I'm not the type to blow money."

"How's business?"

"Tight."

"Maybe you can supplement your income at Gray's Investigations with a side job?"

"Like what? The only thing I've done except be a P.I. is help raise my brother and take in ironing when I was a teenager. I was great at the first, lousy at the second." She gestured to his notes. "What else?"

"If you're questioned about your gun, keep your answers simple. One word—yes, no—if possible. Remember, I don't want the—"

"Focus on me. I got it, Oscar."

He adjusted his glasses, nodded. "Did I mention not wearing your .357 when you take the stand?"

"What makes you think I have it on me?"

"How do I know the Rockies won't crumble," he muttered, glancing back down at his notes. "Another thing. Don't let Kringle's lawyer trip you up on the Good Samaritan slant." He looked up. "The old man needs to be hospitalized before he does something else rash, possibly killing himself *and* others."

She looked around for Kringle, who stood across the foyer in an ill-fitting suit, his white beard freshly trimmed. It had to be real. Men didn't wear beards these days, especially longer ones. "Who's representing Kringle?"

"Probably Victor Lancaster." Oscar dipped his head toward several men standing near the drinking fountain. "He's next up in the rotation."

The rotation referred to who was at the top of the list of court-appointed attorneys. "The guy in the checkered jacket?"

"Yes."

As she removed her gloves, she checked out the thirtyish man, whose dark hair and boyish charm reminded her of the actor William Holden.

"So that's Victor Lancaster," she murmured, tucking her gloves into her coat pockets. Good Lord, the man oozed presence. "He doesn't look stuffy enough to have a wing of the Denver Public Library named after him. His family, I mean." Aimlessly rubbing her fingers along her arm, she watched Victor nod a greeting here, a smile there. Most attorneys seemed to flash contrived, insincere smiles, whereas Victor's looked genuine. Warm, even. "He seems so friendly."

"Don't let the Lancaster charm fool you. Victor, like his attorney father, has a dark side. Both can be killers in the courtroom. Word is he'll be running for D.A."

As Oscar returned to his notes, she observed Victor. So, he'd set his sights on a political career. Now she understood the ready smiles and nods. If he had the brains to match that slick charm, he'd be a shoo-in. "I'm going to check out the docket."

Oscar looked up. "I told you we're second."

"Well, then, I'm going to get a drink of water."

He gave her a warning look over his glasses. "I don't want you bothering opposing counsel."

"Bothering? Me?" She straightened the collar of her coat. "Why, I'm just a sweet, innocent P.I. hanging around the halls of justice, Oscar."

As she walked away, she heard his snort of disbelief behind her.

"WHO'S THE DOLLY?" asked Danny, a criminal defense attorney who'd been Victor's best pal since they'd roomed together in law school.

"Don't know." Victor watched as she paused and placed one hand on the wall to steady herself. "Looks like she hit the bottle before court. Most people wait until *after* they hear the judge's ruling to imbibe."

Danny laughed.

The woman's strawberry-blond hair was short and softly curled. It emphasized her heart-shaped face and big green eyes. Underneath her oversize tweed coat—he hated those shapeless coats, although more and more women seemed to be wearing them—were a pair of shapely legs that stretched forever into a pair of black high-heeled shoes. Now, *those* he didn't mind on a gal, although now that he saw her attempting to walk in them, he realized it wasn't the bottle that made her tipsy.

"Why would a woman wear shoes she can't walk in to court?" he asked Danny.

His friend, craning his neck to better see the front doors, shrugged. "I'm the last person to ask why women do things. I'm still trying to figure out why my wife planned for us to take a vacation to Montana next week. Do you know how cold it is in Montana right now? My wife forgets that Denver's climate is much milder. I'm not sure what we're going to do besides huddle by a fire."

"Could be romantic."

"Yeah, as long as there's plenty of firewood." He glanced at his watch. "My client's late."

"Relax, Danny, there's still time." In law school, Danny had been early for everything, whereas Victor liked to take his time. The only fight they'd ever had in their years-long friendship was when Victor had been late picking up Danny for a Fourth of July party.

He returned his gaze to the woman with the big green eyes. "Couldn't be a litigant. She doesn't look scared or nervous."

"Eh?" Danny followed Victor's line of vision. "No, she looks too purposeful. Except for those shoes."

"Could be a lawyer. Purposeful intent, unsteady premise."

Danny laughed. "Think I'll go to the clerk's office and call my client, make sure he remembered today's his court date. Did I mention my investigator quit?"

"Sounds like you're having a rough week." Victor patted him on the back. "Let me know if there's anything I can do."

"Send firewood to Montana," muttered Danny as he walked away.

Smiling, Victor turned back and watched the woman as she got a drink at the water fountain, then dabbed her fingertips at the corner of her mouth. Their gazes caught.

He smiled.

Her lips curved slowly into a smile that had an I've-got-a-secret quality.

That did it. Court started in, oh, five minutes. Plenty of time to make an introduction, find out what was on the lady's mind.

A few moments later, they stood facing each other. She didn't wear much makeup, except for bright red lipstick. He caught the light, powdery scent of her perfume. Noticed she didn't wear a wedding ring.

"I don't believe we've met," he said, extending his hand. "Victor Lancaster."

"Stella Gray." She shook his hand.

He frowned, trying to recall where he'd heard that name before.

"Gray's Investigations," she said.

He snapped his fingers. "I remember Pete Gray. Great guy. So, you're his daughter."

She nodded, her eyes darkening to a gray-green that reminded him of the eucalyptus trees he'd seen years ago in Santa Barbara.

He remembered something else. "You're here to testify in the Kringle case, right?"

"That's right."

"I wish you wouldn't."

To his surprise, she burst out laughing. "Sorry," she finally said, "I wasn't expecting us to cut right to it."

"What did you expect?"

"Me standing near the drinking fountain, observing you, feeling ahead of the game before we ever entered the courtroom."

"I like how you think, Miss Gray." He gave her a look she felt all the way down to her toes.

The man was utterly, undeniably masculine. For all his polish and sophistication, he had a raw, earthy presence that shook up her senses, disrupted her equilibrium. And from that look on his face, he knew he'd had that effect on her, too.

A smile played on his lips. "Are you in front of or behind the game now?"

Even as she told herself she knew better than to tangle verbally with a lawyer, especially one who'd be cross-examining her, she answered, "In front of. After all, my taking the stand is to ensure Mr. Kringle gets the help he needs."

"Help?" Victor straightened, suddenly all business. "Have you ever had an opportunity to speak with him one on one? Because if you had, you'd find Mr. Kringle to be a gentle soul who cares about others. It's funny how people want to immediately label somebody who cares about the intangibles, such as joy and love and peace, as crazy."

"Intangibles tend to sound crazy when one starts sharing them with a guy who's pointing a gun at you."

Nearby, the bailiff unlocked the doors to the court, which creaked as they swung open. The low-level hum of conversation rose as the small crowd migrated toward the courtroom.

The man she'd seen Victor speaking to earlier walked up. "My client *still* isn't here," he fumed.

"Did you call the county jail?" Victor asked him.

"Yes. He's not there." He rolled his eyes. "Should've done water law," he muttered, walking toward the courtroom.

"I need to go, too," said Stella, turning to leave.

Victor cupped her elbow and leaned close. "What might convince you not to take the stand, Stella?"

She hadn't realized until this moment how important the case was to him. But it made sense. Successfully defending Santa could win a lot of popular votes if one were running for D.A.

Pete Gray had always said it never hurt to ask for what you wanted—worst that could happen, you were told no. "Let me handle your law firm's key investigations," she answered.

Victor puffed out a breath as he stared intently into her eyes. "Can't do that," he finally said. "You know how it works. Senior partners have had their investigative teams in place for years. I can't bring someone new on board, out of the blue."

She gently tugged her arm loose. "Then I'll see you in court, counselor."

CHAPTER TWO

A FEW MINUTES LATER, Stella slipped into one of the wooden spectator benches in the court. The room was filled with whispered conversations, the scraping of feet, an occasional muffled laugh. On the far wall, tall rectangular windows offered a view of the overcast November sky, its somber gray setting the tone for the proceedings about to begin.

At the front of the courtroom, the bailiff stood. "All rise for the honorable Judge Wallace Gerash."

Oscar, slightly out of breath, moved in next to Stella as she stood. "Saw you and Victor talking," he whispered, shoving his glasses back up his nose.

She smiled, shrugged, as though it was nothing. If she told Oscar about the last-minute bargaining she and Victor had gotten into, he'd only worry.

Judge Gerash, a feisty bantamweight of a man, strode into the courtroom, his hair starkly white in contrast to his black judge's robe. He commanded his seat at the raised podium, casting a grumpy look around the room. Her dad, whose friendship with

Wallace had spanned over thirty years, had often said Wallace Gerash viewed himself as the caped avenger of justice.

The two men had enjoyed working together as investigator and lawyer, but it was their mutual love of chess that had cemented their friendship. Her dad had often complained about Wally's "experimental" style of playing, to which Wally had retorted that unlike the courtroom, he could play chess with only his own interests at heart.

"First on the docket," announced the bailiff, "is people of the state of Colorado in the interest of Bobby Myers and concerning his guardian, St. Mary's Orphanage."

The judge looked around his desk, frowning. "Where's my pen?" He glanced from the bailiff to the court clerk. "Does someone have one I can borrow?"

After the clerk handed him a pen, he nodded to the prosecutor, a dour-looking fellow in an ill-fitting blue wool suit. "Ready, Mr. Bauer?"

"Yes, Your Honor."

The clerk handed the judge a piece of paper. He scanned it and looked out over the courtroom, his gaze finally resting on Victor.

"Mr. Lancaster, you're first up in the rotation for appointment to juvenile delinquent cases and, I see, also for mental competency cases. Are you willing to accept appointment on this juvenile matter and also the competency matter about to be called?"

"Yes, Your Honor." As Victor approached the defense table and sat down, the deputy sheriff escorted a boy from the jury box to a chair next to Victor's. A sullen lad, who Stella guessed to be Bobby Myers, he wore patched pants and a long-sleeved gray wool coat with rolled-up sleeves. Although he looked to be eleven or twelve, he walked with a swagger older than his years.

For a moment, she saw her brother Stephen at that age. He'd had that same brooding, angry-at-the-world persona. Their mother had recently died, and their father had turned into a ghost as he sought out the bottle to drown his grief. Sixteen-year-old Stella had filled in as mom and dad as best she could for her brother, but it hadn't been easy. One night she'd overheard Wallace Gerash lecturing her father to get his act together or his kids could end up in foster homes. The thought of losing even more of her family had terrified her for months.

Mr. Bauer loudly cleared his throat, bringing her back to the present.

"Eleven-year-old Bobby Myers," he began, "is a juvenile delinquent with a history of convictions involving assaults. Most recently, he hit—with a book—a nun at the St. Mary's Orphanage. Therefore, the nuns refuse to take him back because they view him as a poor risk for rehabilitation. The state suggests Bobby be committed to the Lookout Mountain School for Boys until he is eighteen."

While he continued to itemize more of Bobby's misdeeds in a droning monotone, the boy sat stiffly, staring straight ahead. Stella noticed a cowlick sticking up from the crown of his head, as though someone—an angry nun?—had slathered Brylcreem on his hair to subdue it, but that stubborn lock refused to be tamed. Kind of like the boy.

She leaned toward Oscar and whispered, "What is Lookout Mountain School for Boys?"

He grimaced, kept his voice low. "A long-term, lock-down maximum-security facility for boys who've committed serious crimes."

"Theft?"

"And worse."

"Murder?"

He nodded.

Murder? The kid had wielded a *book,* not a gun. "Isn't there an alternative?"

"Foster care, I suppose." Oscar gave her a knowing look. "There's your extra income, Stel. Denver Welfare Department pays eighty dollars a month for a child."

"I'm single, Oscar."

"A single woman can't *adopt,* but nothing says she can't be a foster parent."

As Victor pushed back his chair, the legs scraped loudly against the marble floor. He stood, smoothing a hand down the front of his jacket. Stella caught a glimpse of his gold cuff links and wondered why a man accustomed to wealth didn't practice something more lucrative, like personal injury, instead of defending those less fortunate. *Oh, right. He's running for political office.*

"Your Honor," he said, the rich timbre of his voice rolling through the room. "Bobby Myers deserves another chance. The defense recommends the court place Bobby Myers in foster care one last time pending final sentencing. After Bobby was orphaned when he was four, he lived with an aunt and uncle who, claiming they didn't need another mouth to feed, signed him over to St. Mary's Orphanage. He was almost adopted at seven, but at the last minute the parents decided they wanted a younger child. It was only after these rejections and losses that Bobby began exhibiting aberrant behavior at the orphanage, which suggests an emotionally hurt child, not a criminal one. As this is the season where we, as adults and as a society, see the best of what we can be mirrored in a child's hope, let's give Bobby Myers a second chance. He deserves that. One last chance at rehabilitation before he's interned at the Lookout Mountain School for Boys."

Stella felt as though someone had squeezed her heart as she listened to Victor's eloquent pleading. His words made her think back to her kid brother again. He'd been emotionally hurt, devastatingly so, but fortunately he'd had a caring older sister to watch out for him.

Bobby had no one.

Judge Gerash removed his wire-frame spectacles and stared up at the ceiling for a long, drawn-out moment. The court reporter's typing had stopped, as had all murmured conversations. A small gray bird landed on one of the outside window ledges and chirped, its song muted through the thick glass.

Eventually the judge sucked in a long, weary breath, straightened in his chair, and slipped his glasses back on.

"I want to pass this for further review while we hear the next case." He nodded curtly to the court clerk, who handed him a file that he read out loud. "The city and county of Denver in the interest of and concerning the welfare of Kris Kringle." He looked up. "Counsel, enter your appearance for the record please."

Oscar, all business, carted his papers and briefcase to the prosecution table. Bobby Myers was escorted back to the jury box by the deputy sheriff while, from the defense table, Victor motioned for Kris Kringle to join him.

After everyone had taken their places, the judge motioned for Oscar to begin. He stood and adjusted his thick-framed glasses before speaking.

"The government is asking that Kris Kringle be deemed mentally incompetent and be placed in a state institution for the mentally ill. Mr. Kringle has demonstrated repeated behaviors that show he acts without regard for his own safety and the safety of others. Furthermore, Your Honor, he actively engages in flights of fantasy about who he is and what he can do. Institutionalization is the foremost option to ensure the safety of this gentleman and the community." Oscar sat down.

Victor stood, nodded pleasantly to the judge. "To the contrary, Your Honor, Mr. Kringle is a benefit to the community, not a danger to it. His 'flights of fantasy,' as counsel has phrased it, are nothing more than a seasonal retelling of the Santa legend. Further, his conduct at the robbery showed bravery, not foolishness. The fact that he is different does not entitle the state to a finding of incompetency. We ask for a less restrictive alternative for his placement, such as outpatient visits to the city mental health treatment facility, just down Bannock Street."

Victor had barely sat down when Oscar again stood.

"Your Honor," he said, "I wish to call a witness who can provide evidence that Mr. Kringle requires a more restrictive placement, such as in the locked ward of a mental health hospital, at least until a final hearing. I'd like to call private investigator Stella Gray to the stand."

She stood, crossed to the witness box. After taking her oath, she and Oscar ran through their questions and answers just as they'd practiced. It went smoothly.

That is, until it was Victor's turn to cross-examine her. He approached the box with a pleasant smile, no doubt ready to dazzle the court with more eloquence.

She had to stay alert, not fall for his charm. Tough task, considering, in her private heart, she already was falling.

"Miss Gray," Victor said, strolling toward her, "let's quickly review the circumstances. You were at Neusteter's department store on Friday, November eleventh, the day of the attempted robbery, correct?"

"Correct."

He stopped. "Why were you there?"

"Shopping." She slid a glance at Oscar, who looked relieved.

"Not following any bad guys? You are, after all, a private investigator."

"Private investigators, just like lawyers, sometimes go shopping."

Somebody snickered.

"True," agreed Victor. "But I'd wager your shopping makes you far more attractive than my attempts at shopping." He stepped closer, his eyes boring into hers. "Did you make yourself especially attractive today, Miss Gray, because you hoped your photo might be taken?"

Heat crawled up her neck. "No—"

"Really? There was a story about you on page one of the *Post* recently. Did you get any new clients from that?"

"Yes, but—"

"Because I think the *real* reason you're here is not

to help an elderly man," he said, raising his voice, "but to get all the publicity you can." He walked away several feet, then turned. "It's pretty tough being the only female P.I. in town, isn't it?"

A sickening wave of apprehension washed over her. So this was his dark side.

"Objection," said Oscar. "Badgering the witness."

The judge leveled Victor a look. "Sustained."

"Miss Gray," Victor continued, "please tell us about the attempted robbery."

She shifted in her seat. "I saw a man in his late thirties, dark hair, approach the store owner and demand he open the cash register. Because I was standing out of the robber's line of sight, I was able to call the police from a store phone. As I was finishing, I saw Mr. Kringle approach the robber and begin talking nonsense—"

"Nonsense?" Victor interrupted, looking surprised. "You mean when he talked about Christmas being a time of peace and goodwill?"

When Stella nodded, Victor looked at the judge. "That *nonsense,* Your Honor, was actually a calming, rational message meant to dissuade the robber, and in fact was working until—"

"Objection," interrupted Oscar, "There's no evidence to show Kris Kringle was doing anything other than escalating a dangerous situation."

"Overruled," called out the judge. "Continue, Mr. Lancaster."

"If Mr. Kringle was defusing the situation, why did you pull out your gun, Miss Gray?"

She paused, taking a moment to gather her wits. "I was afraid for Mr. Kringle's, and others', safety."

"Are you trained as a police officer?"

"No."

"Yet you pulled a gun in a public place and pointed it in the direction of innocent bystanders—"

"I was pointing it at the robber—"

"Who was within a few feet of the bystanders, yes or no?"

She paused, not liking the implication Victor was making, but knowing she had to answer. "Yes," she said quietly.

"*Innocent* bystanders who might have lost their lives if you'd shot your gun, which, by the way is a…?"

"Smith & Wesson .357."

Victor gave a low whistle. "Impressive. Are you carrying it right now?"

Oscar was not going to like this. She cleared her throat. "Yes."

"May we see it, Miss Gray?"

She eased it out of her coat pocket and showed Victor. "Safety's on."

"Good to know! Would hate to have the gun accidentally go off, shoot an innocent bystander in the courtroom—"

"Objection, Your Honor," cut in Oscar. "Defense

is grandstanding. She knows how to take care of a weapon, has for years. This is inflammatory!"

"Sustained." The judge motioned for the clerk to retrieve the gun. "The court will return your firearm when you leave, Miss Gray."

Victor made a great show of watching the gun being carried away before returning his attention to Stella. "Did the police charge you with anything?"

She blinked, surprised at the question. "No."

"No?" he repeated, incredulous. "You weren't charged with menacing with a deadly weapon?"

"No, they didn't—"

"Your Honor," he said, looking at the judge, "she's testifying about a crime for which she is still under investigation. I am going to ask you to advise her of her right to a lawyer and her right to remain silent—"

The rest of Victor's words were drowned out by the banging of the judge's gavel. By the time he finally stopped, the room was stone-cold quiet.

"Counselors," he said peevishly, "approach the bench. *Now.* The purpose of this proceeding is to determine whether that white-haired gentleman is going to continue to jump into the middle of armed robberies, endangering himself and others. Its purpose is *not* to harass witnesses and insist charges be pressed."

As Wallace Gerash, his face stern, talked quietly to Victor and Oscar, Stella looked over at the defense's table, where Kris Kringle was drumming his fingers on the wooden tabletop, his bright blue eyes filled with curiosity and worry. She felt bad for the old man, whose only crime was playing with less than a full deck. It was an act of kindness for the state to provide him food and shelter. Surely Victor had to know that.

Judge Gerash banged his gavel again, quieting the room. "Rather than sanction Mr. Lancaster for grandstanding or for impeding justice by making this case about the witness instead of the defendant, the court instead opts to be compassionate." For the first time today, the judge smiled. "Being the start of the holiday season, I will give all parties an opportunity for a *new* hearing the day after Christmas *if* they accept the following terms."

He nodded to Oscar. "If your key witness, Stella Gray, agrees to be a foster parent to Bobby Myers and be responsible for his safety and well-being until December twenty-six, then the Court will, at that time, make the final decision as to whether Bobby Myers's next residence is the juvenile prison. In addition, the court will order the standard eighty-dollar foster-care payment plus an award of financial assistance for living expenses for both her and the boy, from the Denver Welfare Department."

Stella felt her stomach drop, the same dizzying feeling she remembered having as a kid when the Ferris wheel ride would suddenly plummet. Oscar, still standing at the bench, looked over his shoulder at her and smiled, which said it all. He'd proposed the idea to the judge.

"Also," Judge Gerash continued, looking over at Kris Kringle, "the court will not institutionalize Mr. Kringle if the defense finds adequate housing for the elderly gentleman until December twenty-sixth, when again I will make a final decision on Mr. Kringle's mental competency."

Oscar returned to the prosecution table, where he motioned for Stella to join him. As she sank down onto the seat next to him, he murmured, "Great deal, eh?"

She slipped a look over Oscar's shoulder at Bobby Myers, who appeared to be carving something into the back of one of the jury seats. "I don't know…"

"Trust me, it is. Being a foster mom to Bobby for a few weeks means extra income, plus you'll have company over the holidays. And when you again take the stand on December twenty-six, no matter what tactics Victor tries, you're going to look like a saint for taking in an orphan at Christmastime." Victor gave a self-congratulatory grin. "You're gonna come out smelling sweeter than Evening in Paris perfume, which means your lawyer will, too. We'll both be getting great publicity."

"What about his schooling?"

"The nuns have forbidden Bobby to attend any more classes at Saint Mary's, so the point is moot. Besides, schools are closing soon for Christmas vacation, so he won't be missing much."

She chewed her lip. "I'm working a surveillance,

just got a retainer on another case. How am I supposed to work with a kid around?"

"Thought you and Mrs. Marshall were good friends."

"She'd probably help out, but I can't take advantage of her good-heartedness."

"You'll work something out." Oscar stood, clicked shut his briefcase. "It's a great deal, Stel. Plus think about how good you'll look in the papers."

She scanned the courtroom for Jimmy, who sat in the corner scribbling something in his damn notebook. "He didn't sound so P.I.-friendly outside when we talked."

"The day after Christmas, Santa will be old news. Holiday fever will be ebbing. A reporter will want to kick off a New Year's story with a fresh angle—say, how the only woman P.I. in Denver is making it in a man's profession. On the twenty-sixth, I'll suggest the story to Jimmy myself. He owes me one."

She looked over at the court clerk and Judge Gerash, both of whom were staring at her. "They're waiting for my answer?"

"Yes."

"I'm as certifiable as Santa," she muttered. "Okay, tell them I'll take the deal."

A SHORT WHILE LATER, as Stella and Bobby walked out of the courtroom, they ran into Victor with Mr. Kringle.

"Hello, Bobby," said Victor.

"Hi, Mr. Lancaster." Bobby slid a look at Stella, then back to Victor.

Kris Kringle's eyes twinkled as he met Stella's gaze. "Hello, my dear. Good to see you again."

"Hello, Mr. Kringle." She felt guilty that the old man was so nice to her, considering she'd taken the stand against him. "So, did Mr. Lancaster find temporary housing for you?"

He nodded exuberantly. "Oh, yes, quite. I'll be staying in Mr. Lancaster's spare guest room. We'll be seasonal bachelors, so to speak." The old man chuckled, the staccato exhales sounding a bit like ho-ho-ho.

Ho-ho-ho. The old guy was really pushing it. Stella looked at Victor. "Is that true?"

Victor nodded. "I have a spare room that's empty. I'm gone so much, the kitchen is never used. It'll be fun being—" he looked at Kris and smiled "—seasonal bachelors for a few weeks."

"Can I join you guys?" muttered Bobby.

Kris Kringle blinked his bright blue eyes at him. "No, Bobby, you're in the best place you could be."

As if it wasn't enough for the judge to decide what'd be best for her and Bobby, now the Santa-wannabe was getting into the act.

"We need to go now," she muttered.

"Did the clerk return your gun?" asked Victor.

"Yes." She gave him a look. "Don't worry, I

won't be brandishing it at any innocent bystanders on the way home."

After an awkward silence, Kris chimed in, "Yes, yes, we should go, too." He rubbed his hands together against the chill. "I have a lot to do—reviewing lists, planning my delivery route, double-checking back-ordered toys. Plus this year, I have an additional quest." He grew serious. "I want to put the spirit back into the season. Joy, peace, love for one another—those are the true gifts of the holiday, the ones we should carry with us all year long."

If there really were a Santa Claus, this old man would be perfect for the role. But if that was the message he wanted to broadcast, he should send it in a Christmas card. Far more practical approach.

Victor patted Kris on the back. "Listen, I need to stay at court, so I'll get you a taxi to take you to my place and I'll catch up later. Stella, you and Bobby want to share the taxi? My treat."

"Yeah!" said Bobby.

"No, thanks," Stella said at the same time. Looking at Bobby's disappointed face, she explained, "I live just a few blocks away. Plus I thought we'd grab lunch at Nate's around the corner."

The boy shrugged, his smile fading.

"Nate's?" Victor blew out a low whistle. "Best hot dogs this side of New York, Bobby. If I didn't have to work, I'd join you."

The boy perked up. "You've been to New York?"

Victor nodded. "Been to London and Paris, too."

"Crazy, man!"

"Fortunately," said Victor, fighting a smile, "I'm not so old to know *crazy* means a good thing." He suddenly snapped his fingers. "I just remembered! Stella, my pal Danny's client missed his court date today. Maybe he forgot, got scared and skipped the state…who knows. Danny's a one-man office, is leaving on vacation tomorrow, and his investigator just quit. Think Gray's Investigations could find out what happened to his missing client?"

"Sure." A prospective job. Hot damn, things were looking up.

"I'll call him, let him know. Since he'll be gone for a week, probably easier if I get the information, then give you a call."

She smiled. "Sure."

"Tomorrow good?"

"Sure." Good to call? Good to work? Hell, she didn't care. Either would do.

After Victor and Kris walked away, she looked down at Bobby, who wore a quirky grin. "What?"

"I think he likes you."

"He's a lawyer," she murmured. "They always act as though they like people."

"I think you like him, too. All you could say was 'sure' every time he asked you a question."

She began fussing with the buttons on her coat, wondering if it was that obvious she liked Victor. A good P.I. never revealed her emotions, much less her thoughts, yet an eleven-year-old boy had just read her like a book. Not that she'd let him know he had, of course.

She looked at Bobby. "Ready?"

He grinned mischievously. "Sure."

A SHORT WHILE LATER, as Stella and Bobby were polishing off their hot dogs next to Nate's stand, a Yellow Cab careened past them down Fourteenth Street.

"Hey," said Bobby, pointing at it with his hot dog, "wasn't that Kris Kringle?"

"Probably." Undoubtedly bending the cabbie's ear with stories of joy, peace, love and how his sleigh was too small for this year's gift haul.

She handed Bobby a napkin. "You got mustard on your nose."

He took it and swiped in the general vicinity of his face, missing the dot of mustard entirely.

Taking her own napkin, she reached over and dabbed it off.

He frowned. "Just 'cause you're stuck with me doesn't mean you have to play mother."

"And just 'cause you're stuck with me—" she playfully touched the tip of his nose with her finger "—doesn't mean you have to wear food on your face." As she tossed the napkin into a nearby trashcan, she saw the trucks and ladders across the street. "Look, Bobby, they're putting up Christmas decorations!"

He turned and looked at the workmen stringing Christmas lights in a tree. "Stupid," he muttered.

"You've used that word several times on our walk," she said gently.

"Well, yours seems to be *damn*."

"In the half hour since we've left the court, I don't believe I've cussed once."

"Like hell."

"Hey, you're too young to talk like that." She paused, thinking. "Okay, maybe I said it once."

A chilly breeze whipped past, lifting strands of her hair. Brushing it back, she said, "Let's get something straight—cussing is something children shouldn't do. I'm now your temporary custodian, so I'm laying down the first rule—no cussing over the next three weeks."

He smirked. "If the nuns couldn't stop me, what makes you think you can?"

"One thing you'll learn about me, Bobby, is that I love a challenge." She fished in her purse, pulled out a few bills. "This is your no-cussing retainer," she said, handing it to him. "Every time you cuss, you owe me a dime."

"Maybe I'll cuss when you're not around."

"Maybe, but I have ways of finding out if you do."

His frown deepened. "Like how?"

She didn't have a clue, but she'd be a lousy P.I. if she didn't know how to bluff. "Trade secret. Now, are you accepting the deal or not?"

He bent his head, toed a crack in the sidewalk. Finally, he looked up at her with such a probing expression, she sadly realized no one had ever challenged Bobby to be a better person.

But he didn't answer. Instead, he turned and looked at the department store display window they stood in front of. It'd been decorated like a family's living room on Christmas day. Two children, dressed in pajamas, were unwrapping presents. Nearby, the family dog chewed on a ribbon-wrapped bone. The mother, in her bathrobe and wearing slippers, sipped coffee while the dad, also dressed in pj's, smoked a pipe. A black boot topped with a fluff of red and white dangled from inside the chimney. Santa making an exit.

Bobby made a broad gesture with his hand to take in the entire window. "That's all a fairy tale. Except for the dog."

She looked at the stuffed animal's cloth fur, leather nose, button eyes. Even the plastic Santa in the red velvet outfit and fake white beard looked more real.

"Have you ever had a dog?" As soon as she asked, she wished she hadn't. When would a kid who'd spent most of his life in an orphanage have had a dog?

"Kinda. There was a stray that sometimes hung around outside the fence at St. Mary's. I'd give him some of my lunch, toss sticks over the fence for him to catch." He grinned. "Goofy dog. Once I threw a stick and he brought back a rock."

Stella laughed. "I know some people like that. Did you name him?"

"I called him Lassie."

"He was a collie?"

"No. A brown mutt with half a tail. I just liked calling him Lassie. Maybe he didn't like it 'cause one day he wasn't there. Never saw him again." He blew out a puff of air, frowned. "How far is your place, anyway?"

"Not far." She nudged her head toward the street. "Left at the light, walk a block, and we're there." She started to put the bills back into her purse.

"Hey," Bobby said, "that's my retainer."

She looked up. "You didn't say anything, so I didn't know." She handed him the bills.

He folded them neatly before slipping them into his pants pocket. "Thought you said you liked a challenge, Stella."

As they headed down the street, she had to smile. She could shoot a Smith & Wesson better than most men, had a knack for picking locks, had once cajoled a tough court clerk into giving over a confidential file.

But Bobby Myers just might be Stella's biggest challenge yet.

CHAPTER THREE

"GRODY, MAN." Bobby stood just inside the door to Gray's Investigations, staring down the room as though he'd just stepped into something that smelled bad.

"Yeah, well, I'm too busy to clean." Not quite the truth, but she felt the urge to save face.

She slipped out of her heels, nearly moaning at how good it felt to wriggle her freed toes. She pressed her stocking'd feet against the worn hardwood floor.

"You should toss those magazines," Bobby said. "They're a fire hazard."

He was staring at the stacks of *Life, Newsweek* and various pulp detective magazines that trailed along the back floorboard, stopped at the bathroom door, then picked up again on the other side, ending in a lopsided pile against the filing cabinets. Most had been her dad's, and she hadn't had the heart to toss them.

"I'll, uh, work on that."

"When's the last time you dusted?"

Who would have thought the little toughie was a neatnik. "Nineteen fifty-three."

His jaw dropped. "You're kidding."

"Yeah, I am." She shifted the lampshade so the burn spot didn't show. "Even if the place is a bit dusty, it's still your home sweet home these next three weeks."

"Whoa." He did a double-take at the room. "This is where you *live*?"

And just when she thought she couldn't feel worse about her abode. "Yes, I live *and* work here."

He looked back at the glass-paneled door, decorated with the words *Gray's Investigations* in black stenciled letters. "Man," he said, turning back with a shake of his head, "even Sam Spade had his own apartment."

"That's because men make more money than women," she muttered under her breath.

Maybe she shouldn't have sold her parents' home after her dad died, but it had seemed silly for her to live in such a large place all by herself. Plus, the money made it possible for her kid brother to go to college. Anyway, moving into her dad's studio office hadn't felt like such a big deal. In some ways, it was comforting. This was where Pete Gray had crashed many a night, and if it was good enough for him, it was good enough for her.

But obviously it wasn't good enough for Bobby Myers.

"Feels a little chilly. I'll turn up the heat." She crossed to the radiator.

He sauntered through the space, touching the

bull's-eye dial on the radio that sat on top of the metal filing cabinet before heading to the globe. He stared at its pea-green oceans and the red lines marking nautical distances. "Where have you traveled?"

Leaning over the radiator, she looked over her shoulder at Bobby. "Several trips to New Mexico and Kansas. Once to Arizona."

The globe creaked as Bobby turned it. "Victor said he's been to London and Paris."

"I'm sure he has," she murmured, fiddling with the radiator knob. "There," she said, straightening. "Heat will be on any minute."

Bobby walked over to the paper-strewn desk, picked up a framed photo. "Who's this?"

"My dad."

"His arm's bandaged."

"That picture was taken during World War I. He'd been wounded by shrapnel."

"Wounded and he's still smiling? Unreal."

"I think he'd been hurt a week or so prior to that picture being taken. He was, at heart, a wild, devil-may-care Irishman. Not much got him down."

The boy stared at her.

"He died." She leaned over and adjusted a corner of the oval rug. "Not then. Much later."

"His name was Pete?"

She paused, straightened. "How'd you know?"

He pointed at the door. "It used to say 'Pete' over 'Gray's Investigations.'"

"That's right." She'd kept his name on the door for over a year, then one day she'd had it removed. The photo warmed her heart, but sitting behind the desk and looking at her dad's name every day had hurt. Why, she didn't know. It just had.

Bobby set down the photo. "My dad died, too. 'Cept I never knew him. I mean, I was somethin' like six months old when he kicked the bucket." He plopped down in the swivel chair behind the desk and did a spin.

"If we're going to be roommates," she said, crossing to him, "we need to get one thing straight. When I need to do work, I'll need that chair. You're free to sit here." She gestured to the roseback dining-room chair, a loaner from Mrs. Marshall, that faced the desk.

Bobby frowned. "What am I supposed to do when a client's here?"

"You can go into kitchenette—" she gestured to the area behind the bookcase "—or to my bedroom."

"How 'bout the hallway?"

"Sure, as long as you stay there."

"Gee, that sounds like a hell of a lot of fun."

"You owe me ten more cents." She pointed to the yellow pad next to the phone. "Write it down there. We'll keep a tally."

She explained how showers needed to be short so they'd both have hot water, where food was kept in the kitchenette—a fancy name for the small space behind the bookcase—and how to change the ice tray in the window-ledge icebox.

After she finished, Bobby stared at her fixedly.

"Where's my bed?" he asked.

"You'll sleep on a cot outside the kitchenette."

"You mean, next to the bookcase, which means I'll be sleeping in *this* room." He said "this room" in the same tone he'd said "grody" earlier.

"Right."

There followed a long moment of silence where the only sound was the hissing of the radiator.

"Because this is my office space," she said, determined to keep her cool, "we'll have to put your cot away each day. But you're free to sit in one of the chairs and read any of the detective magazines or listen to the radio."

He didn't say anything, just continued staring at her.

"Here's the rules," she continued. "Don't answer the phone, ever. Don't leave without asking me first. Mrs. Marshall is a very nice landlady, but she won't be if you play the radio too loudly. No rummaging through the desk drawers. If you get bored, I'd love help organizing my files in the cabinets or perhaps you'd like to dust." She paused. "Any questions?"

"Yeah," he finally muttered, "can I go back to the orphanage?"

KRIS WALKED INTO the living room, halting when he saw Victor sitting on the couch, reading through a stack of papers. "Sorry, didn't realize you were still working."

Victor finished scribbling a note before looking up

at the metal sunburst clock over the fireplace. "Seven-thirty?" He capped his pen, set it on the coffee table. "Didn't realize it was getting so late. Time to call it a day."

"Nice pen," commented Kris. "What kind is that?"

"Parker 51," he said. "It was a birthday gift."

Kris's eyes twinkled. "I noticed you didn't offer it to Judge Gerash today."

Victor chuckled. "Over my dead body. Although considering how often the judge borrows pens, maybe I should keep a cheap one handy." He shuffled a stack of papers on the table. "So, are you settled in?"

"Yes, your guest room is very nice, Victor." He gestured to his shirt. "Thank you, too, for loaning me your father's shirt, which is quite comfortable."

Victor looked up, momentarily taken aback at the sight of Kris in the old red gabardine shirt. It seemed as though Kris's white beard was even whiter and, if Victor's eyes weren't deceiving him, fuller. The old man's cheeks seemed rosier, although maybe that was a side product of the bright red shirt being so close to his face. If Kris were wearing boots and smoking a pipe, he'd almost look like…

"Something wrong, Victor?" asked Kris.

He blinked, shook his head. "It's been a long day," he muttered. "I'm tired, not thinking too clearly."

"You need to relax," said Kris. "How about I make you a hot toddy?"

Looking at the kindly old man, so eager to please, Victor knew, at a gut-deep level, that Kris Kringle would die from neglect or a broken heart if he were shut away from the world. Whatever it took, Victor couldn't let that happen.

"Let me put these reports away, then I'll be ready for a martini."

"I should have guessed you're a martini man. Myself, I stick with milk." He patted his stomach and feigned a wince. "Ulcer. Have to watch spicy foods, too, but I enjoy playing bartender for others." He looked over at the stack of logs on the tiled hearth next to the fireplace. "Say, how about I build us a fire? Nothing like a martini in front of a crackling fire to ease a man's worries."

Victor watched as Kris crouched down in front of the hearth and began arranging logs. "Flue's open," he offered.

"Oh, yes, I saw that," Kris said over his shoulder. "Chimneys made in this particular style are especially easy to navigate."

Particularly easy to navigate? The old man had it bad.

After he finished assembling the wood, Kris straightened, patted his pants pocket and pulled out a matchbook. "What you did in court today bought my freedom at a critical time of the year." He struck the match, which flared to life. "I really appreciate that, Victor."

He watched the old man as he lit the fire, fanning sparks to life. He knew what Kris meant by "critical time"—time to be Santa, deliver toys to the children of the world—which left Victor unsure whether to feel sorry or amused by the older man's delusions. Victor's own grandfather had gone around the bend in his later years—talking, more often arguing, with casts of imaginary people. Some of the arguments got heated, with his grandfather yelling and shaking his fist in the air.

Victor smiled to himself. If he had the choice between growing into a crotchety, mean-spirited old man or a delusional but goodhearted one, hell, he'd pick the latter any day.

Kris finally stood, dusting his hands as he stared at the growing fire. "Not bad, if I say so myself." As he turned to face Victor, his gaze stopped on the multitiered storage unit against the far wall. It was filled with books, several college baseball trophies and, in the middle, a large Motorola television.

Kris took a few steps toward the television, peering inquisitively at it. "Where's the antennae?"

"Built in."

"Is this one of those color models?"

Victor laughed. "I like the finer things in life, but those color sets cost as much as a car. I decided Jack Benny and Sid Caesar are just as funny in black and white."

Kris blew a low whistle of approval. "Moving

pictures in one's own living room. What will they think of next?"

He moved closer to get a better look at the framed photos on one of the shelves. "Your family?"

"Yes, that's the Lancaster clan."

"Cheery-looking lot."

"For the most part. My father has his moods."

"Who's the young lady standing next to you?"

He paused. "Linda."

"Girlfriend?"

"Ex."

"May I ask what happened?"

"I got cold feet."

Kris nodded, crossed back to the hearth. He held out his hands, warming them against the heat of the flickering yellow and red flames. For the next few minutes the only sounds were the ticking of the clock and the crackling fire.

Kris suddenly cleared his throat. "No current lady friend?"

"No."

Kris picked up a knickknack on the mantel, turned it one way, then another. "Stella seems like a nice girl," he said nonchalantly.

So that was where this was going. "Yes, she does."

"Different. You know, being a private investigator and all."

Victor thought back to her pulling that gun out of her pocket in the courtroom. "She's different, all right."

He also recalled her light, subtle scent. She didn't load on perfume the way some women did, drenching themselves in strong floral fragrances. For a woman who packed a gun, she also had a surprising softness about her.

Kris was checking out his reflection in a gold-veined mirror on the wall. "Not only do I make great drinks—" he fluffed his beard "—I happen to be a good cook, too."

"Are you hinting you'd like to make dinner tonight?"

"Oh, I'm always happy to throw something together. But I was talking about a more formal, sit-down affair. Maybe next Saturday night?"

"Can't. I'm speaking at a Denver Bar Association dinner."

"What on?"

"The Enforceability of Marital Agreement Provisions Concerning Timing of Filing of Divorce Petitions."

"You lawyers sound like a fun-loving bunch."

Victor laughed. "Touché."

"Then perhaps the following Saturday." Kris put his finger to his forehead and closed his eyes. "Let me see, that'd be…"

"December tenth."

Kris opened his eyes and smiled. "Excellent. Any special requests?"

"Well, we could use the frozen venison a client gave me. It's in the freezer—"

"Oh, no, no, no," Kris said with a wave of his hand. "Too much like reindeer. How about turkey?"

"Turkey works," he said, not missing the venison-reindeer connotation. "You'll be the first chef to finally break in my kitchen."

"What?" Kris's bushy white eyebrows rose. "You've never cooked in your kitchen?"

Victor shrugged. "Too busy."

He made a tsking sound. "Good thing we're seasonal bachelors together, Victor. I'll help you open up your life, your kitchen, even your heart to all the wonderful things ahead of you."

"That's quite a promise."

After a pause, the older man said casually, "I thought perhaps we'd invite Stella and Bobby."

"Is this you trying to open my heart to something?"

Kris's face was a study in naiveté. "I just thought it'd be pleasant. That Stella looks to be a bit on the skinny side. And anyone can look at that boy and see he hasn't had a decent meal in months. Plus—" Kris picked up a fire poker "—you know you like her."

"Kris, I'm having enough trouble defending your claims to be Santa Claus. Don't tell me you've now become a matchmaker, too."

"Let me tell you a secret, my boy." The older man jabbed at a log, which released a flurry of sparks. "We're all what we believe we are."

THE NEXT MORNING, Victor was at work in his down-town office, finalizing a motion. He liked working on Saturdays because it was easier to get work done without ringing phones and the ongoing client crises, but today was different. The quiet and peace seemed to work against him, left too much room for idling thoughts and questions.

Such as wondering about Stella. Was she an early riser? Did she like to make breakfast or was she the type to grab a doughnut and coffee? He had a hard time imagining her cooking, so he guessed the latter. Maybe, with Bobby there, she'd stocked up on cereal and milk. Which led him to wondering how the P.I. and the boy were doing.

By eleven, Victor decided to stop second-guessing how they were and just call. Besides, he'd told her he'd be calling to discuss Danny's lost client.

"Gray's Investigations," answered a boy's voice, "where your case is made in the shade just like Sam Spade."

Victor bit back a smile as he looked out his office window at the distant view of the Rockies. "Good morning, Bobby, this is Victor. I'm guessing Stella's not around." Or you'd be answering the phone a hell of a lot differently.

"She's, uh, down the hall at Mrs. Marshall's. Should be back any minute—oh, here she is."

In the background, he heard muffled voices, as though someone had put a hand over the receiver.

"This is Stella Gray," she finally said, her words clipped.

"Hi, Stella. It's Victor."

"Oh, hi." She sighed. "Sorry if I sounded tense. I asked Bobby not to answer the phone while I was gone and…" Her voice trailed off.

Although she'd caught the boy *on* the phone, he guessed she didn't know how Bobby had answered it. He decided not to enlighten her. Not right this moment, anyway.

"I'm in my office," he said, "which is near yours, so I thought maybe you'd like to grab a cup of coffee, discuss Danny's lost client case?"

"Sure!"

Was her exuberance for the new case—or for him? He hoped the latter, but he'd go for fifty-fifty.

They made arrangements to meet in half an hour at The Wishbone, a nearby diner within walking distance. If he'd made such plans with Danny, or any other of his pals, they'd know thirty minutes meant forty or fifty to Victor. It wasn't that he was chronically late—he had no problem being on time for court—it's just he felt no desire to rush when it came to his personal life.

But not today. Not with Stella.

He was out the door and on his way in five minutes flat.

EXACTLY THIRTY MINUTES later, Victor sat in a corner booth at The Wishbone, nursing his second cup of coffee as he anxiously watched the front door. The scent of burgers and fries lay thick on the air, the short order cook with the Jersey accent kept sniping at the waitresses, and in the corner some sad-faced teenage boy kept filling the jukebox with nickels, playing Pat Boone's "Ain't That a Shame" over and over.

Victor was wishing he'd picked any other place to meet when the front door opened.

It took him a moment to recognize Stella.

Yesterday, she'd looked professional in her skirt and heels. Today she looked more like a tomboy—albeit, a sexy one—in her flats, jeans and sweater. Although her clothes weren't exactly tight, they hugged her body, revealing her trim, compact form. The way her peach sweater caressed her small, pert breasts, it'd be a sin for her to wear anything but sweaters for the rest of her life.

He bumped the table as he stood, sloshing coffee onto the Formica top. Grabbing a napkin to mop it up, he knocked over the bottles of salt and pepper, which clattered loudly. He didn't have time for this. Blowing out an exasperated breath, he managed to extricate himself from the booth without further mishaps.

By the time he reached her, his mind had turned to mush. All he could do was take in her luscious red mouth, her windblown hair, her flushed cheeks. Had she run all the way here? Crazy thought. It was chilly outside, with winter winds picking up. But his male ego liked entertaining the thought he could be so important in Stella's world, she'd race to meet him.

Belatedly realizing he'd carried the soggy napkin with him, he smiled sheepishly. "Had a coffee mishap."

"I saw."

"Call me Grace."

She laughed. "I'd rather call you Victor."

He loved her laugh. Spontaneous, real. The kind of laugh a man could get used to. Suddenly, he could care less about the noises and smells that he'd found so irritating before.

He glanced over her shoulder. "Where's Bobby?"

"He's spending the afternoon with Mrs. Marshall, my landlady. She and I made a deal this morning where in exchange for free background checks on prospective renters, she'd babysit Bobby these next few weeks when I have work outside the office."

Disappointment washed over him. "You have to work today?"

"This said from a man who called me from his office?"

"Touché." Cupping her elbow with his free hand, he steered her toward their booth.

"To answer your question," she said as they walked, "I have a stakeout this afternoon and didn't want to leave Bobby alone. He was rarin' to go with me, of course."

"Of course."

They reached the booth and sat down. Victor flagged down their waitress, who brought Stella a cup of coffee.

"Bobby confessed how he answered the phone," said Stella, reaching for the cream.

"I'm surprised he confessed."

Stella smiled. "I told him I have listening devices in my office."

"You do?"

She flashed him a look of disbelief. "Of course not. I'm just trying to stay a step ahead of Bobby. I thought I knew a few tricks about raising boys after playing mom to my kid brother, but Bobby is a whole other story." She poured cream into her coffee. "He's part kid, part Al Capone."

Victor laughed. "Now, now, he's not as bad as Capone."

"No," she said quietly, "he's not. And I hope he never is." She set down the creamer. "So," she said, "tell me about Danny's missing client."

"Last name's Marlen. First name is either Elmer or Edward—sorry, I didn't remember to bring the notes." He'd been in such a damn hurry to get here, he was lucky he'd remembered his coat.

She stirred her coffee. "Does Elmer or Edward Marlen live in Denver?"

"Yes."

"That's enough to go on."

He paused, surprised. "That's all the information you need?"

She shrugged, set down her spoon. "The name is unique enough I can start with that, anyway. You can call me with the additional information tonight, after I get back from the stakeout, or tomorrow."

"Or I can drop it by your office."

"Sure," she said softly.

He watched as she took a sip of her coffee, her red lips puckering on the edge of the cup. He cleared his throat, suddenly not trusting his voice to work properly.

"By the way, Kris—well, Kris and I—would like to have you and Bobby over for dinner soon."

She swallowed, smiled. "Sure. When?"

"Saturday the tenth?"

"Sounds good."

"I'll call you later with the specifics." That made two more reasons to call or drop by soon.

"How's Kris doing?"

"All settled in."

"I have to admit something," she began, her fingers lightly poised around her cup. "Yesterday in court, it surprised me how impassioned you, a man who grew up privileged, were in defending those less fortunate."

He knew why, but it was something he rarely discussed. That's how it was with those who'd returned from World War II. What happened back there stayed there, in their minds, anyway. Or maybe they didn't talk because most people didn't ask.

Stella, being a P.I., was obviously accustomed to asking questions. And this story wasn't horrific, not like other memories. It was easy enough to share.

"Back in the war, I was in a detail searching for abandoned artillery, when I stumbled upon a young girl, maybe seven, hiding in a burned-out home. She just stared at me with those big eyes, too tired to cry. I gave her my rations, tried to figure out if she had relatives, friends, someplace where she could stay, but nothing." He picked up the fallen saltshaker, set it upright. "I ended up carrying her on my shoulders to the next village, found a family who took her in. Of all the things that affected me the most in the war, that walk with that little girl was one of them."

"Because you saved her life?"

He took a sip of his coffee, set down the cup. "Hate to shoot down your expectations, but I was hardly a hero. After I had given her my rations, I'd walked away. I was rendezvousing with my regiment, didn't want to risk being left behind. But I couldn't get her face out of my mind. Those big, solemn eyes in a child's face. Maybe it was guilt about being, as you so aptly phrased it, a man who grew up privileged, but I knew I'd live the rest of my life regretting not helping that child. So I turned back and carried her to the village."

Stella watched Victor as he took another sip of his coffee, thinking how easy it was to misjudge a man like him.

She reached over and laid her hand on his. After a moment, he turned his hand, causing her fingers to slip into his palm. He closed his hand over hers, his touch gentle, yet firm. Vulnerable, yet masculine.

She watched their hands, mesmerized by his warmth, by how hers felt tucked inside his. Such a simple act, holding hands, yet his touch opened up something deeper inside her, feelings so sweet and primal, it made her ache for more.

From this angle, she saw the time on her watch. Eleven-fifty-five. Of all times to have to go to work.

She looked up, met Victor's gaze. "I told my client I'd start a surveillance around 12:30, so I need to go."

"Now?"

"Yes." She smiled apologetically. "Rain check?"

He gave her hand a squeeze before releasing it. "Absolutely."

He stood, extracted a quarter from his pants pocket and left it on the table. "That should do it."

As he helped her up, she murmured, "You're tipping more than what both of our coffees cost."

"Waitresses work hard."

"Wish P.I.s got tips," said Stella drolly, "other than the informant variety."

Victor chuckled and put his hand lightly on her back as they headed toward the front door. "So what is it you'd like to do after this?"

"I have my stakeout," she reminded him.

"No, I meant…" He opened the entrance door, ushering her outside first. Joining her, he wrapped an arm around her shoulders against the outside cold "…after doing investigations, what are you going to do? And please tell me you're wearing a coat on this stakeout. That sweater won't be enough to keep you warm."

"I will." She looked up into his face. "What do you mean *after?* I plan to be Gray's Investigations until I can no longer do the work."

"Until you're eighty?"

"Well, that's a bit far-fetched, but who knows. I could probably do a stakeout at eighty as long as I was warm, had a Thermos of hot tea with me." She smiled.

But Victor remained serious, his blue eyes probing hers. "It's just...the P.I. business is tough enough without being a woman. Seems you're setting yourself up for a lot of struggle."

It took her a moment to understand what he was really saying. "You think I should want something bigger, better than Gray's Investigations, right? Get out of my cramped office and, I don't know, go to law school or something?"

"Something like that."

"Hate to shock you, but that's the last profession I'd choose for myself."

"Stella, I didn't mean to insult you—"

"But you did," she said quietly. "Just because you want to be D.A., maybe after that mayor, and after that...well, it doesn't mean others don't like exactly where they're at."

She dragged in a deep breath and let it go, the cold filling her chest, numbing her heart. She should have known better than to start having feelings for Victor. Their ideas of success were as different as the sun and the moon, day and night. He wanted to climb the ladder into the clouds, she wanted to stay grounded on her patch of the earth. Not so different from their beliefs on life's intangibles and realities.

Rather than say anything more, she gave a tight-lipped nod, turned and began walking away, her heart as heavy as the cold air around her.

BY WEDNESDAY, Stella valued talking over being tight-lipped, a friend over her wounded pride and, surprisingly enough, intangibles over reality, as sharing the latter with Bobby was driving her to the edge.

That afternoon, while Bobby was down the hall making cookies with Mrs. Marshall, Stella called Victor at his office, ostensibly to forward him the results of her investigation of Elmer Marlen, who she'd found visiting a sick brother in Colorado Springs.

After they wrapped up that discussion, they both got quiet.

"I have a problem," she finally said.

"What is it?"

"Bobby. He likes to break rules. Especially the one about never answering the phone when I'm not there."

"'Made in the shade like Sam Spade'?"

"He also has one about Dashiell Hammett reaching his limit. It doesn't even rhyme."

Victor chuckled. "Sorry. It's not funny."

"He not only breaks the rules I laid down in the beginning, he breaks rules I haven't even made yet!"

"Such as?"

"Drinking coffee. Smoking cigarettes."

"Where'd he get the cigarettes?"

"Says he found them. I think he lifted them from the corner liquor store, but nobody saw him do it." She sighed heavily. "He's not a bad kid all the time. I mean, he's organized my files, dusted, even fixed the globe so it doesn't creak when it's spun. It's just he has this hardcore rebellious streak and…" This was harder than she thought. She hated to be a quitter. "I don't think I can do this any longer. Several times he's disappeared for hours, and I have no idea where to find him. It's too much for me right now."

"I thought Mrs. Marshall was helping out."

"She does, but I can't lean on her all the time."

If Victor had ever wanted a clean run at permanently removing Stella Gray from being the key witness in the Kringle case, now was it. If she backed out on the foster-parenting deal, Judge Gerash would view her in a less positive light, not be so easy on her when she took the stand against Kris Kringle again. She'd look bad, Victor would look good, Kris would go free. The perfect happy ending for a lawyer's case.

"I guess I should call Oscar," Stella said, "tell him I can't do it."

Victor started flipping through his address book.

"Or call the judge. I have his number right here." He stopped on the page with Judge Gerash's office number and stared at it.

He imagined how it'd be to come out on top, ride the wave of publicity right into his announcement that he was running for D.A. And then he heard Bobby's voice play in his head. *"Gray's Investigations, where your case is made in the shade just like Sam Spade."*

A tough kid with the soul of a bebop poet. This was the boy Victor had argued deserved a second chance. Problem was, as good as it'd be for Victor and Kris if Stella pulled out, it'd be lousy for Bobby. This time of year judges were overwhelmed with packed dockets—rather than find another custodial parent on such short notice, Bobby would most likely be packed off to juvie hell on the eve of Christmas, the first of many holidays spent behind bars at a maximum security lockup.

Victor had asked for the boy to have these next few weeks as a test to see if he could be rehabilitated. If he supported Stella's giving up, he was ultimately giving up on Bobby, too. Deserting him would be no different than deserting that little girl.

"Let me talk to him," Victor said. "Maybe I can get through."

"Thank you, Victor," she said, obviously relieved.

After a moment, he asked, "Still mad at me?"

"No. Well, a little."

"I'm sorry."

"Apology accepted."

"I'll drop by around five-thirty?"

"Sure."

"One other thing. It's just a suggestion. Maybe if you gave Bobby a task, something where he got to make a few phone calls, he might temper his urge to be the biggest, baddest receptionist this side of Chicago."

Stella laughed softly. "If that would make him less Al Capone and more little boy, it's worth a try."

CHAPTER FOUR

CLOSER TO 6:00 P.M., Victor walked up to the door marked Gray's Investigations and knocked. From inside, he heard faint strains of Bing Crosby crooning "White Christmas." A moment later, Bobby opened the door.

The boy's hand-me-downs from the orphanage had been replaced by a new pair of jeans, a T-shirt with broad horizontal stripes and a pair of Keds. Stella was putting the stipends to good use.

Victor smiled. "Is this Gray's Investigations, where your case is made in the shade just like Sam Spade?"

The boy rolled his eyes, although not before Victor had caught a smile in them, then opened the door wider.

As Victor stepped in, his first thought was how masculine the office looked, then he realized Stella probably hadn't changed a thing since she'd lost her old man. Victor, on the other hand, had been eager to break loose of his father's law firm and set up his own office.

Bobby crossed to a door behind a battered desk and knocked. From the other side, Stella called out. "Yes?"

"It's Victor," Bobby said.

"I'm busy…ironing. Tell him I'll be a while."

Bobby turned back to Victor. "She said—"

"I heard." Victor took off his fedora and sat on the rosewood-back chair in front of the desk. That ironing line had to be her alibi for leaving him alone with Bobby. Okay. He'd run with it.

Bobby took the seat on the swivel chair behind the desk and spun slightly to the left, then the right, the chair creaking with his movements.

Victor glanced down at the desk covered with papers, notes, coffee cups. His gaze stopped on a photo of a lanky young man in a World War I uniform, grinning despite his arm being in a sling. Had to be Pete Gray. Lying in the middle of the desk was a copy of the pulp magazine *Strange Detective Mysteries*.

"Interesting reading?" Victor asked.

Bobby grinned. "Yeah." He lowered his voice. "Stella's a pack rat. She had a ton of magazines stacked along her wall, but I cleaned them up, gave a bunch to Mrs. Marshall. She loves those movie star stories in *Life* magazine."

"I'm sure Stella appreciated the help."

"If I hadn't come along, she'd have kept pilin' magazines in stacks and more stacks until clients wouldn't have had anywhere to sit."

Victor chuckled. "Well, good thing you're here."

Bobby shrugged, picked up a pencil. "I'm not here much longer, though."

Victor was at a loss for words. Funny how he could work up a speech at a moment's notice in the court-room, but one-on-one with Bobby, and suddenly Victor felt somewhat insecure. Could he pull this off? Convince a hard-luck kid to shave off some of that log he carried on his shoulder before it was too late?

"Bobby," he began, "the short time you're here can make the difference between spending the next few years in a foster home, another orphanage, or in Lookout Mountain for Boys."

Bobby turned somber, his gray eyes fixed on Victor.

"So, let's talk about you abiding by Stella's rules. Like, you can't slip away for hours at a time. I've rep-resented clients who were robbed, beaten up, even shot at on some of those streets late at night. Besides, it's not fair for Stella to not know where you are. She worries about you."

That seemed more impressive to the boy than being robbed, beaten or shot. "Okay," he muttered, "I'll ask if I can take a walk."

"And no smoking while you're out on a walk, or back at the office or anywhere in the world for that matter."

Bobby suddenly found his Keds to be of the utmost interest. He scuffed them back and forth across the hardwood floor.

"Bobby, you have two-and-a-half more weeks to show the court you're capable of being rehabili-tated—"

"What's that mean?"

"Capable of being healthier, more useful. If you can do that, I'll fight like hell—" He shook his head. "Sorry." He noticed Bobby jotting something down. "I'll fight hard for you to not be sentenced to Lookout Mountain. I can't promise we'll win, but you'll make our chances better if you start acting like a boy who wants a better life."

To Victor's surprise, Bobby's eyes grew moist. The boy quickly looked away, swiped his hand across his face. When he looked back, he was all accommodation. Or so Victor hoped.

"So, if I follow the rules," Bobby said quietly, "what do I get?"

"What do you want? We could go shopping, look at toys. Or tell me what you like and I'll, uh, tell Santa."

Bobby frowned. "You believe Kris Kringle is Santa?"

"I didn't say that." He didn't want to say yes, didn't want to say no, so he denied saying anything. Typical lawyer response.

"I don't believe in Santa, either," said Bobby. "But since you asked, there's something I want. I've wanted it for a long time." He stood, started to reach into his pants pocket, then stopped.

"What?" Victor finally asked.

"Never mind." Bobby dropped his hand. "I like you, Victor, but…it's my secret."

Victor nodded, looked at the magazine cover.

"So," he said, changing the subject, "been reading a lot of those?"

Bobby shrugged. "Twenty or thirty, I guess. They didn't have anything like that at St. Mary's."

"Thinking of becoming a pulp fiction writer?"

"Nah, I'd rather be the real thing."

"A P.I.? That'd be a great profession for you, Bobby. You're fearless, inquisitive…" He thought about how the boy had cleaned up the stacks of magazines "…and well organized."

The boy looked so surprised and pleased, Victor guessed he had gotten little positive feedback at the orphanage. Hard to make good choices if everybody's always saying how bad you are.

Bobby gestured to the globe. "I want to be a P.I. who travels. The way Stella did."

The door behind the desk opened, and she stepped out.

Maybe it was a trick of the light, or the deep-throated yearning of Bing Crosby's voice in the background, but for a moment Victor thought, "She's the one."

She wore a blue sweater that complemented her strawberry-blond hair. As usual, she wore little makeup, except for a slash of red on her lips. The dungarees would be nondescript if he hadn't noticed the outline of a gun in her front left pocket. Talk about a woman packing heat…

He stood. "You look nice."

A look of appreciation washed over her.

"Thanks." She looked at Bobby. "The way Stella did?" she prompted.

"I'd like to be a P.I. and travel, the way you did." Bobby hopped up and crossed to the globe. He turned it, eyeing the land and oceans as he talked. "You know, on cases with your dad."

Stella stared at the boy, her face softening. "*With* is the key word, Bobby. When it comes to traveling and following a case to another city, a smart P.I. travels with a buddy." She glanced down at the desk. "You cussed again?"

Bobby laughed. "No, *Victor* did!"

Stella feigned shock. "Looks like you owe Bobby ten cents."

"I do?" Victor grinned, a confused look on his face.

"Whenever Bobby cusses, he loses ten cents from his retainer."

"Oh." Victor stood, picked up his fedora. "Well, I have an idea how to pay up. How about the three of us go out for hamburgers?"

"Yeah!" Bobby said, bounding over. "You're made in the shade like Sam Spade."

A FEW HOURS LATER, the three of them stood again in the office of Gray's Investigations, their faces flushed from the walk home after gorging on burgers, fries and shakes.

Stella began unbuttoning her coat. "Would you like me to make some coffee?"

"If it were earlier, I'd say yes," answered Victor. "But this late, I'll have trouble sleeping. Thanks, anyway, Red."

He'd started calling her that on the walk home, a teasing reference to her hair color.

"I'm going to hang up my coat," she said. "If you'll help Bobby get set up for bed, I'll take a few minutes to put away my ironed clothes."

"Sure," said Victor, watching as she entered her bedroom, shutting the door behind her. He turned to Bobby. "What did she mean by set up—"

Bobby was dragging a folded cot across the room. He stopped. "Setting up my bed. I sleep on it next to the kitchenette."

"There's a kitchenette?"

The boy pointed to the bookcase. "It's back there. She turned a bookcase so its shelves are like cabinets where she puts canned foods, cereal, plates and stuff. There's an icebox on the window ledge. We make coffee and sometimes soup or hot dogs, using the hot plate."

Victor peered around the bookcase. "Very practical," he murmured. *Just like Stella.* He helped the boy finish assembling the cot, blankets and pillow.

"At first I thought it was weird to be sleeping in the office," said Bobby, "but now I like it. I can look out the window and watch the stars and moon. If I get hungry, I go into the kitchenette and get a snack. Stella has her rules about going outside, smoking, the phone…but otherwise, I have a lot of freedom and I like it. Reminds me of the couple who almost adopted me. They let me feel…well, at home there, too."

Bobby rummaged in the bookcase, extracted a magazine and flashlight, then stood next to the cot, looking expectantly at Victor. "I usually get in and read a magazine with a flashlight."

"Okay."

He fiddled with the flashlight. "Don't mean to be rude, Victor, but I'm going to bed now."

It took Victor a moment to understand. "Oh." He picked up his hat. "Guess you don't want me tucking you in and reading you a fairy tale, eh?"

"I'm too old for that. Besides, I don't believe in fairy tales. They're just lies, the way everything in that window display we saw tonight was a lie. Nobody really lives like that."

It pained Victor to hear a young boy be so callused.

"Well, I'll say good-night then." He looked at Stella's door, debating whether to knock or leave.

"Go ahead," Bobby whispered. "She likes you."

That nudge of encouragement did the trick. Victor knocked lightly.

Stella opened the door, backlit from the light in her bedroom, which set fire to the tips of her strawberry-blond hair and emphasized the curves of her figure. He shifted uncomfortably.

"Are you through putting away your clothes?"

"Almost."

He glanced at Bobby, who still stood next to the cot. Turning back, he put on his hat. "Come outside with me, Red. I want to say good-night to you. Properly."

CHAPTER FIVE

TEN MINUTES LATER, Stella and Victor stood on the sidewalk outside her building. The scent of baking pies from the Puritan Pie Company across the street permeated the chilly night air.

A round-bodied black Chrysler, its tires crunching against the asphalt, cruised down the street, Fats Domino's "Ain't That a Shame" floating through the driver's partially open window.

"Hope he remembers to close that window later," said Victor. "Weather report says an inch of snow before sunrise." He looked at Stella. "I should've told you to wear a coat." Victor slipped off his coat and wrapped it around her shoulders.

She inhaled deeply, catching his scent in the material. Musky and masculine.

Looking up into his face, she studied the angle of his fedora, and how it cut a sharp shadow across the top of his face, hiding his eyes. The neon sign across the street cast a pale crimson glow along the hard line of his jaw and his full lips. In the distance, a dog barked.

"I shouldn't like you," she murmured.

"Why not?"

"December twenty-sixth."

"Stella," he murmured, shaking his head back and forth, "that's business. This is…"

"Intangible?"

A sudden drop of moisture blurred her vision. She blinked, looked up. Tiny flakes of snow airily danced over their heads. Closing her eyes, she felt them land— soft and light—on her face. That's how it felt with Victor. Invigorating, fresh, alive. And, yes, intangible.

"You're so lovely, Stella."

Opening her eyes, she looked into the shadows of his face. "I want to see your eyes." She reached up and removed his hat.

Even in this muted light, she could see a curl of hair that had fallen over his high forehead. She brushed it back with her hand, liking the way he responded with a sensuous curl of his lips.

Something magnetic passed between them—a heady, giddy sensation—and she felt herself grow more vulnerable, more open to him. Sensations poured through, a drizzly tenderness, an achy need.

Stella swallowed.

Victor lowered his eyes to her mouth.

"I didn't mean to dismiss your concern about December twenty-sixth. It's just…we're more than two people on opposing sides in court. We have a lot in common."

"Like bullheadedness," she teased.

"You more than me."

When she playfully went to punch him, he snagged her hand and held it. He grew serious. "We also have the good things in common, Stella. Like how we feel about Bobby."

She nodded, staring into his eyes, sensing everything she was feeling reflected there. Desire, bewilderment, happiness.

The snowflakes had increased, the tiny dancing dots of white blowing, dancing, shimmering in the air around them.

He bent his head, just as she raised up to meet him, parting her lips. They drew closer until she shared his very breath…

"Stella," yelled a boy's voice, "it's starting to snow—you okay?"

She paused for a suspended, surreal moment. "Please tell me that's not who I think it is."

"It's who you think it is."

With a small, strangled groan, she pulled away and dropped Victor's hand.

"He can't see us over here," explained Victor, "so he thinks you're out here alone. Probably thought you were locked out."

She released a prolonged, achy sigh. "I was about to be kissed for the first time in over a year."

"So was I."

"Victor Lancaster, I don't believe you."

"Okay, first time in several months."

"Stella?" called Bobby.

"I'm okay," she answered, raising her voice. "Just saying good-night to Victor."

She returned his coat, planted the hat back onto his head. The snow flurries were picking up, whitening the air.

Victor, his hand on her back, walked her briskly back toward the building entrance where Bobby still stood, his eyes wide as he realized what he'd obviously interrupted.

"Sorry," Bobby said as they got closer.

Victor smiled. "No problem. It's smart for me to leave now. Weather report mentioned the possibility of a foot or more by tomorrow—guess they were right." He suddenly groaned, gave his head a shake. "Kris is going to need a ride home from his temporary job tomorrow and I'll be stuck in court."

"I'll give him a ride," offered Stella, stepping onto the covered porch next to Bobby. After all, Victor had helped her out today.

He looked up, squinting against the snow, pulling up the collar of his coat. "May Company. Toy department. He gets off at five." With a wave, he headed down the walkway.

Stella and Bobby stepped inside, closing the building door behind them. She brushed flakes off her sweater.

"Sorry," Bobby said sheepishly as they headed

toward the stairs. "I'm used to living with nuns, so I wasn't thinking about…I mean, I did think about it earlier. In fact, I told Victor you liked him, but I forgot all that when I saw the snow falling." He blew out an exasperated breath.

"Bobby—" she put a hand on his shoulder as they headed up the stairs "—if you're going to be my P.I. assistant, you have to learn to not say *everything* you're thinking."

He stopped, blinked at her. "You're hiring me?"

"I didn't say that." She caught herself. His cussing had cost him a sizeable chunk of his retainer. Only fair to give him a way to earn it back, give him a sense of accomplishment. "Okay, yes, I'm hiring you."

Bobby whooped so loudly, she had to shush him. "People are sleeping," she whispered.

He pressed his lips together, but the joy still shone in his eyes. "Does this mean I get to answer the phone?" he whispered.

She thought of Victor's suggestion. "Can you answer it 'Gray's Investigations, may I help you?'"

He nodded exuberantly.

"It's a deal."

They continued climbing the staircase to the second floor.

"Now that we're business partners," he suddenly said, "can I answer the phone 'Gray's and Myers's Investigations'?"

No was on the tip of her tongue when she remembered Victor's words in court the other day. *Bobby Myers deserves a second chance.* The boy wasn't asking for much, and it'd give him pride.

Plus, it was a hell of a lot better than that "Sam Spade made in the shade" line.

"Gray's and Myers's Investigations," she repeated slowly. "It has a ring to it."

THE NEXT DAY, at 5:00 p.m., Stella and Bobby entered the revolving door of May Company department store, and headed toward the toy department.

When they reached it, they both stopped and watched a photographer cajoling kids to smile. Employees dressed as elves scurried around the line of parents and their children, the latter waiting to sit on Santa's lap.

"I should have guessed," muttered Stella as she stared at Kris Kringle, dressed in a red-and-white suit, sitting on the thronelike chair. Taking a pouty-faced toddler onto his lap, he gave the child a candy cane. While the little girl gurgled and smacked on it, Kris belted out a hearty *ho-ho-ho.*

"Man, he's really into it," said Bobby.

"Probably been practicing." And driving Victor crazy in the process.

"That beard can't be real." Bobby cupped his hands around his jaw. "Mr. Kringle's beard was, like, this short at court."

"Right, nobody's hair grows that fast."

"He'd make a better Rumpelstiltskin."

She glanced down at the boy. "Thought you didn't know any fairy tales."

"Is that one?" When she nodded, he made a sound of surprise. "I always thought it was called a lesson. The nuns read it to us to teach us about not talking to strangers."

Stella laughed under her breath. "Let's stand closer, where Kris can see us. Looks like there's only a few more kids in line, so it shouldn't be long."

They walked along a plastic gate made to look like a snow-topped picket fence over which cardboard reindeer and elves peeked. They finally stopped in front of a huge display of toys that was in plain view of Santa and the kids, which Stella realized was a very savvy move on the part of the store. If a kid got stymied as to what to ask for, for Christmas, Santa could gesture toward the display and the child could point at a toy, giving the parent the inside scoop on what to buy.

Christmas was, after all, about buying and selling. *That* was the reality.

"Stella, dear!" Mrs. Marshall, coordinated in a black-and-cream weave wool coat and black velvet cap, walked up to them. "Are you here for the big sale, too?"

"I'm here to give Santa a ride home."

Mrs. Marshall laughed, which always reminded Stella of Glenda the Good Witch's bubbly laugh in

The Wizard of Oz. "I imagine the North Pole is a long way to travel," she said with great emphasis, giving Bobby a look.

"Santa Claus doesn't live at the North Pole," he said matter-of-factly, "because there's no such thing as Santa Claus. We're giving the guy *playing* Santa a ride to my lawyer's apartment."

Mrs. Marshall blinked rapidly and turned her attention back to Stella. "I wanted to ask if you'd be interested in an electric icebox this coming year. Frigidaire makes one with, of all things, an ice ejector…"

While they talked, Stella kept an eye on Bobby, who stayed nearby, watching the children take their turns on Santa's lap. At one point, a dark-haired girl shyly approached Kris. The mother, gently nudging her forward, explained something about the little girl having traveled recently from Holland.

Stella tuned out the rest as she and Mrs. Marshall continued talking.

A few minutes later, after Mrs. Marshall left, Bobby looked up at Stella with a funny expression on his face. "Did you see that little girl who only spoke Dutch?"

Stella half nodded as she glanced at her watch.

"What's crazy," said Bobby, "is the mom, who'd just adopted the girl, didn't speak Dutch. Then, just like that—" he snapped his fingers "—Santa, I mean Kris, started speaking Dutch with the little girl. That was, like, magic. For a moment, I wondered if…"

"Bobby, I speak Spanish, but that doesn't make me Carmen Miranda." She paused. "Oh, good, the last child is sitting on Kris's lap. We'll be out of here soon."

THIRTY MINUTES LATER, Stella, Kris and Bobby were driving back to Victor's apartment. Stella, who'd always lived in Denver, prided herself on being able to handle any vehicle in the snow, although her old Caddy was getting grumpier every winter. She turned onto Colfax, tugging hard on the steering wheel.

"Maybe you'll get a car with power steering one of these days," said Kris, sitting in the front seat.

He still wore his Santa suit, which irked her. He hadn't wanted to "break the spell" for children who might see him leaving the department store. Which meant she looked like a taxi service for Old Saint Nick.

"Yeah," Bobby said enthusiastically from the backseat, "maybe you'll get a Thunderbird or a Chevy Bel Air flip-top!"

"Maybe." She grunted as she wrestled the steering wheel to straighten out the tires again. "If business keeps going well."

"Oh, it will," said Kris, "it will."

She wanted to say that *telling* her that her business would keep improving was a world apart from her *working* to make it so. But she didn't. Kris was a sweet-tempered man who believed he was a fictional character. Being practical and realistic had no place in his world, so she'd save her breath.

"I understand how it is to worry about business," he continued, stroking his beard. "Every year my gift list gets longer and longer, and I wonder how I'll ever get them all distributed by the end of Christmas day."

The silence in the car could have been cut with a butter knife.

Stella squinted through the dirty windshield at the street sign. "I think I turn right here."

"That's correct," said Kris. "Turn right, then drive three blocks to Stout Street. So, I'm similar to you, Stella, because I manage my own office and employees."

"Except your employees are elves and reindeer," chimed in Bobby.

Stella looked into the rearview mirror and caught the boy's eye. She gave him a please-tell-me-you're-not-serious look.

He smiled sweetly back. Which made her more worried than relieved.

"I wish," Kris continued, "that children weren't encouraged to make lists in the first place. It'd be much better if everybody only asked for one thing."

"Yes," Stella said, maneuvering down another snow-packed street, "I imagine that's a lot of work." Were these the kind of conversations Victor and Kris were having every night?

"Fortunately," said Kris, patting her on the arm, "I know what you want, and I'm working on it."

She fought hard not to roll her eyes. It was one

thing to discuss Kris's concerns about coordinating all the wish lists for the children of the world, but telling her what she wanted for Christmas was crossing the imaginary line.

"And what might that be?" she asked testily, slowing to a stop at a red light.

"Something you've wanted for several years."

"Like that's so hard to guess." The light turned green and she shifted into First. "I held on to Gray's Investigations when nobody wanted to hire a woman, even though I was Pete Gray's daughter, so building my clientele is something anybody who's spent more than fifteen minutes with me knows."

Kris's voice softened. "I was speaking of something else. Something less factual and more indescribable. Something that goes to the very heart of who you are, and what you want to have."

"Oh, this is good," she murmured. "Okay, I give. What is it that goes to my very heart?"

"It's what you lost when your father died," he said gently. "What you've wanted ever since and fear you'll never find again."

An old hurt pierced right through her, one she thought she'd conveniently put away, out of sight, out of mind, but obviously not out of her heart.

"Stella," said Kris, "I—"

She held up a silencing hand. "Can't drive if I can't see," she said hoarsely, blinking back a well of emotion.

They drove slowly, no one talking for a few blocks

through downtown, past store windows with brightly blinking red and white lights, past the incessant ringing of a Salvation Army bell ringer, past scents of popcorn and hot dogs from a street vendor.

She heard a rustling noise in the backseat.

Looking again in the rearview mirror, she saw Bobby, his face serious, pull a folded piece of paper from his shirt pocket. For a moment he held it midair, as though debating something.

"If you're really Santa," he said solemnly, handing it to Kris, "you'll get this for me for Christmas."

They'd stopped at another light. Stella, still somewhat numb after her exchange with the older man, looked at him as he accepted the paper and opened it. He read it carefully, his finger to the side of his nose, making an occasional thoughtful noise. Finally he looked over at the boy.

"It's one of my tougher orders this season." He paused. "But I promise to find it."

The light changed and Stella punched the gas. As the car lurched forward, Kris and Bobby laughed in surprise, but she stared straight ahead, her jaw tight, fighting a tumult of feelings. She felt hurt and defensive that Kris had recognized a deep-seated pain within her. But more than that, she felt furious that Kris would purposefully mislead a young, needy boy whose entire future hinged on how he managed his world, and his dreams, for these few weeks.

She looked over at Bobby, who leaned over the

front seat, a big grin splitting his face. She'd never seen him look so happy. Or hopeful. And although she wanted to give Kris a piece of her mind about making promises he couldn't keep to a child, now wasn't the time. Nor was he the one to say it to.

She'd talk to Victor, explain that the old man's delusional world was in danger of breaking a boy's heart.

FIFTEEN MINUTES LATER, Stella looked around Victor's living room. It reflected the man, all right. Classy, smart and yet down-to-earth. On the coffee table were a fountain pen and an empty martini glass. My, Victor certainly knew how to slave away with style.

"Wow," exclaimed Bobby, "he has a television!"

"You must come over and watch it sometime," said Kris. "There's a new cartoon show starting next Saturday, *The Mighty Mouse Playhouse*."

Bobby shot a look at Stella.

"We're coming over that night for dinner—" Stella began.

"Let's get here early, then!"

"I wouldn't mind at all having the company," said Kris. "Bring him early. He can stay the day, help me cook dinner."

"Can I?" asked Bobby, his eyes gleaming. "Please?"

It was that look of hope again. No way could she say no, not for something she could promise *and* make come true. "If it's okay with Victor, it's okay with me."

"Cool!"

"Let's go to the kitchen now," suggested Kris, rubbing his stomach. "I'm famished after a hard day of work. I'll make us a light snack to hold us over to dinner."

"Go ahead, Bobby," Stella said, "I'll wait here."

She wandered around the living room, stopping to check the books, mostly mysteries, shelved on the room divider, what looked to be a family photo and several college baseball trophies. On the mantel of the fireplace she picked up a matchbook and read its cover: *Ship Ahoy, Atlanta's Leading Restaurant.*

She heard the front door open.

Victor stepped into the room, wearing the coat and fedora from last night, carrying a briefcase. After hanging his hat on a rack next to the door, he turned and saw Stella.

He gave her that familiar boyish grin. "Look who we have here," he said. "Am I a lucky man or what?"

She stood, feeling a rush of heat fill her face. "You're a charmer, that's what."

Bobby's and Kris's laughter rolled down the hallway.

"Kris is making Bobby a snack," she explained. She stepped closer to Victor and lowered her voice. "Before they come back, we need to talk."

Victor nodded, suddenly serious. They stood so close, it reminded her of last night, how it'd felt in his embrace, how it was to almost kiss…

She eased in a breath. "Kris's delusions are going to crush Bobby."

Victor raised an eyebrow. "What happened?"

She glanced toward the kitchen, back to Victor. "He's promised to get Bobby what he wants for Christmas."

Victor looked confused. "What does he want?"

"I don't know. It's on a piece of paper—looks like a page ripped out of a magazine. I think he's been carrying it with him for quite a while, and now Kris has it."

Victor nodded. "He started to show me, but changed his mind. It seems to hold great significance to Bobby."

She dragged a hand through her hair. "I'm concerned because Kris has gone over the edge with his delusions, Victor. He not only promised Bobby he'd get whatever is on that paper, but he also claimed to know what secret wish I've nurtured since…well, since Dad died." This was harder to talk about than she'd expected. "Forget that last part. What concerns me is that Bobby's put his trust in Kris, probably believes he might really be Santa, and he's going to get hurt. He could give up, fall back into his old ways, end up at that maximum security school for boys. You and I both know that years spent there most likely mean…"

"I'll handle it," he said quietly. "Keep in mind he's a harmless old man who means well. The key is to find where he's from, reunite him with any family members."

She glanced at the fireplace, remembering the matchbook. "Have you traveled to Atlanta?"

"No. Why?"

She looked back. "He might be from there. It's something to check out."

Victor studied her face for a long moment. "All right. But let's get back to you. What did he say that affected you so deeply?"

She laughed uncomfortably. "It's silly, really. He mentioned something about a secret in my heart, and who doesn't have secrets?"

"But it upset you."

She paused, nodded.

Victor pulled her close. "Maybe you have a lot going on in your head, and in your heart, and it's time some of that came out, Red."

She sank into his embrace, her face buried inside his coat, against his soft cotton shirt. The warmth of his chest invaded her body, making her feel safe and protected. It felt good to not be in control, to let herself lean on someone else's strength.

He bent his head so his lips were near her ear. "Tell me the secret in your heart," he whispered huskily.

He cupped her chin with his warm hand and turned her face to his. His blue eyes, so warm and caring, probed hers. And in that moment, she realized hope was many things, from the wish in a child's heart to the secret ache in a woman's.

She flashed on her parents' faces, thought back to

the last time she'd seen her brother. He was so busy with college and his new fiancée he never visited Denver anymore.

"I miss hearing my dad's stories," she whispered, "smelling my mom's meat loaf baking for dinner. I even miss my kid brother's dumb pranks. The four of us were a team, our home a refuge, and it's gone." She swallowed back the emotion crowding her throat. "My secret is…I want back what I lost. I want my family."

He pulled back slightly and, cradling her jaw with his warm hand, tilted her face up to his. His gaze fell to her mouth. He drifted his thumb across her lower lip, then slowly back again.

"Can't give you back the past," he murmured huskily, "but I can offer the future."

And with that, he kissed her.

CHAPTER SIX

"CAN YOU BELIEVE IT?" Kris, walking with Victor down Sixteenth Street, did a double-take at a young man they passed. "He's wearing a T-shirt, and it was snowing just the day before yesterday!"

It was Saturday morning, and Victor had offered to walk Kris to his Santa gig at the department store. It had been several days since he and Kris had talked, and Victor wanted to find out what the older man had promised Bobby.

"I've seen people wearing parkas in June," commented Victor.

"Denver weather can never seem to make up its mind," Kris said. "One day snow, next day sunshine. Quite unlike the North Pole!" He chuckled heartily.

"North Pole, eh?" Victor dug his hands into the pockets of his Ricky jacket. It was time to dig deeper into Kris's delusional world. "So, what's it like up there at the North Pole?"

Kris tipped his head to a passerby. "Consistent weather every year. Sun rises in the early evening at spring equinox and finally sets just after autumn equinox. It isn't seen again until the spring equinox."

He was impressed by the old guy's research. "Must be difficult to get ready for Christmas in all that darkness. I mean, you have toys to make and…" hell, he had no idea what Santa did besides that "…and whatever you do."

"The workshop fires burn around the clock— plenty of light to make toys, tune up the sleigh, take care of Rudolph and the other reindeer."

If anyone heard this conversation, they'd make arrangements for both of them to visit the mental institution. "So, how'd you end up in Denver?"

Kris shook his head dejectedly as he stroked his beard. "I thought it'd be a good idea to take the sleigh on a test drive." He sighed heavily. "Hate to admit it, but I got lost, ended up in Red Rocks Park. Beautiful area, by the way."

Victor tried not to do a double-take, but *Red Rocks Park?* A majestic natural park just outside Denver, it boasted towering red stone formations that had been a popular tourist spot for years. It was difficult, however, to imagine Kris accidentally landing there.

"Yes, Red Rocks is beautiful," Victor agreed. "So, you left your sleigh there?"

"Had no choice. Hate to leave it outside in the elements, but…" He shrugged. "Fortunately, the reindeer are used to the North Pole, so I know they're fine. Plus, there's lots of vegetation at Red Rocks for them to eat, plenty of sheltered places to sleep. They'll be quite healthy when I pick them up again on Christmas Eve."

Victor nodded. "Not earlier?"

"Oh, no. That'd be impossible. The magic of the journey starts on Christmas Eve." He looked perplexed. "Thought everyone knew that."

"Oh, we do." Victor paused. "I thought perhaps you might want to go to Atlanta."

"Atlanta?" Kris looked surprised. "Certainly. There, as well as many other towns on Christmas Eve through Christmas Day."

"When the magic occurs," Victor repeated.

"Right." Kris stopped, patted his pocket. "I hate to pry, Victor, but I can tell something's troubling you." He pulled out a matchbook and his pipe. "Want to stop for a minute and talk?"

Just the opening he was looking for. "Yes, I would."

They stood in front of an ornately designed brick building that had been turned into retail shops, including a jewelry store whose window was filled with sparkling items laid out on a red velvet background.

"Go ahead." Kris lit his pipe, looking into the window.

"It's about Bobby."

Kris nodded, puffing on his pipe.

"He gave you a piece of paper that contains a picture or a description of something he wants very much."

Kris blew out a cloud of sweet-smelling smoke. "Quite right."

"Well, Kris…" This was the hard part. "I'd like for you to not extend promises that can't be fulfilled. Such as promising Bobby whatever is on that piece of paper."

Kris smoked his pipe for a few moments, a contemplative look on his round face. "But I'm going to fulfill that promise."

Victor paced a few steps. "Kris, I'm speaking as Bobby's lawyer. He's a troubled child who is going to be in the judge's crosshairs for sentencing in a few weeks, and he doesn't need any more disappointment than he may already be receiving from Judge Gerash. The Santa Claus act is really nice, and quite inspiring at times, but I'm counseling you as a lawyer who deals with people all the time—people who have to face consequences without peppermint sugarcoating. I'm thinking about both of you when I tell you to cease and desist from leading Bobby to believe in Santa Claus to the extremes you're taking it. Do you understand the plain meaning of my words?"

Kris glanced at the ground, then back to Victor. He nodded sagely. "I understand. I won't say another word."

"Thank you, Kris."

The older man smiled, nodded. "Is that all?"

Victor laughed uncomfortably. It hadn't been easy

laying down the law, literally, with the gentle old man. "Isn't that enough?"

"Good." As he tapped his pipe against the brick wall, he looked into the display window. "Beautiful, aren't they?"

Victor checked out the display, his gaze landing on a diamond ring. The solitary diamond, at least a carat, was set in a simple gold band. Impressive, yet unpretentious. Made him think of Stella.

"She's a lovely girl," said Kris, putting his pipe back into his pocket.

Victor looked at him. "Who?"

"Why, Stella, of course." He looked up at the sky, blinked, then started walking. "I'm going to have to start planning my menu for next Saturday night. Something impressive but unpretentious would be very good."

"KRIS," STELLA SAID the following Saturday night at dinner, "wherever you learned to cook, I want to go there, too."

Kris, sitting between Victor and Bobby, smiled appreciatively at her. "I learned at the Nor—"

"More potatoes, Red?" asked Victor, handing her the bowl. "These are even better than at that restaurant we ate at the other night."

She bit back a laugh, knowing exactly what Victor was doing. Since the night she and Bobby had dropped off Kris, Stella and Victor had had several dates, during which time they'd discussed how to ensure Kris didn't go overboard with the Santa thing again, especially in front of Bobby.

"Dinner was delicious," she said, pushing back her chair. "Since Kris and Bobby cooked dinner, I'll clear the table."

"I'll join you," said Victor.

Entering the kitchen, she came to a dead stop. "I don't believe it. Not only do you have a television, you also have a dishwasher!"

"Now you're making me feel guilty." He set a bowl on the countertop and opened the dishwasher door. "C'mere," he said. "I'll show you how to load dishes into it."

"What will they think of next," she murmured, watching Victor place dishes in one area, utensils in another.

It didn't take long before their hands were touching more than they were touching the dishes. Finally, they stopped pretending to load the dishwasher and simply stood near each other, less than a foot apart, their eyes not hiding the intensity of what they felt.

Victor reached up and turned on the radio perched on top of the Frigidaire. "Love Is a Many-Splendored Thing" was playing.

He took her hand in his, wrapped his other arm around her, pulling her close.

He began swaying slightly, guiding her body with his.

She faltered. "I'm a terrible dancer."

"I'm sure you would be if you tried doing this in those stilettos." She laughed softly as he tugged her closer. "Just follow me. One. Two. One. Two."

The combination of Victor's murmured encouragement and his body leading hers gave her confidence. She melted against him, finding their rhythm. One. Two. Outside his kitchen window, she watched a full moon rise, its luminous, yellow glow a distant match for the way she felt inside. It was as though her blood had turned molten, flowing sensuously through her breasts, her middle, her thighs, making her feel limp and exhilarated at the same time.

I'm in love, she thought hazily. It had never been this way before. And it would never be this way again because there would never be another man for her. Never. She knew that as certainly as the man in the moon was her witness.

Victor put his head next to hers. "Stella…"

"Hmm?" One. Two.

"You know, I've been thinking about announcing my candidacy in the next district attorney's race."

She stilled for an instant, then fell back into step. "Yes."

"If I win, I'd like to hire you to be my senior investigator."

Something inside of her chilled, but she tried to ignore it. "That's…very generous."

"You deserve it. It's not easy being a woman in

your profession." He held her closer. "But there's more. I'd like for us to be side-by-side, not only in our professional careers, but also in our personal lives."

Even as a giddiness washed over her, the chill grew colder. "But…you want the splashy newspaper coverage from winning the Santa Claus case to be the launching pad for your announcement, right?"

"Well, yes. It's an affirmative, popular story. Perfect backdrop for making an announcement."

She stopped, looked up into his face. "In order to have that, you need me to *not* take the stand against Kris, right?"

He didn't have to answer. She saw it in his face.

"But," she said softly, "we've talked about Kris needing help. Plus, my taking the stand helps my career."

"Stella, I need you."

"No—" she stepped back "—you're manipulating me."

This was all about his political career. Sure, he was offering her a job, but to work for *him*. He was telling her how much he needed her, professionally and personally, but again, how much of that was about *him?*

Emotion, hard and hostile, thickened the air. She braced herself against the cold, slick countertop as a bluesy, lovelorn Sinatra tune started playing on the radio. It almost made her want to laugh, hearing such a melancholy song at such a heartsick moment.

"You're not happy," he said quietly.

"Got that right."

Victor hung his head momentarily, then looked back at her. "You're determined to put Kris away, aren't you?"

Stella felt dumbstruck. Angry. Betrayed.

And of course, there was Bobby.

She thought back to the boy's face when he'd handed Kris the folded piece of paper, and how he'd never have that look of hope again after his heartfelt Christmas wish was shattered.

"This isn't about putting a delusional old man into an institution, it's about finding a homeless, elderly man a safe facility where he won't endanger himself and others. Or don't you remember the reason for the trial? It happened because Kris blundered his way into an armed robbery!"

"An armed robbery you want credit for resolving," Victor said coldly.

"If I were a man, you'd never have thrown that at me. The truth is, I did resolve a potentially life-threatening crime in progress, Victor. And for that, I deserve the credit *and* the press coverage."

They stared at each other for a long moment.

"It's no different than it was that day before we went into the courtroom," she finally murmured. "You want to deal in intangibles, while I prefer practicalities."

"Maybe those intangibles are the only things that are worthwhile, Stella."

With a heavy heart, she left the room.

"I CAN HEAR YOU PUTTING gifts under the tree, Santa Stella."

She stopped and smiled. "So all this time I was stumbling around in the semidark on Christmas morning, trying not to wake you, you were watching me?"

"What'd you expect?" He laughed sleepily. "I'm a P.I."

She flipped on the overhead light. "Merry Christmas, Investigator Bobby!"

Lying in his cot, he blinked and grinned. Then, tossing back the covers, he shuffled in his flannel pajamas toward the small Christmas tree they'd set up in the corner next to the globe. Bobby had liked it there, said its twinkling lights could be seen all over the world.

He crouched next to the tree and began shaking boxes. She found a radio station playing Christmas tunes, and she turned up the volume.

"Don't you dare open anything until I bring back the eggnog!" she warned.

While in the kitchenette, she poured two glasses of the thick, creamy mixture, hating the thought that tomorrow was the court date. Over the past few weeks, she and Bobby had become a team. She wanted him to stay with her, but no way would the court let her, a single woman, adopt Bobby.

As she sprinkled nutmeg on top of the eggnog, she

reminded herself to make the best of today, Christmas, because tomorrow would come all the same.

"What do you want me to open first?" asked Bobby as she walked back in with the drinks. "Frosty the Snowman" began playing on the radio.

Thirty minutes later, they sat in piles of ripped wrapping paper and bows. Bobby was reading the back cover of a detective paperback while Stella pluncked a few strings on his *The Lone Ranger* guitar.

"Hey, Bobby," she said, setting down the guitar. "There's one more gift."

He looked up, grinned. "I knew he'd remember!"

This was what she'd been worried about. Whatever it was Kris had promised hadn't happened, although Bobby had kept hoping it would.

"This is from me," she said gently, standing. "It's not wrapped, so close your eyes."

After he did, she took him by the hand and led him to the globe.

"Okay," she said, "open them."

He did, blinking at the globe.

"It's yours," she said, gently turning it. "Wherever you are, you can look at it and know wherever I am, I'm thinking of you."

Bobby gingerly touched it. "Will we travel together someday?"

She put her arm around his shoulders. "No way I'm doing out-of-state cases without my business partner. Absolutely, we'll travel together!"

He spun the world slowly, watching the countries and oceans. "Is that a promise?"

For a dark moment, she hated Kris for breaking his word to Bobby. "That's a promise, Bobby."

Knock, knock, knock.

They turned. Bobby, seeing the rotund silhouette through the frosted glass, yelped with glee as he rushed to answer the door. "It's Santa!" He threw open the door.

Kris Kringle stood there, his Santa outfit looking plusher, more vibrant than the one he'd worn at the department store.

"Ho-ho-ho!" he bellowed, carrying a large canvas bag.

Bobby looked anxiously at Stella. "Do we have any of those cookies left over that Mrs. Marshall made?"

"In the kitchenette." As Bobby ran out of the room, she leaned toward Kris. "If you hurt him," she whispered, "you're going to have to answer to me, buddy."

As Bobby ran back into the room, holding a plate with several cookies, Kris blinked in surprise at Stella.

"Here, Santa!" Bobby said, setting the plate on the table in front of him.

"Thank you, Bobby." He continued digging into his bag of gifts, finally pulling out a small box wrapped in shiny silver paper. "For you, Stella," he said, grandly handing it to her. He reached in again and pulled out an envelope. "And this, my dear boy, is for you. It took some work, but I got what each of your hearts most desires."

He helped himself to a cookie while heading out the door. "Hate to rush, but still have a lot of homes to visit." He paused in the doorway. "Remember to keep Christmas alive in your hearts all year long, and not just for a day."

The door clicked shut behind him.

Stella released her held breath. "Bobby, we don't have to open…"

But he already had. The envelope had dropped to the floor, and he was looking at the piece of paper that had been inside. After a moment, he looked up, a wounded expression in his eyes.

She took the paper from his hands. It was a flyer for a house for sale over on Bannock Street. She stared at the address, realizing it was near the courthouse. Not so surprising an orphan might dream of a home, but how cruel to tease him with this ad.

She looked at him.

"Let's see what you got," he said, acting as though nothing had happened.

"Sure." She set the ad on the edge of the desk and opened the box. "A ring?" she whispered, staring at what appeared to be a diamond ring in a gold band. Why would Kris think she wanted costume jewelry? Hardly what was foremost on her mind since her dad had died.

A clattering sound on the roof. "Rudolph,"

Kris's voice called out, "head *west* toward the mountains!"

Stella and Bobby looked at each other.

"He's going to hurt himself," Bobby said, worried.

"It's an old trick," she mumbled. "He's just tossed some pebbles on the roof so we'll *think* they're reindeer. My dad did it every Christmas."

She sighed, ruffled his hair. "Well, buddy, it's still *our* Christmas, so tell me what you'd like to do. Go see a movie? Read your new detective novels? Shoot, if you want to cuss, it's on the house. No charge."

Knock, knock, knock. Behind the frosted glass was the outline of Santa's hair and beard.

"That's it," she growled, making a beeline to the door. "Mr. Make-Believe is going to get a real piece of this lady's mind." She jerked open the door. "How dare you…you?"

Victor had topped off his slacks and shirt with a Santa hat and the worst-fitting white beard she'd ever seen. He held up a bag. "I suppose I dare to bring gifts?" He smiled sheepishly. "I've practiced this speech a few times, so here goes. Merry Christmas, I'm sorry, and I'm not here as the lawyer or politician, just Victor, who happens to be crazy about you. May I come in?"

He did a double take at the box in her hand. "That's the ring I saw in a jewelry store window. How'd you—?"

"Kris gave it to me." She blinked at the sparkling stone. "You mean…it's real?"

"If it's the one I saw, yes," he murmured, stepping inside. "But he doesn't have that kind of money."

"When did you last see him?"

"I found a note on Christmas Eve thanking me for my hospitality and that he'd see me soon. Which I took to mean tomorrow at court." He looked at the ad lying on the desk. "What's that?"

Stella and Bobby shared a look. Finally the boy said, "Kris dropped that off for me."

Victor picked it up. "It's an ad for a home for sale." He looked at Bobby. "Is this what you gave Kris?"

"No, but it *looks* a lot like what I gave him, which was a picture of a home I ripped out of a magazine several years ago."

"Tell you what," Victor said, tugging off his beard. "Let's go see if this home is really for sale."

FORTY MINUTES LATER, they stood in front of the house. A big red and white For Sale sign was stuck in the lawn.

"It's even more picturesque than described in the ad," said Stella, admiring the gabled roof, bay windows and turret.

Bobby, who had run ahead, yelled, "The front door's open!"

Victor looked at Stella. "Shall we?"

Minutes later, the three were exploring the house.

"You should see the room off the dining area," Stella called out as she walked back down the hallway. "It'd make a great office."

Victor, looking at the backyard through a picture window, shook his head in amazement. "That yard could fit a small football team, a gazebo *and* a barbecue grill."

Bobby came tearing down the stairs, his face flushed. "The upstairs bedroom has a view of the Rockies! It's *exactly* what I've always wanted!"

He nearly stumbled to a stop in front of Victor and Stella. "Holy cow!" He pointed at the fireplace, swallowing hard.

They turned and looked. There, on the stonework above the grating, was a tuft of red material.

"Was Santa here?" whispered Bobby.

Morning After Christmas, 1955
Denver City and County Court, Bannock Street

AT THE FRONT of the courtroom, the bailiff stood. "All rise for his honorable Judge Wallace Gerash."

Judge Gerash, in his black judge's robe, strode into the courtroom and sat at his podium. Adjusting items on his desk, he suddenly paused, then picked up something.

"Is this for me?" He held up a pen with a red bow around it.

The court clerk shrugged. The bailiff shook his head.

Judge Gerash looked at it more closely. "It's a Parker 51," he said approvingly. "Someone trying to bribe the judge?"

Laughter rippled through the courtroom.

Victor, sitting at the defense table, suddenly recalled his and Kris's discussion about the judge's pen-borrowing habit. Kris, in fact, had said the judge should have a Parker 51. Coincidence? Maybe.

Victor had been here this morning when the doors first opened, and he hadn't seen anyone deliver such a present. Which meant it was left yesterday, Christmas, except the courthouse had been closed. It would have taken inventive, if not extraordinary, means to put a bow-wrapped pen on the judge's desk.

Judge Gerash cleared his throat. "The city and county of Denver in the interest of and concerning the welfare of Kris Kringle." He looked at Victor. "Ready, Mr. Lancaster?"

Victor stood, smoothed a hand down his suit jacket. "Your honor, my client Kris Kringle is, unfortunately, not here."

"Do you know where he is?"

Victor thought about Bobby's secret dream, the ring, the pen. Crazy as it seemed, it all added up. "I think I do, your honor."

"Can you bring him here now?"

"No."

Judge Gerash gestured with the pen as he spoke to the court clerk. "Issue a bench warrant for Mr. Kringle." He shuffled some papers. "Let's see, next on the docket is people of the state of Colorado in the interest of Bobby Myers and concerning his guardian, St. Mary's Orphanage." Judge Gerash looked over the top of his glasses at Bobby. "I see *this* client is present."

Dressed in a suit, his hair slicked down, a nervous-looking Bobby joined Victor at the defense table.

Oscar, at the prosecution table, started to stand.

"Your Honor," said Victor, "may I proceed?"

Judge Gerash looked surprised, then nodded. "Irregular, but acceptable. Mr. Lancaster, you have the floor."

"Thank you." Victor walked toward the bench, stopped.

"That pen—" he motioned to the one in the judge's hand "—is a gift from Kris Kringle. Weeks ago, he told me you should have it, and now you do. The presence of that pen and the lack of any other plausible explanation for its appearance on your bench compels only one conclusion. The man who failed to appear before this honorable court has traveled back to the North Pole because he is, without a doubt, Santa Claus."

"That's hardly foolproof evidence," commented the judge.

Victor gestured toward Bobby. "Bobby Myers has carried with him a secret—a picture of a house that he ripped out of a magazine. No one has known about it. Not the nuns at St. Mary's, nor the court, nor Stella Gray. But he trusted Kris Kringle with it, and on Christmas day, Kris found such a house for sale for

Bobby. What better evidence is there than the granting of a child's secret dream?"

"Mr. Lancaster," interrupted the judge, "what does this have to do with a juvenile delinquency placement hearing?"

"Everything. I'd like to call Miss Gray to the witness stand."

Stella headed to the witness box, took her oath.

After she sat, Victor approached. "Miss Gray, you were previously sworn to tell the truth, the whole truth, were you not?"

"Yes."

"Do you love me?"

Her mouth dropped open. She closed it, blinked. "Yes."

They held each other's gaze. "I love you, too," he said gently. "Do you love Bobby Myers?"

She nodded, her eyes moistening. "Yes."

"Did Kris Kringle correctly guess your dream when he said you wished to regain what you lost…" his voice dropped "…when your father died?"

"Yes."

"Stella, would you mind telling the court what that dream is?"

She wasn't one to open up that easily, not even to spill her innermost secrets to a friend, much less a room filled mostly with strangers.

"I can't," she said softly.

He stepped closer, a look of tenderness like she'd

never seen before on his face. "I know it's hard, Stella. Please trust me."

Taking a leap, blindly trusting, was also not her style, but she instinctively knew if she didn't take the chance, she'd lose more than her silence could gain. She took a deep breath and released it.

"It's to hear my dad telling his stories, to smell Mom's dinner cooking, to put up with my brother's practical jokes. It's to have my family back."

He reached into his jacket pocket and pulled out a box Kris Kringle had given to her on Christmas day. Then, dropping to one knee, Victor opened it for her to see. "Stella, I'm asking you to marry me, but only on the condition that doing so fulfills your dream."

She sucked in a breath, momentarily struck dumb by the sight of Victor Lancaster on his knee, in front of his peers, asking for her hand.

"Stella," blurted Bobby, "say yes!"

She laughed, her vision blurring with joy. "Yes," she said, her voice breaking. "I'll marry you."

Victor stood, put the ring on her finger. "Your Honor," he said, holding Stella's hand. "I move that the court place Bobby Myers in Stella Gray's custody pending an adoption hearing, which should be set after our wedding on February 14, 1956. I also move that Kris Kringle, whose business is making dreams real, is Santa Claus. As such, he is no more a danger to society than hope or love or joy are, and therefore his case should be dismissed."

The court reporter, whose hands had been moving furiously on her machine, stopped to wipe her eye.

Judge Gerash looked for a long, drawn-out moment at Victor and Stella. "As a judge, and on behalf of my good friend and Stella's father, Pete Gray, I grant your requests. The Myers adoption hearing is set for February 15, 1956." He fumbled around his desk. "Where is my new pen? Oh, there." He lifted it, paused. "Before I sign off on this request, I have one question for Stella Gray, our witness bride. Do you, my dear, also believe Kris Kringle is really Santa Claus?"

She looked at Victor, then Bobby, her dreams come true.

"I believe," she whispered.

* * * * *

IT'S A WONDERFUL NIGHT

Kathleen Long

CHAPTER ONE

ALL MEREDITH DOWNEY ever wanted was to get out of Dodge. Dodge, New Jersey, that was.

She'd always had a vision. Big cities, bright lights, excitement. Love. But on this particular Christmas Eve morning, she'd settle simply for the ground opening up and swallowing her whole.

The small medical clinic she ran seemed more dingy than usual. Maybe it was the contrast of old paint against holiday lights, or out-of-date equipment against faded informational posters, but the offices looked as tired as Merri felt.

With insurance reimbursements growing smaller and smaller and her wish list for new equipment and technology growing longer and longer, most days she wasn't sure why she showed up and shrugged into her lab jacket.

This morning she'd given the entire Moose Lodge their flu shots, and her sister had called from yet another fabulous European city where she'd photographed yet another fabulous fashion show. Merri had had to tell Belinda Murphy her breast cancer was back, and now Matt Riley stood staring at her with only one thing in his eyes.

Murder.

And Merri knew exactly why.

She studied the thick waves of his close-cropped brown hair, visually traced the sharp lines of his jaw and steeled herself beneath the intensity of his dark gaze.

She recognized the expression he wore. Heck, he'd sported the stubborn, headstrong expression for as long as she could remember, back to the day he'd given another Dodge Grade School student a bloody lip for calling Merri short.

She bit back a smile and focused on the present… and the fury in Matt's gaze.

She'd never installed a back door in the clinic, and it was at moments like this she realized that particular budget cut hadn't been too smart.

"Something I can help you with?" She forced a bright tone, hoping it would defuse the anger plastered across his rugged features.

"You can start by minding your own business." Matt's expression grew even darker, not that Merri had thought that possible.

She turned and headed quickly down the hall toward her office, hoping she could shut and lock the door before he could plop one of his big boot-covered feet in the doorjamb.

"Did you have an appointment, because I don't remember seeing you on the schedule?"

Matt grasped her elbow and Merri turned to glare at him. She raised a single eyebrow and he dropped his hand from her arm.

"Why?"

His one-word question stunned her momentarily. She'd expected a rant, a rave, a tirade. But regardless of the brevity of his question, she understood exactly to what—or rather whom—he referred.

His daughter, Rosie.

"Didn't you ever have a dream?" Merri asked. "Didn't you ever want something so badly you could taste it?"

An emotion she couldn't quite put her finger on flashed in his dark brown eyes, momentarily softening his expression, but he shook his head, his features growing stern.

"We all know you've had a chip on your shoulder ever since your daddy dropped dead and you got stuck running this clinic, but don't transfer your high-and-mighty dreams to my daughter."

Obviously, word had gotten back to Matt about Merri's recent heart-to-heart with Rosie. Heat fired in her cheeks and she bit back the urge to launch into a diatribe about letting children follow their hearts.

Matt and Rosie Riley had been through enough. It had been barely five years since Matt's wife, Claire, had drowned in the small shore town's surf.

The man had a point.

Merri didn't have any right encouraging his daughter to stretch out of her comfort zone. To follow her heart. To chase her dream of becoming an actor. To audition for the school musical.

Merri caught herself mid-mental-ramble.

Wait a minute.

If she didn't encourage Rosie, who would? Certainly not Mr. It's-a-whole-lot-safer-hiding-back-at-the-farm Riley.

She spun on him.

"Maybe if you'd take more time to encourage her, I wouldn't have to."

The murderous look in his eyes deepened and he reached for his inside jacket pocket.

Merri resisted the urge to make a quick check for any obvious weapon bulges. This was Matt, after all.

He pulled out a single, glossy brochure, handed it to her without saying a word, then turned to walk away.

She glanced down at the title. Triboro Health Systems. She'd heard the large hospital chain was moving into the state, but a job there would require she leave the clinic. Require she leave the area.

Exactly what she'd always wanted to do, but she wasn't about to let Matt Riley decide for her.

"Oh, no, you don't." Merri raced down the hall, catching up to Matt as he pushed against the exit door.

A waiting room full of patients looked up, fascination and small-town curiosity painted across each face.

"Good morning, everyone," Merri called out in her best holiday season singsong voice.

Then she put one hand flat against the hard plane of Matt Riley's back and pushed him outside. She followed him onto the sidewalk and reached into her own pocket.

"You showed me yours."

He looked surprised.

"Now I'm showing you mine." She handed him a carefully folded sheet of paper. A note she'd promised Rosie Riley she'd keep to herself. But surely Rosie would understand the reasoning behind Merri's transgression.

Merri hoped.

Matt's gaze never left hers, and she nodded toward the note. "Open it. You think you know it all. You think you have everything all under control. Open it."

And he did, carefully unfolding the sheet one section at a time. Slowly. Meticulously. Infuriatingly slowly.

Merri snatched it from his fingertips and shook it open.

"Read it."

Matt focused on the handwritten words on the paper. Merri knew he'd reached the vital part when his angry features fell slack.

At age thirteen, Rosie Riley already dreamed of

leaving Dodge, fantasized about living in New York City, longed to sing and dance on Broadway.

And yet she knew her father would never give her his blessing. He wouldn't let her try out for the school musical, let alone leave Dodge someday. And she wasn't about to hurt him.

He'd been hurt enough.

At her tender age, Rosie Riley felt trapped, doomed to a life in Dodge she didn't want.

"Think on that for a bit," Merri said as she pushed back into the clinic.

As she crossed to the sign-in sheet to call her next appointment, she listened for the jingle of the door to indicate Matt had followed her back inside, finally ready to talk about his daughter.

The sound never came.

Merri shoved away her sense of disappointment, even though she knew she shouldn't feel an ounce of surprise. Matt had shut her out of his life years earlier.

First, when she'd pursued college instead of a life in Dodge. Second, when she'd failed to save his wife's life.

But based on the flash of emotion she'd seen as he'd read Rosie's letter, Merri might have achieved something she'd thought impossible.

Maybe, just maybe, she'd cracked Matt's wall of grief long enough to plant concrete proof of his daughter's dreams in his large, callused hands.

And while Merri hoped he'd put the information

to good use, she feared he'd do nothing more than tuck Rosie's dreams away somewhere out of sight.

MATT CAREFULLY REFOLDED the note and tucked it into his jacket pocket, working to keep his frustration at bay.

Frustration at the audacity of Merri Downey to give him parenting advice, and frustration at Rosie. Why would she confide in Merri Downey instead of him?

His heart sank.

Because the good doctor was a woman, and the girl missed her mother. He didn't need an advanced degree to figure that one out.

"Morning, Matt." Earl Norton nodded a greeting as he walked past. "In town for a checkup?"

Matt resisted the urge to snarl at the clinic's front door. "Something like that."

"Well—" Earl slapped him on the shoulder "—hope everything's all right. Merry Christmas."

"Merry Christmas."

Matt fought his desire to spit.

Christmas.

He and Rosie hadn't had a Merry Christmas in five years. Not since Claire had...left them. His eyes shut momentarily, as if of their own volition.

Hell, he couldn't even bring himself to think the word *died*. No wonder Rosie had been seeking Merri's advice.

Matt drew in a deep breath and headed for home. Rosie was off from school and he wanted to spend some time together before they headed over to Katie and Jack Caldecott's for an early dinner.

Maybe Matt would try his hand at baking the cookies Claire had always made on Christmas Eve.

Crisp and sugary, shaped like snowmen and reindeer, covered in powdered sugar and candied cherry halves.

Emotion grew so tight in his throat it threatened to strangle him. He leaned against a lamppost, glaring up at the oversize candy cane that hung in decoration.

"Merry freaking Christmas," he muttered at the sky.

"It is, isn't it?"

The voice that answered wasn't one he recognized. Female. Relatively young.

Matt turned to locate the source and stared into a pair of warm brown eyes peeking out from a white cotton wig and a fluffy beard. His eyes trailed down the standard getup. Red jacket, black buttons, red pants, black boots.

Santa.

"At your service." Santa gestured to the street-corner setup. "This is just a temporary gig."

Matt frowned as he studied the person before him.

Had he said the words out loud? And where had this particular Santa come from? She hadn't been there a moment before. Or was it he?

"She," Santa answered, patting her belly. "It's the stuffing. Throws 'em off every time."

Myriad thoughts whirled through Matt's mind. Was he losing it?

"How did you—" He blinked and shook his head. "I didn't—"

"You did." The female Santa nodded. "I heard every word."

Matt squinted.

The woman finished unpacking a portable Santa station and plopped down into her chair. She patted a knee. "You look like you have a Christmas wish or two you need to unload."

He stared at her. Hard. "Who are you?"

"Tewanda…er…I mean, Santa." She shrugged, then said, a definite tone of indignation in her voice, "Christmas? Elves? Reindeer? Surely you've heard the story."

Matt smiled despite himself. A smart-aleck Santa. Go figure.

"Nice to meet you, Tewanda." He waved over his shoulder as he turned away, headed for his parked pickup. "I've got to get home."

"You'll come back," the young woman called out after him. "They always do."

Matt slowed momentarily, turning back to steal another glance, but the woman had vanished. Only her chair remained behind.

He frowned, scanning the sidewalk for any sign of the red suit, red hat, white hair.

Nothing.

He pulled open the door to his truck and climbed in.

Somehow this was all Meredith Downey's fault. The woman made him so mad he was seeing Santas where there were none.

He could only hope Merri would take the brochure he'd given her and start driving—straight into her new life and out of his. The sooner the better.

His gut caught and twisted as he remembered the first time Merri had driven out of his life.

They'd grown closer and closer the summer after she'd graduated from Dodge High. When he'd kissed her during the last night of the annual carnival, he'd flashed forward to a life in Dodge.

Their life in Dodge.

Together.

But Merri had been quick to set him straight on that count. She'd wanted no part of the town or her father's clinic.

She'd set out for college and left Matt behind so quickly his head had spun.

Fate had handed her a surprise years later when her father had died suddenly. Just as fate had handed Matt a cruel surprise the day he lost Claire.

Seeing Merri day in and day out provided a constant reminder of just how different Matt's life had turned out from the one he'd planned.

What would have happened if Merri had skipped medical school and stayed in Dodge? And what would have happened if she'd left after her father died?

Matt steadied himself, drew in a long breath and cranked on the truck's ignition.

He needed to leave the past behind and focus on the present…and Rosie.

Perhaps then this year would be a Merry Christmas after all.

As soon as she rounded the corner to Katie and Jack Caldecott's house later that afternoon, Merri recognized Matt Riley's truck and groaned.

She'd wring Katie's neck if she'd invited the man to their annual Christmas Eve get-together in yet another attempt to introduce romance into Merri's life.

Merri checked her ego as she climbed the steps to the old Victorian.

Whatever romantic notions she and Matt had once shared were long gone. The relationship had been nothing more than a sweet summer flirtation between two people who hadn't know any better.

Her insides panged in protest.

Barely a day passed that she didn't wonder what might have been if she'd followed her heart and chosen Matt over her dreams of medical school.

She shook off the notion.

Any hope she'd held out about ending up with Matt someday…somehow…had been dashed when Claire Morgan had breezed into town, visiting for the summer with Merri's sister, Melody. Melody and

Claire had studied photography together and had become fast friends.

Matt had set eyes on Claire—as brunette and beautiful as Merri was blond and average—and never looked back. Claire had never returned to school, and Rosie had come along exactly nine months after the wedding.

Matt had never again looked at Merri with affection in his eyes. And she had no one to blame but herself.

Merri blew out a deep breath and steeled herself, bracing for the holiday bedlam of Katie and Jack's home.

Matt and Jack had become fast friends since Jack had moved into town to marry Katie. Chances were Matt's being here was nothing more than a coincidence. No doubt he'd merely stopped by to wish the family a Merry Christmas.

She realized differently when she saw the number of place settings at the Caldecott dining room table.

"Merri's here," Katie called out as Merri shrugged out of her coat.

"Why is Matt Riley here?" Merri ground out the question through clenched teeth.

"Why not?" Katie took Merri's coat and pulled the closet door wide. "He's our friend as much as you're our friend. You know—" she waggled her eyebrows "—I actually remember a time when you two got along."

"I do my best to block that out," Merri answered, her tone so curt she surprised herself.

"What's with you lately?" Katie frowned, disapproval blatant in her expression. "You used to be so positive about everything and now you're just… well…you're not."

Merri winced. "Sorry. It's been a long day."

She wanted to say it had been a long seven years since she'd taken over the clinic, but she wasn't about to unload her woes on her best friend on Christmas Eve.

"Merri." Rosie Riley's voice filled the house as she came down the steps, carrying Katie and Jack's newborn, Elizabeth, in her arms.

"Hey, honey." Merri dropped a kiss to Rosie's cheek and caught Matt's eye as he rounded the corner from the kitchen. "Mr. Riley." She kept her tone curt but civil.

"Dr. Downey."

Truth be told, he put a little too much emphasis on the word *doctor* for Merri's taste. He'd never trusted her abilities, and obviously that hadn't changed.

"Hey, first names only in this house. Got it?" Jack Caldecott stepped from behind Matt, expertly holding two-year-old Connor on his hip.

A twinge of regret nipped at Merri's insides but she shoved the sensation away.

As happy as she was for Katie and Jack and the life they'd created for themselves, romance and family wasn't a priority in her life. She didn't have time. More importantly, she didn't have the inclination.

She glanced quickly at Matt but shoved away any remaining trace of *what if.* The past was the past. She needed to deal with the life she had now. The life she'd chosen.

Katie and Jack steered the conversation during dinner, avoiding dangerous topics like the clinic or the school musical. Instead, they talked about the weather, the new dessert menu at Parker's, and Connor's latest developmental feats.

During the evening, Merri saw the caring, kind facets of Matt's personality that she'd always admired. He helped Connor with his food and encouraged the youngster's conversation skills. He smiled warmly at Rosie as she talked about her studies, and he nodded politely as Katie babbled on and on about the baby's sleeping habits.

It was only when Matt and Merri's gazes met that his icy reserve snapped back into place.

They stayed on their best behavior through the entire meal, neither mentioning a word about their earlier argument.

The gloves came off, however, after dinner. While Merri and Katie cleaned up the kitchen, Rosie disappeared to give Connor his bath. The baby had been snug in her crib in the nursery the whole meal.

"So, Merri." Matt's voice startled her and she

bobbled a cup. "Did you tell Katie about the new hospital?"

"Hospital?" Katie's focus shifted from the sink to Merri's face, her brow creased with worry. "You're not leaving, are you?"

Merri shrugged. "I wasn't planning on it, but you know I've always wanted to do more than what I'm doing here."

"Yes," Matt said, hoisting a soda to his lips. "I'd say you've done enough here."

"Matthew Riley." Katie's tone was unforgiving and critical.

Merri stiffened, inhaled slowly, then turned to face Matt. "At least I have an open mind, Mr. Riley. You should try it sometime."

Matt's eyes narrowed just as the phone rang, setting off a round of crying from the nursery.

Merri took full advantage of the distraction. She grabbed her coat, called out a thank-you to Katie, gave Jack a quick kiss goodbye, cast one last glare over her shoulder at Matt and left.

"NICE GOING." Jack chuckled as he reached for his beer.

"That woman needs her head examined." Matt sank into the sofa and crossed his legs, ankle to knee.

Jack grinned, saying nothing.

"What?" Matt asked.

"You two are more alike than you know." He gave a quick shrug. "That's all."

"Don't take her side in this." Matt took a long draw on his bottle of soda.

"How is that taking her side?"

Matt's only response was to squeeze his eyes shut and drop his head back against the sofa. After a minute or two of utter silence, he cracked.

"I'll bite. How are we alike?"

Jack leaned forward, lifting a finger to tick off each point he made. "You're both smart, opinionated, stubborn as hell, and—" he straightened, his features growing serious "—you want what's best for Rosie."

"Bull." Matt climbed to his feet. "That woman doesn't know a thing about my daughter."

Jack responded with a lift of his eyebrows. "Doesn't she?"

Rosie reappeared, toting Connor, a blanket and a book.

She hesitated as she entered the room, looking from her father to Jack, then back to her father. "What's going on?"

Both men shook their heads.

"Just talking." Matt cast a warning look at Jack.

"Mind if I read to Connor in here?" Rosie asked.

"Of course not." Jack shook his head and reached to clear a pile of wrapping paper off an overstuffed chair.

Matt was too busy studying his little girl to say a word. She'd grown up seemingly overnight. How had that happened? She'd lost all traces of baby fat, leaving her tall and lean.

He looked away, flashing back on the evening and his earlier argument with Merri.

The woman was infuriating. He didn't care what Jack said.

Matt had to admit the closeness he'd seen between Merri and Rosie tonight had seemed natural and genuine. Just when had they grown so chummy? And was this his future? A teenaged daughter who preferred confiding in a stranger to confiding in her father?

His heart gave a twist and he longed for Claire to be at his side, guiding him through this. What did he know about raising a daughter?

He'd always thought the best thing for Rosie would be to stay in Dodge, working the produce farm beside him, taking over once she married and had a family of her own.

But her letter had left him full of doubts.

What if Rosie wanted nothing more than to leave, to explore life outside the small, safe town?

He steeled himself, determination welling inside him.

Too bad, that's what.

Rosie would get over her schoolgirl dreams. The time would come when she'd be old enough to realize the best place for her was where she'd been all along.

Dodge.

He stole another glance at his daughter, reading softly, smiling brightly as she snuggled with Connor.

She was growing up too fast.

Matt suddenly longed for fresh air, for a chance to clear his mind.

"Jack, you mind if I take a quick walk?"

His friend smirked knowingly. "Merri Downey's got you thinking, hasn't she?"

Matt glared at his friend. "Merri Downey doesn't have me doing anything."

Jack smiled, handing Matt his coat. "Take your time. We'll keep an eye on Rosie for you. Make sure she doesn't hop the next bus to Broadway."

"Very funny," Matt mumbled as he stepped out into the crisp night air, but then he froze.

Did Jack and Katie know about Rosie's dreams?

He frowned, turning around to ask Jack, but his friend had already shut the door.

Had Rosie confided in the Caldecotts, as well as Merri?

Was he the only person in Dodge who didn't know Rosie's hopes and dreams?

A fresh wave of doubt about his parenting skills washed through him as he stepped outside. He shook his head, pulling the collar of his coat tight around his neck.

He had a lot to learn about Rosie, but he knew everything he needed to know about Merri Downey.

The sooner the interfering woman left town, the better.

CHAPTER TWO

A LITTLE BEFORE six o'clock, Merri poured herself a second cup of eggnog and resettled on the hardwood floor in front of her Christmas tree—her barren, less-than-desirable, pathetic excuse of a Christmas tree.

She shrugged.

Who cared how sad the tree looked?

There was no one to see her decorating efforts.

She'd slapped on a few handfuls of tinsel and hung the ornaments that had once been her mother's. Ornaments her father had cherished after her mother's death and before his own.

Merri's vision misted over and she put down the cup of eggnog. This holiday cheer was killing her.

Having two arguments with Matt Riley in one day was bad enough. At least she'd had a little time with Katie and her family before their *discussion* had taken place.

She smiled at the memory of the sheer joy glowing in her friend's face. Katie deserved the life she'd found with Jack.

According to Matt, there wasn't much Merri did right, but introducing Katie to her favorite pharmaceutical sales rep had been genius.

They'd married six months later.

Merri had come home to another phone message from her sister Melody, this one obviously from some fabulous party, based on the noises in the background.

Oh, well.

At least one of the Downey sisters had a life.

The other had stayed behind to take over the family practice in the town she'd worked so hard to escape.

Merri sighed and reached for the package Belinda Murphy had handed her that day at work. Belinda had insisted Merri open the box *before* Christmas morning.

Merri studied the package, wondering what surprise the owner of Belinda's Boudoir had tucked inside.

She took another swallow of eggnog for good measure, ripped open the end of the wrapping paper and slid the box free.

She pulled off the top, flipped back the perfectly creased tissue paper and blinked.

Underpants?

Belinda had given her underpants? *Christmas-themed underpants?*

She understood the woman's fondness for lingerie. Belinda had opened her shop after undergoing a mastectomy and not being satisfied with the selection of apparel in Dodge.

No surprise there.

The town put the word *small* in the phrase *small town*.

Belinda's Boudoir had opened two years ago, and Merri admired both Belinda's enthusiasm and her hard work, but undies?

Merri pulled out a pair, unfolded them and held them high. Santa and his eight not-so-tiny reindeer danced across the front of the largest pair of cotton panties Merri had ever seen.

Really. Could this day get any worse?

She got up and crossed to the center hall, standing on her tiptoes and twisting to get a good look at her derriere in the mirror.

Surely Belinda didn't think these panties were the correct size. Did she?

Maybe Merri needed to stop wearing her lab coat at work.

She blew out a sigh and headed for the front door, suddenly needing to put as much space as possible between her and all signs of Christmas.

She slipped her feet into her sneakers, pulled her zip-front fleece over her head, and yanked her hair into a high ponytail. She picked up the Triboro Health Systems brochure from the spot where she'd dropped it on top of the mail and headed outside into the raw night air.

Snow.

The air definitely felt like snow.

Dodge sat so close to the salty ocean, the town rarely saw much in the way of the white stuff, but maybe this Christmas would be different.

She caught herself, stifling the perky, unrealistic holiday thought.

White Christmas. *Right.* Like that could happen.

Merri blew out a sigh, glanced down at the brochure and shoved it into her jacket pocket. She pulled the zipper tight against her throat and broke into a run, not knowing where she was headed, just knowing she needed to be anywhere but here.

But then, she'd been thinking that for the past seven years—ever since her father's sudden death had sent her fondest hopes and dreams down the drain.

Finishing up her surgical residency.

Securing a position with a university hospital in Philadelphia.

Saving lives.

Merri blew out another sigh and quickened her pace, running hard.

Her life plan had been so straightforward. Solid. Yet here she was. Approaching yet another Christmas in Dodge, New Jersey.

Merri headed for Main Street, surprised by the number of last-minute shoppers bustling in and out of the local toy store, department store, candy store.

Residents zipped in and out of Parker's Diner, no doubt dropping off gifts for Bert and his wife, Sally. The two served free meals on Christmas Eve and loved the holiday more than anyone in town, which was saying something.

Snow or no snow, Dodge knew how to do Christmas right.

Merri slowed to a stop, bending to catch her breath, then stared up into the night sky. She shot a glare at the multicolored lights strung from lamppost to lamppost.

"Bah, humbug," she muttered to no one.

"Not feeling the love?"

The female voice sounded close and Merri jumped, turning to locate the source.

A young female Santa stood smiling in her direction, warm eyes winking out from beneath the fluffy white edge of her red cap.

"Merry Christmas." Santa smiled brightly. "You look like you could use a Christmas wish."

Christmas wish. Now that was a joke.

Merri shook her head and turned to walk away, then hesitated. She thought about her life, her work, her frustrations at the clinic, her pathetic Christmas tree and her jumbo panties.

"I wish I'd never stayed." She spoke the words without turning around.

"Stayed?"

Merri nodded, shifting to meet Santa's questioning look. "After my dad died." She straightened, forcing a weak smile. "I wish I'd left Dodge forever."

Santa narrowed her eyes. "That's a mighty big wish."

Merri drew in a deep breath, then blew out a sigh. "Yes, it is." She started walking, this time without hesitation, headed for home. "Merry Christmas," she called out over her shoulder to Santa.

She broke into a jog, then a run. She ran day in and day out, yet she always ended up exactly where she'd started. In Dodge.

Maybe this Christmas things would turn out differently.

Maybe her Christmas wish would come true.

Even though she'd stopped believing in Christmas wishes a long, long time ago.

MATT MENTALLY CHASTISED himself as he neared the center of town. He hadn't worked up the nerve to talk to Rosie about her note.

Maybe the cold night air would clear his head and he'd know exactly what to say when he headed back to Jack and Katie's.

Matt turned toward Main Street and the street-corner Santa just as Tewanda had predicted he would.

She looked up as he approached, as if she'd been sitting there waiting for him since he'd left. "Long time, no see."

Matt smiled at the young Santa's confidence. "What if I said I was doing some last-minute shopping?"

Santa pursed her lips and shook her head. "You're here for your wish."

"My wish?"

"Your Christmas wish."

Matt rubbed a hand across his tired eyes, glancing up and down the street as he did so. When he spotted Merri Downey, anger and frustration began to tangle anew deep in his gut.

"Do you know what I want for Christmas? I want her—" he pointed down the sidewalk toward Merri's departing backside "—to go back to the day she decided to stay in Dodge, then I want her to leave."

Santa's expression softened and she nodded ever so slightly. "So you think that particular change will make your life…what? Better?"

Matt thought of Claire, lying lifeless on the beach, Merri working frantically to save her and failing miserably.

If only Merri hadn't been the first responder. If only Claire's rescuer had been someone…anyone else. But she hadn't been.

Cold resignation settled over him. Claire was gone. He could think only of Rosie now.

He leveled a look at Santa's friendly brown eyes, tracing a finger across the folded note in his pocket. "I need to focus on what's good for my daughter."

Santa nodded as if she knew everything Matt was thinking, everything he'd never voiced to another living soul.

"Like the school musical?" she asked.

Matt's only response was a questioning frown.

He looked down the sidewalk toward Merri, compelled for some reason to check on her. He started when he realized she'd turned back and stood within earshot, cheeks flushed with color, strands of blond hair fluttering loose in the night breeze where they'd slipped from her ponytail.

For a split second, their eyes locked and he relived the moment she'd walked away. The moment he'd asked her to stay at the end of a long-ago summer and she'd said no.

Funny how much your wishes could change over the years. Back then all he'd wanted was for Merri to remain in Dodge. Now, all he wanted was for Merri to leave.

Had she heard everything he'd said to the street-corner Santa?

Based on the tight set of her mouth, she had. No matter. Matt wasn't about to apologize. No way.

"I wished for the same thing." She nodded as she spoke the words, eyes sparkling vividly.

Her words and the sure tone of her voice stunned him.

"You what?"

"I wished I could go back to the day we buried my father and never look back." She waved one arm dramatically, gesturing to the overhead lights and decorations. "If I could leave all this behind and never, ever come back, I'd be the happiest woman alive."

But the sudden moisture glistening on her lower lashes belied her words.

Matt turned back to Santa, but she was gone.

Suddenly, last-minute shoppers and overhead decorations vanished. The holiday lights disappeared. The storefront windows grew dark. Trash tumbled down the once pristine Main Street.

Freezing rain began to fall, sheeting down onto the dark, deserted street, spreading bitter cold instead of sparkling holiday cheer.

"What the—?"

A slender hand pressed Matt's elbow and he jumped.

"Sorry."

He looked down into Merri's eyes. At least they were the same beautiful blue-green they'd always been. His stomach tightened, thankful for the familiar sight.

"What happened?" she asked.

"So you see it, too?"

"Everything's…different. Everything's gone."

Matt reached into his pocket for Rosie's letter, finding nothing but the empty lining and a ball of lint. Her letter was gone.

Merri must have read the surprise in his eyes. "What?"

"Rosie's letter's gone. I put it right here."

As he watched, Merri reached into the pocket of her pullover, frowning.

"What is it?" he asked.

"The brochure you gave me. I shoved it into my pocket when I left for my run. I'm sure of it."

"Gone?"

"Gone." She nodded.

"Just what you wished for." Santa's voice called out to them, but not from the corner behind them. Instead, she sat in the driver's seat of an old-fashioned sleigh, pulled up to the curb across the street.

"The life you knew is gone." Her smile crinkled the skin around her dark eyes. "The life you wished for awaits."

She jerked a glove-covered thumb toward the sleigh's seat. "Let's get a move on. You two are about to take the ride of your lives."

CHAPTER THREE

THEY MOVED FORWARD SLOWLY, powered by what, Merri couldn't tell. The vehicle had to have some sort of engine, but there was no telltale hum. No roar. Nothing. She also couldn't see the driver operating any sort of steering wheel.

The Santa cast a glance over her shoulder. "Name's Tewanda, by the way."

Surely Merri had to be imagining this.

She sneaked a look at Matt's profile, momentarily taken aback by his nearness and flashes of that one wonderful summer, so long ago. She seldom saw him like this—from close up—without being in the midst of an argument.

If they weren't in the middle of being escorted God knew where by some young woman in a Santa suit, she'd rather enjoy the moment.

But the reality was that Dodge had morphed into a ghost town.

No one ventured outside.

No music played.

There was nothing.

Nothing but dark storefronts and empty sidewalks.

What on earth was going on?

She reached over and pinched Matt's arm. Hard.

He jumped at the contact, jerking his arm away from her offending touch.

"What the hell are you doing?" Anger flashed in his dark eyes. Now there was the Matt she knew.

"Making sure this isn't a dream." She dropped her voice low.

"Aren't you supposed to pinch yourself?"

Merri gave a slight shrug. "I figured if you were real, then this was real. But, what *is* this?"

Matt shook his head, brow furrowed. "I have no idea."

Merri surveyed the street on her side of the sleigh as Matt did the same. When they turned back to face each other, the disbelief in his eyes shone as blatantly as the disbelief in her heart.

What on earth had happened to downtown Dodge?

Belinda's Boudoir sat empty, its windows covered in thick plywood spray-painted with a jumble of colors and offensive words. The corner grocery store had been replaced by a national chain not known for its hometown approach.

Storefront after storefront sat unrecognizable from the downtown Dodge Merri had been part of just moments ago.

She sank back against the seat. Sure, she'd spent

countless hours fantasizing about a more glamorous life anywhere but here, but she'd never wish this fate on the quaint little town.

Heck, she couldn't even imagine it.

"This is not Dodge. It can't be."

"But it is," Tewanda answered. "This is the Dodge of your wishes."

"Not possible," Matt grumbled.

"Very possible." Tewanda made a clucking noise with her tongue. "People tend to forget how one tiny change—one wish granted—can alter an entire life or family…or town."

This time, Merri pinched herself, then mumbled an expletive under her breath.

Matt shook his head and looked away. "You're not dreaming, neither am I, and I intend to find out exactly what's going on."

"I granted your wishes," Tewanda answered. "Just as you wanted."

Merri scanned the street. Empty. Not a pedestrian or holiday shopper in sight. Not a light. No holiday ornaments, no candles in the storefront windows.

"Where is everyone?" she asked.

"Folks don't mingle so much since the flu swept through this time last year."

"The flu?" Matt asked, his voice ringing with incredulity.

"How many?" Merri asked, sensing exactly what had happened. The flu had spread through the town, and without a clinic the town's senior population hadn't received the vaccinations or the care they needed.

"Twenty." Tewanda spoke the word flatly, sadly.

"Twenty folks got the flu?" Matt asked. "What about their shots?"

"Merri wasn't here to insist they receive vaccinations. Hundreds of Dodge residents became seriously ill. Twenty died."

A tangible hush fell over the sleigh.

Merri felt as though Tewanda had broken her heart with her words.

Twenty residents. *Gone.*

"The Moose Lodge was hardest hit," Tewanda explained, gesturing to the bare streetlamps. "Jim Cooper was the first to die, then twelve more members followed." She shook her head. "No one's hung a single holiday decoration since. Matter of fact, rumor has it the decorations were destroyed when everything inside the lodge was burned to rid the place of germs."

Jim Cooper.

Merri blinked back sudden tears.

The man's enthusiasm for life had been contagious. His visit for his annual flu shot had always made Merri's day, even though she griped about the chaotic schedule she followed at that time of year.

Just as she'd done earlier today.

She turned away from Matt to hide her tortured expression. "No one got their shots?"

"No one." Tewanda's next words might as well

have driven a knife through Merri's chest. "You weren't here to remind them or to battle for an adequate supply of the vaccine."

Merri swallowed down the knot of emotion choking her throat. "But that's senseless."

"Yes." Tewanda nodded. "It was."

"Why are you doing this?" Matt asked, his face tight with shock and anger.

"Because you asked me to." Tewanda turned her attention back to guiding the sleigh down the street. "You *both* asked me to. I did my job."

Frustration and skepticism edged out Merri's sense of defeat. "You're making this up to scare us, and it isn't appreciated. Take us back to Dodge. Now."

"This is Dodge." Tewanda slowed the sleigh, turning in her seat to meet Merri's angry glare. "This is the Dodge you wished for."

"I never would have wished for this."

Tewanda's dark eyebrows lifted. "Maybe not, but this is the Dodge you left behind."

"Surely someone else would have taken over the clinic." Matt's voice was also tinged with anger. "You can't blame this on Merri."

Was he defending her? Merri couldn't believe her ears. Matt hadn't defended her since she'd worn hot-pink pajamas and bunny slippers for pajama day her freshman year. Trouble was, it hadn't been pajama day.

The memory warmed her, bolstering her a bit against the new reality they faced.

"The town wouldn't have allowed the clinic to stay closed," Matt continued.

"But it did," Tewanda answered.

Merri couldn't bear to think any wish she'd made had cost a single Dodge resident his or her life, let alone twenty to a flu outbreak.

She found the prospect too painful to imagine.

Wishes like the ones she and Matt had made didn't come true, did they? And surely not at the hand of a street-corner Santa.

"Hold tight," Tewanda said. "We're about to move on."

Tewanda's words sent a renewed dread tumbling to life inside Merri.

What on earth had she and Matt done?

THE SLEIGH LURCHED forward and the stark store-fronts blurred into unrecognizable flashes of color. The rain stopped, replaced instead by a cold burst of air rushing past Matt's face and through his hair.

He drew in a deep breath and steeled himself, trying to process what he and Merri had just been told. He hadn't once stopped to think what Merri's leaving might mean for the town.

Twenty dead?

Surely this Tewanda person must be exaggerating.

The sleigh slowed as quickly as it had sped off, jolting Matt to attention.

He scanned their surroundings. The sleigh still

sat on Main Street, but this time there was one crucial difference. At the end of the block, a light glowed, pouring brightness out into the gloomy night.

Parker's Diner.

Relief flooded through Matt at the familiar sight, but as they pulled closer, dread edged aside the momentary sense of calm. He leaned forward and squinted.

The building had fallen into a state of disrepair, shutters hanging loose, paint peeling.

Bert Parker would never let his place look like this. And it was Christmas Eve. The diner typically bustled with activity until the wee hours of the morning.

Matt searched the building for Parker's sign but found nothing. Then he spotted the lettering, faded and chipped on the front window.

Buddy's.

Matt pushed out of the seat, climbing to his feet.

What on earth had happened to Parker's?

"Are you sure we're still in Dodge?" Matt worked to keep his alarm out of his voice.

The young woman in the Santa suit said nothing, her only response a quick nod. She pulled the sleigh to a complete stop and climbed down onto the street.

Merri cast a questioning look at Matt, then hurried after the Santa. Matt followed slowly as he took inventory of their surroundings.

This couldn't be Dodge. This had to be a dream. One hell of a dark, depressing dream.

Didn't that just figure?

He should have known Merri would play a lead role in the worst nightmare of his life. Hell, it wasn't as if it were the first time.

"Merry Christmas," the street-corner Santa called out brightly to the restaurant's manager as she pushed through the door. "Name's Tewanda. What's your special tonight?"

Matt moved inside the restaurant, stunned by the interior. Not one thing was as he remembered.

"We're closing," the manager answered gruffly. "That's the special."

"Nothing for Santa and a couple of her elves?"

"Lady, if you're Santa, then I'm Mrs. Claus."

The man moved forward menacingly, leaning his thickly muscled arms against the grubby counter. His eyes may have once been a vivid blue but they were now cloudy, as if the same layer of grime that covered the tables and stools covered his irises, as well.

Merri stood back cautiously, several feet behind Tewanda. Matt couldn't say he blamed her.

There wasn't another soul in the restaurant, save one.

Earl Norton.

At last, a familiar face.

"Earl," Matt called out, crossing to where the older man had just emerged from the men's room.

The burly manager slammed a fist against the counter. "I thought I told you to take that outside. My restaurants are for paying customers. Not bums like you."

Earl winced as if he'd been slapped. "I don't remember you saying that."

"Your problem," the manager continued, "is that you don't remember a thing."

Matt reached for Earl's arms as he passed. The man was a bag of bones, wearing clothes that reeked of filth.

"Can I drive you home, Earl?"

Earl blinked, his stare vacant. "I don't know you, son, but thank you just the same."

Matt's heart twisted. "You don't know me, Earl?"

The older man shook his head. "Am I in trouble?"

"No—"

"The hell you aren't." The manager rounded the corner and barreled straight toward Earl and Matt. Raw fear shimmered in the older man's eyes.

Matt stepped in front of him, blocking the restaurant manager's path. "This man's done nothing to you. He's an upstanding citizen of this town."

The manager's chuckle started low in his belly, building to a full-out rolling laugh. "You're one to talk. You still owe me for the chair you broke the last time you were in here."

Matt took a quick look around the interior of the unfamiliar establishment, then turned back to the manager. "I've never been in here since it changed hands."

"Your memory's just as bad, pal." The manager

held open the door as he spoke, a clear signal he wanted them out. "Maybe you need to cut back on the drinking."

Drinking? Matt had spent much of his youth watching his father sink into the dark abyss of alcoholism. If there was one thing he prided himself on, it was his restraint when it came to drinking.

"Earl." The plaintive tone of Merri's voice captured Matt's attention as she rushed past him.

Earl had vanished, slipping out into the unforgiving night.

"His medicine," Merri said softly. "He must not be taking his medicine."

Tewanda planted her hand against Matt's back and steered him through the doorway out into the cold before he could say another word.

"What's going on?" Merri asked.

"That's what I'd like to know," Matt growled, casting an angry glare in the direction of the manager, now peering out through the glass door.

"And what's wrong with Earl?" Merri stepped between Matt and Tewanda. "I have to find him. He needs to be examined."

"Won't help." Tewanda shook her head.

"Well, I just want to be sure he's taking his medicine."

Genuine concern shimmered in Merri's eyes as she turned away, apparently searching the deserted, cold street for any sign of Earl.

"It's too late for that," Tewanda answered, gesturing toward the sleigh.

Merri's only response was a confused frown.

"There never was any medicine. You weren't here to diagnose his Alzheimer's. He never got the help he needed."

Surprise washed through Matt, and he flashed back on his earlier, happier encounter with Earl on the sidewalk outside the clinic. Earl had been as alert as always.

"Earl has Alzheimer's?" Matt asked, disbelief dripping from his words.

Merri nodded. "Early stages."

"But I just saw him—"

"He didn't want anyone to know, and he's been responding nicely to the prescription I gave him."

Tewanda pursed her lips and shook her head.

"I gave him that prescription." Merri's tone grew insistent, impatient.

"And I saw him this morning and he was fine." Matt moved next to Merri, scanning the street. "Where did he go?"

Tewanda studied Merri. "You never gave him the prescription." She turned to Matt. "And you never saw him this morning. All of that was erased the moment I granted your wishes."

Tewanda made a grand gesture, sweeping her arm in the direction of the darkened storefronts and the wet, deserted street. "Time to accept that Dodge as you knew it is gone."

Merri inhaled sharply. "It can't be."

"That's just it." Tewanda made a snapping noise with her mouth as she walked toward the sleigh. "It is."

Matt didn't say a word as he climbed back into his seat. Cold dread eased through his every muscle. What if the Santa named Tewanda *had* erased the past seven years?

What then?

And where was Rosie?

His pulse kicked up a notch.

"Where's my daughter?"

"You'll see," Tewanda answered. "All in good time."

Anger tangled with impatience and dread deep inside Matt's gut.

He didn't want to see where Rosie might be, didn't want to think about how *this* Dodge might have affected his daughter. He only wanted to think of her safe back at Jack and Katie's. Nowhere else.

With any luck at all, Matt would awaken any moment and this would be nothing more than a bad dream.

A very bad dream.

CHAPTER FOUR

"DID YOU SET THIS UP?" Merri's voice rang tight with anger. "I always knew you hated me, but this is ridiculous."

Matt blinked, stunned by her words.

Sure, she'd broken his heart once upon a time, and he blamed her for Claire's death. He supposed he hadn't done a stellar job of hiding his emotions, but *hate?* Dr. Merri Downey wasn't someone anyone could hate, much as he'd tried over the years.

"Why do you look so surprised?" she continued. "You wince every time you see me around town."

Matt sat back, crossing his arms. "Maybe if you'd let me worry about raising my own daughter, we wouldn't have to do battle on a constant basis."

"For your information—" Merri leaned close, close enough to make his pulse quicken unexpectedly "—your daughter came to me with her problem, not the other way around. And I'd imagine she came to me because I listen, unlike others riding in this sleigh."

Matt uttered a bitter laugh at her last statement. The phrase riding in this sleigh sounded too odd to be true.

Yet here he sat, next to Merri, watching the street-corner Santa's back as she led them who knew where.

He held up a hand to buffer his eyes from the flashes of light and the harsh winter air. "Do you honestly think I had anything to do with this?"

"Didn't you?" she asked. "You were talking to *her*—" she jerked her thumb toward the front seat "—before this started."

"Tewanda," the woman called out from the front seat. "I told you to call me Tewanda."

"Good ears." Merri tipped her head to one side.

Matt grimaced. "I don't think she needs ears."

Confusion twisted Merri's features.

But instead of explaining, Matt focused on Merri's accusation. He grasped her hand, hoping to push past the anger and frustration blazing in her eyes. "Merri, I want you to leave. Why would I arrange this to scare you into staying?"

Merri flinched, her bravado fading as she slid her hand from his.

But before Merri or Matt could say another word, the sleigh came to a stop at their next destination. Merri visibly tensed, and Matt followed her gaze.

Her father's clinic sat dark and shuttered, just as it had the day the town of Dodge had buried the man.

In the vision, Merri stood slump-shouldered, locking the front door, her long blond hair plastered flat against her head from the damp weather. Someone had draped Dr. Downey's shingle in ribbon as black as Merri's suit.

Matt stared at the scene before them, remembering the day clearly and feeling a surge of sympathy for the effect the sight must be having on Merri.

Her father's sudden death had stunned her. Hell, his passing had stunned the town, shaking it to the core.

Dr. Downey had been a revered physician and a beloved resident of Dodge. He was a man a person could trust. A man who never turned away anyone in need.

A lot like his daughter, actually.

Matt shoved away the unwanted thought, working to regain the conviction he'd felt earlier that day—that the sooner Merri left Dodge, the better off he and Rosie would be.

Matt straightened, picturing Merri racing after Earl back at the restaurant. She'd diagnosed and treated him for the early stages of his Alzheimer's and no one had known. She'd helped the man *and* kept his secret.

He shook his head.

The woman was a doctor. Of course she could keep a secret. It was minding her own business where she fell short.

Just look at how she'd interfered in Rosie's life, encouraging the girl to try out for the school musical.

Anger heated his neck and face as he reached into his pocket for Rosie's letter.

Still gone.

Just like the town he knew and loved.

Matt concentrated on the scene unfolding before them as if some unseen person was running a video for their benefit. As he watched, Merri's sister Melody stepped to Merri's side, dabbing a handkerchief to her eyes.

Merri reached her arms around her younger sister and pulled the woman into a hug, gently patting Melody's back.

Something deep inside Matt's stomach tightened.

For all of the faults he could find in Merri, he had to admit one thing.

She had a kindness streak a mile wide.

He'd seen it in her actions with Rosie, with her patients and, most of all, with her sister, Melody. Hell, he'd seen it throughout their childhood, in her defense of the so-called unpopular kids in school, in the string of stray animals she'd forced her father to adopt and shelter.

In fifth grade, Frankie Jackson had stolen Katie's ring from her desk and presented it to Merri as a gift. Merri had returned the item before Katie had realized the ring was missing, then she'd smiled and squeezed Frankie's hand. Nothing more. No telling the teacher.

No telling Katie. Just a quiet refusal made without publicly humiliating Frankie.

No one could say Merri wasn't a good-hearted person, but similarly, no one who knew her could deny that the thought of leaving Dodge was ever-present at the back of her mind.

Wasn't it better to make the way clear for her to leave Dodge now? To set up a plan to keep the clinic open and avoid a nightmare vision like tonight's?

After Santa's charade was over, Matt vowed to press the issue of Triboro Health Systems. In the meantime, he concentrated on the sight before him, studying the image of Merri's younger sister Melody.

Last he'd heard, Melody was off in Europe some-where, photographing an endless stream of fashion shows. Merri no doubt resented the fact Melody had escaped Dodge, leaving her far behind.

Truth be told, Claire had resented Melody. Melody had forged the photography career Claire had hoped for before their marriage. Before Rosie's birth.

Even though she'd never said so, Matt knew Claire had had moments in which she wanted to leave Dodge as much as Merri once had. But Claire had chosen to stay, to be his wife, to be a mother to their daughter until the day the ocean had swept away their life together.

Matt shook his head, bolstering his resolve to watch the scene before them.

"I can't go." Melody's voice reached him,

carrying across the space between the clinic vision and the sleigh.

"You have to," Merri answered. "You've dreamed of this your whole life."

"And you haven't dreamed of getting out?"

"I'll get my chance."

Next to Matt, Merri stiffened. She pressed her fingertips to her lips, visibly shaken by what she saw.

"What if you don't?" Melody asked. "What if you're stuck here forever?"

Beside him, Merri's breath audibly caught and Matt flattened his palm against her arm. "You okay?"

She started, lifting her luminous eyes to his. "I don't know *what* I am right now, do you?"

He shook his head, shifting his hand away from her skin, aware of the chill he felt at the loss of contact.

Merri leaned forward, closing the space between her and Tewanda.

She pointed toward the clinic. "This is what happened. I didn't leave. So why has everything changed?"

"You left the next morning," Tewanda answered. "You left after you woke up and found your sister gone, even after she'd promised to stay on for a month or two to help you deal with your father's affairs and get settled in at the clinic."

Merri's throat visibly worked and she sat back, shoulders sagging as if Tewanda's words had let the air out of her body.

"She did promise me," Merri said softly. "And then she left me all alone. She phoned me the next day to say goodbye."

"Why did you stay?" Matt surprised himself with the question and the genuine interest in his voice.

"I couldn't let my father down, couldn't leave his patients without care. I wanted to honor his memory."

"But Melody didn't?"

"Melody was a photographer, not a doctor," Merri answered. "She wanted to be anywhere but Dodge." She hesitated before saying anything more. "I forgave her. She knew I would."

"But what if you hadn't?" Tewanda asked.

Merri straightened once more. "If I hadn't forgiven Melody?"

Tewanda twisted in the front seat and nodded. "What do you think she would have done?"

Merri laughed. Even though her tone was more nervous than joyous, Matt's breath caught. The sound of her distinctive laugh never failed to affect him.

Even when Merri was stressed, as she was now, her good nature came through in her laughter. It was as if none of the twists and turns life delivered could fully take away her underlying joy at being alive.

He'd been a fourth-grader the first time he'd ever heard her laugh and, although he'd never told a soul, he'd been mesmerized by the little blond first-grader with the toothy grin and booming laugh.

Merri shoved her hands up into her hair, shaking

loose the strands of her ponytail as she looked to the sky. "Melody would have done exactly what she did. She would have chased her dream and been a success. Photographer to the stars." She shook her head, lowering her gaze. "Trust me when I tell you my approval never meant a thing to my sister."

"That's where you're wrong." Tewanda pursed her lips. "Without your approval, Melody faltered, disbelieving in her abilities and turning to others for approval. She fell in with the wrong man and her career was ruined." She grimaced. "Your sister hasn't taken a photograph in years."

Matt watched in amazement as the images before them faded, first Melody's and then Merri's.

Merri inhaled sharply as if the sight pained her.

"Where is she?" she asked.

"She faded away. Forgotten. A pretty face to answer phones at a third-rate advertising agency in Pittsburgh."

Merri squeezed her eyes shut. A single tear escaped and rolled down her cheek. Matt lifted his hand to brush it away, but Merri wiped her face before his fingers reached her skin.

She snapped her eyes open and pulled herself taller in the seat. "So what are you, my guardian angel or something?" Her pale brow furrowed.

Tewanda shook her head, sending her thick, white artificial beard bouncing from side to side.

Merri frowned and Matt waited for Santa's

answer, wanting to make sense of what was happening. When Tewanda shot a smile in his direction and pointed directly at his chest, he tensed.

"I'm his." A teasing note danced in her voice.

"My what?" Anxiety tinged the impatience welling up inside Matt.

Tewanda leaned close and placed her hand on Matt's knee. A sense of calm enveloped him and he realized he'd experienced the sensation before in his life.

The day Rosie was born.

The day he'd buried Claire.

The day he'd first heard Merri laugh.

Matt knew what Tewanda was about to say even as she opened her mouth to speak.

She chuckled, brown eyes twinkling. "I don't have to say it, do I?"

He shook his head.

"What?" Merri moved so close her arm brushed against Matt's, sending heat flashing through him. "What's going on?"

One of Tewanda's eyebrows lifted toward the fake fur trim of her hat. "I'm not your guardian angel, Merri." She tipped her chin toward Matt. "I'm his."

"I don't understand." Merri scrubbed a hand across her eyes. "If I'm the one that made the life-altering decision to leave Dodge, why is Matt's guardian angel here?" She dropped her voice to a mumble. "And when did I start talking about guardian angels like they were real?"

"You'll see." Tewanda nodded tightly. "If all goes well tonight, I might even earn my wings."

"Wings?" Matt's tone reeked of disbelief.

"Mmm-hmm." Tewanda pursed her lips and nodded. "Let's just say I have a little control problem. I'm very good at showing the possibilities, I'm just not very good at stepping back and letting my charges make their own decisions and take their own actions.

"My job is to provide the tools and the guidance," she continued. "But then I'm supposed to back off."

Matt laughed, unable to believe what he was hearing. Not only had he and Merri been kidnapped by a wingless angel, they'd been kidnapped by a wingless angel with control issues.

"You can laugh all you want." Tewanda shook her head. "But I'm all yours, so you'd better get used to the idea."

Unbelievable.

He'd argued with Merri one too many times, and he'd completely lost his mind.

The sleigh came to an abrupt stop and Tewanda was out of her seat and walking away before Matt could say another word. He stayed put, wishing there was a way to wake up and put this night behind him.

"Pinch me again." He turned to Merri.

Her beautiful eyes popped wide. "You weren't terribly receptive to the idea the first time around."

"Just do it." His tone bordered on an order.

Merri made a face but reached forward, taking his

hand in hers. She cradled his fingers while she squeezed a chunk of his flesh between her thumb and index finger.

The pinch hurt like hell, yet it was the comforting warmth of her skin pressed to his that kicked Matt's inner turmoil up a notch.

What was going on? After all these years of denying he had any residual feelings for Merri, his attraction to the woman had roared back to life.

Merri's gaze lifted to his and he spotted the same question in her eyes.

For a fleeting moment he pictured pulling her close and apologizing for the way he'd acted earlier. He imagined how it might feel to hold her, just as he'd done so many years ago, before life had hardened his heart and his soul.

His every instinct longed to promise her he'd get them safely out of whatever sort of time warp they'd become stuck in.

Instead he broke contact, pulling his hand free from hers before he did something he'd regret for a very long time. Matt had trusted the woman with his heart once. He had no plans to make that same mistake again.

"Thanks," he said as he climbed out of the sleigh, wanting to put as much distance between the two of them as possible. "Definitely felt something."

As he walked toward their destination, he fought down the question niggling at the base of his brain.

Which was a more frightening prospect?

The fact that everything they'd seen tonight might be real?

Or the fact that he still had feelings for Merri, even after all the heartache the woman had brought into his life…and his family?

CHAPTER FIVE

MERRI RECOGNIZED THEIR surroundings instantly.

They were still at the clinic, only this time, the clinic wasn't the clinic at all. Far from it.

Huge windows had been inset into the walls, their glass covered with numerous construction-paper cutouts of letters, numbers and holiday shapes.

The fenced-in yard boasted an assortment of playground equipment fit for climbing, swinging and sliding. An area of asphalt showed traces of pastel chalk drawings.

"A daycare center?" Merri asked.

Tewanda nodded.

Merri squeezed her eyes shut, letting her mind conjure up the sound of happy laughter and children playing. At least the clinic had been turned into something positive, a place full of hope.

Through the windows, Merri spotted a lone figure taking down holiday decorations and rearranging furniture. She recognized the woman's profile instantly.

Katie.

Her heart leaped at the sight of her dear friend, but an anxious curiosity pushed down her initial sense of joy. She turned to Tewanda. "Why is she here so late on Christmas Eve?"

Tewanda smiled, the gesture forced, the expression not reaching her eyes. "She has nowhere else to be."

"What about Jack?" Matt asked. The deep rumble of his voice startled Merri. She hadn't considered Matt's reaction to the scene.

"You've been gone for seven years, Merri." Tewanda's breath brushed Merri's ear. "With the clinic closed, there was no need for a visit from a pharmaceutical sales rep." She shook her head. "No Jack. No Katie and Jack."

Merri pictured the Christmas Eve meal she and Matt had shared with Jack and Katie. Was it possible it had been only hours earlier?

"No Connor? No Elizabeth?" Merri's heart broke as she asked the question, and she intently studied Tewanda's reaction.

The young woman shook her head, her eyes turning sad. "This is the only life Katie knows. Her little charges are her family. The daycare is her home."

"But I just saw her." Merri cringed at the desperation in her own tone. "*We* just saw her." She reached for Matt, wrapping her fingers around his arm and holding tightly. "Jack and Katie are our friends. They love each other. They're happy."

Tewanda shook her head. "Jack works somewhere up in North Jersey. He never married." She gave a slight shrug. "You never introduced them. They're both alone."

Merri drew in a breath, shaken by the possibility Tewanda's words were true. A shiver danced down her spine, and Matt pressed a hand to her shoulder as if she might lose her balance.

Merri turned again, hoping to catch a glimpse of Katie, but her friend had stepped out of sight. Instead, Merri noticed a framed portrait hanging on a nearby wall.

Belinda Murphy.

Confusion swirled inside her. "Why is Belinda's picture here?"

Tewanda stepped to Merri's side, the red felt of her sleeve brushing against Merri's arm, sending an odd tingling sensation outward from the point of contact.

"She worked here before…" Tewanda hesitated.

"Before what?" Merri's voice climbed several octaves.

Matt stepped closer, and Merri longed to turn into him, to wrap her arms around his waist and ask him to make the nightmare end. Instead she stared straight ahead, willing herself to be comforted by his nearness alone.

In the blink of an eye, the three were back in the sleigh, sliding to an abrupt stop, sending Merri and

Matt slamming against the back of the seats in front of them.

When had they gotten back into the sleigh? And where were they now?

Merri tried to see through the night sky and the rain that was falling once again. Shapes and shadows came into focus. Tombstones. Grave markers. Withered bouquets of flowers.

The old Dodge cemetery.

A large tombstone sat just to her right. The letters etched into the slab of marble were unmistakable.

Belinda Murphy.

"No." Merri whispered the word.

She scrambled down from the sleigh and ran her fingers along the top of Belinda's tombstone, then traced the engraved dates with her fingertips.

She'd been gone for three years.

Three years? Two years before the flu epidemic?

"Breast cancer," Tewanda answered before Merri could ask the question.

Merri straightened defensively, her voice rising in intensity. "Three years ago she battled breast cancer and won. She opened a boutique. She's a happy, vibrant woman."

Merri pictured Belinda's eyes, bright with excitement. Her smile had been radiant, filled with joy when they'd beaten her cancer.

And they *had* beaten her cancer. At least until today.

Merri remembered delivering the news of

Belinda's recurrence earlier that day and felt the weight of the world close in on her.

If only Belinda hadn't put off traveling into the city for her tests. If only Merri had had the equipment she needed at the clinic.

If only.

"You and she would have beaten it the second time—" Tewanda spoke softly as if reading Merri's mind "—if you'd stayed in Dodge. Without you she skipped her annual physicals. Her first diagnosis came too late. The treatment failed to save her."

Merri sank to her knees, not caring that she kneeled in ice-cold water. Not caring that her heart was broken.

She only cared about Belinda—her patient and her friend—who wasn't supposed to die.

"I can't take any more of this." Merri leaned her forehead against the stone momentarily, then looked up at Tewanda, searching the woman's face. "Please. I need to go home."

"I'll take you home." Tewanda thinned her lips, and her gaze narrowed. "But we have one more life to check in on first." She twisted in her seat, looking directly at Matt.

When Merri followed Belinda's gaze, she saw something in Matt's eyes she'd never seen there before. Not once.

Never during the years she'd known him in school or during the summer they'd shared after her graduation—not even in the days and months following Claire's death.

Matt's expression was one of fear, and recognizing that particular emotion scared Merri more than anything else she'd seen tonight.

MATT COULDN'T BELIEVE the level of emotion churning inside him as the sleigh catapulted into motion.

How could one life affect so many others?

He'd always known Merri to be a good person, but even before Claire's death, he'd thought her too young to run the clinic. He'd never thought her worthy of the town's respect, especially not when her lifetime goal had been to leave Dodge far behind.

But now…

Now Matt faced a reality he'd never considered.

Dodge needed Merri—both the woman and the doctor.

A sense of protectiveness rumbled to life inside him, a protectiveness he hadn't felt toward Merri in years. He wanted nothing more than to make this night end and transport her back into the Dodge they both knew.

He longed to wipe the anguish and heartache from her face.

He could forgive her for walking away to go to college. Without her medical training, where would Dodge be today? Would things be as Tewanda had shown them? Or would they be even worse?

And if Merri had never left, Matt would not have married Claire, and Rosie would never have existed.

As many times as he'd caught himself wondering what might have been had Merri stayed after high school, he'd never wish Rosie away. Any heartache he'd once felt because of Merri had been worth bringing his beloved daughter into his life.

Deep inside, Matt knew he should apologize for the way he'd treated Merri for failing to resuscitate Claire on the beach.

The old grief welled inside him, a wound too deep to heal, shoving away all thoughts of making amends.

He gave himself a mental shake.

No matter what he'd seen tonight, Merri *was* to blame for Claire's death.

Matt would do whatever he could to return them both to the Dodge they knew, but he wouldn't forgive Merri for Claire's death.

Some things were too much to ask.

He drew in a deep breath, letting his head slump back against the sleigh's seat. He wasn't sure how long he'd stayed in that position, but when he opened his eyes, they'd stopped once more.

No rain fell, but a dense fog rose from the earth and grass around them.

That odd sense of calm he'd experienced earlier settled over him now and he knew exactly where he was.

Home.

Matt strained to see his property, his farm, his house.

Yet when he did, the feeling that came over him wasn't one of relief but rather one of shock.

The farm had never looked worse.

What on earth had happened?

CHAPTER SIX

MERRI FOLLOWED MATT as he slowly made his way toward the house. Tewanda stood off to the side, as if she wanted Matt to experience by himself whatever was about to happen.

Merri ignored the street-corner Santa and quickened her pace to catch up to Matt.

Reliving the day she'd buried her father had been painful enough, and she'd witnessed that from the safety of the sled.

Matt was about to walk into his ruined home with no idea what lay in wait for him, and she had zero intention of letting him do it alone.

She steeled herself as she followed Matt through the back door, trailing him through a seriously cluttered kitchen—the mess the opposite of what she would have expected from such an orderly man.

Even so, nothing could have prepared her for what she saw when she stepped into Matt and Rosie Riley's living room.

Her jaw fell slack. Shock overwhelmed her. She

knew without looking that Matt's expression must match her own. How could it not? They were looking at a second Matt—a Matt neither of them had ever seen or imagined.

The Matt before them was but a shadow of the proud, handsome, confident man she knew.

The Matt in the vision sat nursing a bottle of beer in the midst of trash and clutter. Judging from the empties sitting on the floor, the beer in his hand wasn't his first and wouldn't be his last.

The man's appearance was beyond sloppy, bordering on slovenly. His shirt looked as though he had slept in the garment night after night. The pair of jeans he wore hadn't mingled with soap and water in a very long time.

But it was his unkempt hair, unshaven face and tortured expression that left Merri feeling bereft. She longed to cross the room and embrace the Matt in the vision.

An inner voice screamed at her to help him clean the house, to toss him into a shower, to launder his clothes and cook him a hot meal. Most of all, her every instinct begged to solve whatever problem had turned Matt into this unfamiliar, haunted shadow of a man.

Was this the Matt the restaurant manager had referred to? Had Matt become an alcoholic?

"It's like looking at my father." Matt's deep voice growled. "I would never do this. Never."

Matt's voice rang out strongly and clearly next to

Merri, and relief whispered through her. She could touch the Matt beside her, and she reached out to do just that. He met her move with a warning glare and she quickly withdrew her hand.

Merri ignored his nonverbal rejection, focusing instead on the brief but solid feel of his arm beneath her fingertips. The Matt beside her might not be happy at the moment, but he was real. He was strong and fit and healthy, and Merri had every intention of doing whatever it took to keep him that way.

"Are you going to answer me?" Matt raised his voice, his anger palpable. "I would never do this."

Tewanda appeared next to them, taking in the scene, then turning slowly away from the second Matt to face the first. "Wouldn't you?"

"Absolutely not." Matt shook his head. "There's not a thing in this world that could make me like *him*." He pointed at the sight before them, his finger trembling with anger. "Nothing."

"What about someone?"

Tewanda turned away once more and the vision faded, blurring into nothingness. They were back in the sleigh, hurtling sideways, careening through space and time.

When the vehicle came to a stop, they were surrounded by another scene of filth and decay, this one the alley between two city streets.

Somewhere in New York, if Merri wasn't mistaken.

She scanned the area, not spotting any sign of life

until a young girl staggered around the corner, un-steady on her feet in a pair of faded stiletto boots.

The girl's features were barely recognizable be-neath her heavy makeup. The sharp lines of her mal-nourished face distorted her appearance, but the moment Matt swore beneath his breath, Merri knew exactly who the young girl was.

Rosie.

"No." She and Matt uttered the word at the same moment.

Merri's insides turned liquid, flipping and rolling at the terrifying implication of the scene before her.

"Yes." Tewanda answered without taking her eyes from Rosie. "Don't you think this might be enough to drive you to drink, Matt?"

Merri shot him a glance, but Matt said nothing, sitting in shocked silence, apparently unable to wrench his gaze from his daughter.

Merri climbed to her feet. "He'd never let this happen. Matt's a good father. *No.* He's a great fa-ther. Sure, he's a bit obtuse sometimes, but what parent isn't."

Matt looked up at Merri, amazement across his features. She babbled on without stopping to let Matt say a word.

"Whether I was in Dodge or not—" she pointed at Rosie, who was now picking through a Dumpster "—this would never happen. Matt would save her."

"What if he couldn't?" Tewanda asked.

"He'd find a way." Merri leaned toward the pseudo Santa, heat firing in her cheeks. She hadn't felt this strongly about anything in…well…ever.

Tewanda shook her head. "She's been on the streets since she turned twelve, and Matt couldn't stop her."

"Twelve." Tears swam in Merri's vision and she sank back onto the seat. "What about school? Her friends? Her singing?"

Matt's expression grew sullen.

"The music inside Rosie died a long time ago." Tewanda clucked her tongue. "She dropped out of school and went in search of what she couldn't find at home."

Matt finally spoke. "What?" his voice cracked on the word. "Why?"

"She felt invisible. She felt abandoned." Tewanda reached up to straighten her cap. "She left to chase the bright lights of Broadway, but like so many young girls, she never made it."

As they watched, Rosie walked on unsteady feet toward a phone booth, lifted the receiver and dropped coins into the slot.

Suddenly they could hear her. Her frightened breathing. The way she murmured to herself, trying to bolster her confidence as she waited for the other party to answer.

"Hello." Matt's voice sounded loud and clear from the other end of the line. "Hello?"

Rosie swallowed but said nothing. A tear streaked down her cheek, leaving a pale trail in its wake.

"Rosie?" Matt's voice asked. "Is that you?"

Rosie pressed a hand across her mouth and lowered the phone back into its cradle. Then she dipped her head toward the booth, her shoulders shaking with her sobs.

Merri felt as if someone had ripped out her heart and torn it to pieces. Matt's face grew so distorted with anguish he became almost unrecognizable.

"What's going to happen to her?" Merri asked, forcing the words through her throat, choked by the fear taking over every inch of her body.

"You did this." Matt pointed a finger menacingly at Merri.

Merri straightened sharply, not believing Matt was about to blame her for what they'd just seen.

Tewanda reached between them, shaking her finger. "You're forgetting the rules. Merri wasn't a part of Dodge. Rosie wasn't much more than a toddler at the time Merri's father died, and Merri was away at medical school years before that fateful day."

Matt held Tewanda's stare momentarily, then turned his attention to Merri. The need and fear in his eyes reached deep inside her and pulled.

"You have to help me get her back," he whispered. "Please."

"That's what I'm trying to do." Tewanda shrugged as if his statement was a no-brainer.

"Not you." Matt shot Tewanda a look but quickly returned his focus to Merri. "You."

Merri hadn't seen such trust and need in Matt's eyes for a very long time. She nodded and a tear slipped over her lower lid, sliding down her cheek.

Matt reached to brush the moisture away and Merri captured his hand in hers, pressing his palm to her cheek, savoring the contact, the feel of his skin against hers.

He wasn't alone in this. She had to make sure he understood that.

"I'll do whatever it takes." She spoke the words slowly and surely. "I love your daughter, Matt. I'd do anything for her."

Matt swallowed visibly and pulled his hand away from Merri's cheek, turning back toward Tewanda, repeating Merri's earlier question.

"What's going to happen to her?"

"That's not for me to say."

The sleigh was in motion before Matt could do or say anything more, and the sudden motion tossed him back against the seat.

When he dropped his face to his hands, Merri reached out to squeeze his knee. While he didn't acknowledge the contact, he also didn't move away.

Merri didn't release her grip until the sleigh came to a halt.

She studied the scene before her, knowing instantly where they were and what was taking place.

The sleigh sat on the beach just outside town.

The beach where everyone went swimming.

The beach where Claire Riley had drowned.

Merri watched in horror as a vision of Claire swam in the waves off the sandy shore. Memories of that dreadful afternoon came back, flashing through Merri's mind like frames from an old home movie.

Tewanda had brought them to the sight of what probably had been one of the worst days in both of their lives.

"Claire." Matt uttered the word on a whisper.

Merri reacted to the grief and loss in his voice by reaching for his hand, catching herself at the last moment. Matt had made his feelings perfectly clear during the years since Claire had drowned. He blamed her for Claire's death.

Surely, the last person on earth he'd turn to for comfort here would be Merri.

The trio sat silently in the sleigh, watching as Claire swam, diving through waves and riding the surf.

"She loved it here." Matt climbed down from the sleigh, his feet sinking into the soft sand as he moved. "She used to take her camera everywhere, as if she were trying to capture something just out of her reach, something she'd missed by living here in Dodge. But here—" he nodded toward the water "—she didn't need her camera. Here, she was happy."

Merri scrambled to follow, but Tewanda raised a hand to stop her.

"Let him go." Her expression grew serene, intent. "He needs to see this."

"Why?" Merri's heart threatened to burst. "No one needs to see this."

Tewanda's features tightened. "He does. Trust me."

"Claire." Matt's shout rang above the crash of the surf, but Claire didn't respond, never looking up from her focus on the waves.

When Claire clutched at the side of her head, Merri straightened, pushing herself to her feet.

Claire faltered, slipping beneath the waves, bobbing to the surface once, then sliding into the unforgiving ocean a second time.

Matt ran, his feet splashing through the puddles left behind on the uneven sand by an earlier tide.

Merri jumped from the sleigh, chasing him, racing as fast as she could.

Matt came to an abrupt stop and slapped at the air around him as if he'd run smack into an invisible wall.

"He has." Tewanda's voice sounded in Merri's ear as she pulled up short next to Matt.

Merri glanced quickly at Tewanda then reached toward the space before them. Her fingers brushed against a hard surface, not visible, but solid.

Frustration and fear twisted Matt's features. "Can't we stop this? Can't we save her?"

Tewanda placed her hand on Matt's shoulder. "No one can." She shook her head, her expression softening. "No one could."

Matt spun away from Tewanda's touch, searching the ocean's surface for several long, silent moments before he turned on Merri, pointing at her, fury flashing in his moist, dark eyes.

"Maybe *she* didn't save her, but someone more experienced could have." He stepped so close Merri could smell the soap he'd showered with that day. "A better doctor would have resuscitated Claire. If your father had been alive, my wife would still be here today."

Matt's words sent remorse and frustration surging through Merri's veins. He'd never voiced his thoughts so bluntly, but the words had hung between them, unspoken since that fateful day on the beach.

Merri had understood exactly how Matt felt from the moment he'd raced across the sand after word had spread that Claire was in trouble.

She could see his face as if it were yesterday. She remembered the smell of his fear and pain as he cradled Claire's lifeless body in his arms.

"Claire didn't drown." Tewanda's words startled Merri back to the present.

The confused look on Matt's face matched the emotions tumbling through Merri.

"She died of a brain aneurysm." Tewanda stepped through the invisible wall to the ocean's edge. "No one could have saved her." She pivoted on one heel, tipping her chin toward Merri. "But because Merri happened to be out for a walk, you were able to know what happened to your wife."

Matt scowled. "I don't understand."

"Neither do I." Merri's mental anguish weighed on her so heavily she sank to her knees. She voiced the thought that had haunted her for five years. "She died because I wasn't good enough."

Tewanda stood above her, smiling gently. "She died because of the aneurysm." She jerked a thumb back toward the ocean, where there was no sign Claire had ever gone for a swim. "This is what happened without you here."

The young woman in the Santa garb moved between Merri and Matt and faced the empty surf. "Without you to pull her from the surf, Claire was swept out into the open ocean. Her body was never found."

Tewanda reached for Matt's chin, forcing him to look at her instead of the ocean. "You and Rosie never knew what happened to Claire. She simply disappeared. As far as you or anyone else knew, she'd abandoned you."

He shook his head. "She'd never—"

Tewanda held up a finger to interrupt him. "You say that now because you know she drowned, but what if you didn't know? What if you walked into the house one day and she was gone? What if you and Rosie spent night after night, morning after morning, day after day wondering where she went? Wondering how she could leave you? And why?"

She placed both hands gently on his shoulders. "Merri might not have saved Claire, but she saved you and Rosie. She let you say goodbye. Sometimes, that's the greatest gift anyone can give."

Merri tried to process Tewanda's words.

Claire had died of an aneurysm?

The old sadness washed over her anew, but she had no time to wallow in it before Tewanda was on the move.

"Let's go," the young woman headed toward the sleigh. "We're burning nighttime."

Merri didn't move as Tewanda walked away. Instead she stood watching the woman. The icy-cold sea breeze caught the pom-pom on Tewanda's red hat, sending it bouncing up and down against her head.

The sight was in such opposition to everything the woman had shown them tonight, Merri laughed. But her laughter quickly gave way to tears.

She dropped her chin, staring at her hands, remembering how hard she'd worked to save Claire.

She squeezed her eyes shut.

Her efforts had been for nothing.

Nothing.

"You saved us."

Merri looked up to find Matt standing over her, his hand extended.

"But I didn't save Claire." She shook her head.

"There must have been something I could have done. I should have known it was an aneurysm. You were right. I was inexperienced and young and—"

Matt quickly dropped to his knees, pressing his fingertips to Merri's lips.

The contact shocked her and she leaned back, putting distance between his touch and her face.

He reached for her hand and she slipped her fingers into his, letting him help her to her feet.

As they walked back toward the sleigh, Matt squeezed Merri's hand.

"All this time I've blamed you. I'm sorry."

"You had no reason not to blame me."

He hesitated, turning her to face him, pulling their joined hands against his chest. The doctor in Merri couldn't help but note the rapid beat of Matt's heart. To say he'd just been through a lot would be the understatement of the century. What he needed now was time to digest what he'd learned. To rest. To recover.

"You did everything you could." Matt grimaced. "I should have trusted you. I was wrong." His words were barely audible above the crash of the surf. "If you hadn't been there, Rosie and I would have never known what happened to Claire. Thank you."

With that he broke their contact, turning abruptly and heading for the sleigh.

Merri stood her ground, touched by Matt's words, yet stunned by the void she'd felt the moment he'd let go of her hand.

She fully understood the role her leaving would have played in Matt and Rosie's life, but what role might her staying *now* play?

Try as Merri could to deny it, she was becoming more and more interested in finding out.

CHAPTER SEVEN

A FREEZING-COLD SLEET began to fall, stinging Merri's cheeks, leaving her feeling raw and exposed.

And angry.

Why had Tewanda seen fit to make Matt witness Claire's death? Wouldn't telling him about the aneurysm have been enough?

"Don't worry. The weather will be better where we're going," Tewanda called out.

Matt's eyes appeared vacant, his features slack. Perhaps he was reliving everything they'd seen, or perhaps he was remembering Claire. Remembering their life together.

A flicker of regret whispered through Merri, even though she did her best to shove it away. What might have been had she not walked away from Matt after high school?

The image of Rosie's face flashed through her mind and Merri felt nothing but remorse. If Matt hadn't married Claire, there would be no Rosie, and that would be the biggest tragedy of all.

"Are you all right?" Merri kept her voice low as she reached out to touch Matt's hand.

He surprised her by capturing her hand in his and giving her fingers a squeeze before letting go.

"Just thinking."

Merri nodded and stared into space as they traveled toward their next destination. No matter how hard she tried, her thoughts immediately went back to Matt. She couldn't help wondering what his thoughts were.

For all she knew, he was grieving the many life events he and Claire would never share.

Rosie's graduation from high school and college.

Her wedding day.

The birth of their first grandchild.

A dull ache took root deep inside Merri, and for the first time in a very long time, she let herself imagine a life where she had all of that. A family. True love. Commitment.

Without warning, the images around the sleigh slowed, becoming clearer and clearer.

Suddenly she and Matt were standing inside the hallway of a hospital. Staff bustled past them and the activity level at the nurses' station hummed just below a frenzy.

"Where are we?" Matt asked.

Merri studied him, worrying about how pale he'd gone and how drawn his features had become. The set of his jaw seemed far more severe than it had earlier that night.

Tewanda swept her hand across the scene. "We're home. Merri's home. And don't worry, they can't see us."

Merri frowned, puzzled. "I've never been here before."

"But you have." Tewanda nodded. "You've been here countless times in your mind. This is the life you've always imagined. The life you gave up to stay in Dodge and run the clinic."

Merri watched herself appear in the scene. A much thinner version of herself, an older-looking version, an exhausted version.

A hollowness settled inside her as she saw herself doing all the things she'd fantasized about over the years. Working at a large hospital. Operating on cancer patients, counseling families, consulting with a team of caregivers.

She saw herself putting her medical degree and surgical training to good use. *No.* To great use.

And yet, she felt as though someone had punched her in the stomach and left her sitting on the sidelines, completely out of breath.

"You're living your dream, Merri."

Tewanda smiled as she uttered the words, but Merri could read the mixed emotions in the angel's eyes. She was holding back. There was obviously far more she wanted to say, but she was using uncommon restraint. Why now?

"What about her personal life?" Matt asked.

Matt had said nothing since they'd first arrived and his voice startled Merri. She blinked, surprised by the intimate question.

The color had returned to his complexion, and relief eased through her.

He'd be all right. They all would. They had to be.

He shrugged innocently when Merri held his gaze. "I want to know if you got what you wanted. If you got it all."

"Mmm—" Tewanda straightened "—I know this one. She's got a great apartment she never spends time in, no friends because she's always at work and three cats who entertain themselves."

Cats?

Merri shook off the image and laughed, thankful she was still capable of enjoying humor. "I never wanted it all."

Matt's eyes narrowed. "I'm not following you."

"I never imagined myself in love or with a family." She tipped her chin toward the scene before them, scowling as it began to fade. "I only wanted this. I wanted life in a big city with a big career at a big hospital."

"How could I forget?"

Matt looked hurt and Merri's stomach dropped. But he'd always known she wanted this, hadn't he? He'd been the one to give her the Triboro Health Systems brochure, for crying out loud.

Had Matt changed his mind? Did he want her to stay in Dodge after all?

Merri's stomach tilted sideways as she took in her surroundings. This was all she'd ever wanted.

Until tonight.

Now, her perspective on life had shifted. She understood how much she'd accomplished in Dodge at the little clinic she'd resented since the day her father had died, yet all the time she'd believed she could be doing more—much more. She'd always imagined she could have a greater impact on medicine and mankind if she were somewhere—anywhere—but Dodge.

But as she watched the last image of the hospital fade away, she realized she'd be hard-pressed to accomplish more than she had in Dodge. She'd made a difference. Tewanda had shown her that tonight.

Acceptance dawned and she knew what the angel had been trying to say with her eyes.

The life Merri had always wanted was the life she already had.

Her work at the clinic was vital and lifesaving. She had the love of her friends and her patients. More importantly, she didn't have a house full of cats, not that there was anything wrong with that.

She had to find a way to erase what had happened tonight. She had to turn back the clock to the moment before she and Matt had made their fateful wishes.

Was she too late?

Was it even possible to change things back to the way they'd been?

"How do you feel now that you've seen what a success you became by leaving Dodge?" Tewanda's eyebrows lifted with her question, kissing the brim of her cap.

"I feel—" Merri bit down on her lip, concentrating, struggling to make sense of the myriad emotions battling for position inside her. "I feel—" she hesitated again, searching for a way to put the hollowness she felt into words.

She finally gave her head a quick shake and blew out an exasperated sigh. "I feel empty."

"Empty?" Both Matt and Tewanda asked the question at the same time, but while Matt's expression grew confused, a smile spread wide across Tewanda's face.

Merri shrugged. "Empty," she repeated.

She thought about the life she'd been shown and the life she'd lived until tonight. Tewanda's new version of reality had been such a shock, Merri could no longer wrap her brain around what she'd seen.

Merri was alone.

Katie and Jack had never met.

Matt had become an alcoholic buried in grief.

Rosie was adrift on the streets and doing heaven only knew what to survive.

"Empty." Merri whispered the word through a knot of emotion.

Tewanda placed a hand on her back. "We're ready for our final stop."

SILENCE BEAT BETWEEN Matt and Merri as they waited to see what Tewanda had in store for them next.

Empty.

Merri's response to the last vision haunted Matt, reverberating through his brain.

He jerked a thumb over his shoulder as if the hospital setting were just behind them. "Wasn't that all you thought it would be?"

"Well—" Merri sucked in a deep breath and forced a smile even though sadness bracketed her eyes "—I always thought I'd be a first-rate surgeon at a large teaching hospital and I'd specialize in oncology. I wanted to give everything I had to saving people's lives and making them feel cared for. Truly cared for. As a person, not a case number."

As she spoke, she shook her head, a glimmer lighting her eyes before fading away. Matt thought about her mother, succumbing too young to cancer, leaving Merri, Melody and Dr. Downey to fend for themselves.

"Oncology?" He squinted. "Cancer, right?"

Merri nodded.

"Like your mother," he said softly.

Merri pressed her lips into a thin line and repeated his words softly. "Like my mother."

"I sense a 'but' coming." He held her gaze.

Merri squeezed her eyes shut and sighed. "You've seen the same things I've seen tonight. My leaving would cause too much pain."

Their gazes locked and Merri searched Matt's face as if she were trying to see into his very thoughts.

"Besides," she continued. "What if I realized everything I thought I wanted wasn't enough?" She let out a sigh. "I just don't know anymore."

She turned away, tucking her head into the crook of her arm as she rested against the sleigh's side.

Matt watched her for what felt like hours, yet was no more than seconds. Confusion swirled through him.

Had Merri decided to stay in Dodge?

An unfamiliar emotion stirred within him.

Hope.

Merri might not be sure of what she wanted, but Matt suddenly realized what had become most important to him.

He wanted Merri Downey to be happy. She deserved that much and more.

If she chose to leave Dodge, he'd prepare the town for her absence armed with the knowledge of what he'd seen tonight. He'd find a way to fix things, to lessen the blow of losing Merri, to keep the clinic alive.

On a personal note, he couldn't deny the hold Merri still had on his heart, but he'd survived her leaving once. He'd find a way to survive again, even though, in just one night, her leaving had become the last thing in the world he wanted.

Merri buried her face in her arm, wishing she could wake up and this entire night would be nothing more than a bad memory, yet she knew that wasn't possible.

Even if everything she'd witnessed returned to normal, she was forever changed.

Someone tapped her shoulder and Merri lifted her head.

Tewanda leaned close, her eyes soft yet serious. "It's rare that people stop to think about how many lives their life affects. How many events one decision alters."

"But I never imagined—"

"Most people don't." Tewanda offered a gentle smile. "Your wish changed not only your life, but the lives of so many others. You thought you could do great things only in the big city, at a big hospital, but the truth is, the greatest things you could have done were all right here. In Dodge."

Matt straightened, shifting toward the edge of the seat. "But what if Merri made a new discovery, invented a new treatment? What if she saved more lives at the city hospital than she'd ever save here? Wouldn't that justify what's happened here?"

Merri couldn't believe what Matt was saying. She took his hand in hers, shock racing through her at the connection she felt when their eyes met—a connection stronger than any bond they'd shared in the past.

"Nothing could justify what we've seen tonight."

She shook her head, filled with sadness and remorse. "Nothing," she repeated.

Much to Merri's surprise, Matt made no move to extract his hand from hers. Instead, he lifted her hand and cradled it between his palms, interlacing his fingers with hers.

She blinked, then held his gaze, again stunned by the emotional bond she felt. She'd always known she still cared for Matt, but tonight's events had shown her how much, just as they'd erased her every regret at staying in Dodge after her father's death.

"I'm so sorry," she whispered. "I had no idea one wish would cause you so much pain."

He shook his head, then leaned his forehead against hers. "I made the same wish."

Matt shifted, pulling Merri close to his side. He wrapped one arm around her and she tucked her head against his shoulder, feeling safe enveloped in his warmth and strength.

They sat in silence for several long moments as flashes of shapes and colors blurred past the sleigh.

Merri was completely unprepared for Matt's words when he broke the silence.

"I'm proud of you, Merri. For all you became and everything you accomplished."

Merri pushed away from their embrace to study Matt's face, reaching to brush her fingertips against his cheek.

She shook her head. "But I can read the pain and anger in your eyes every time I look at you."

"Is it there now?" The hard angles of Matt's face softened.

Merri searched his gaze, her pulse quickening when she realized what she found there now was miles away from the emotions she'd seen there before.

The only thing reflected in Matt's eyes now was a mixture of acceptance…and attraction. Did he still care for her? Even after all these years? After his marriage to Claire?

Matt leaned toward Merri, his lips close to hers.

"Next stop, Dodge."

Tewanda's sudden words broke the spell between Merri and Matt. They each moved to their respective ends of the bench seat but maintained eye contact.

The heat and desire in Matt's stare sent a raw need spiraling to life inside Merri.

She'd never stopped to make room for romance or love in her life, yet there was no way to deny what she felt now.

Her attraction to the man had started the day he'd first defended her on the playground as a child. Her feelings had grown throughout the years, yet she'd never admitted how deeply those feelings ran, not even when Matt had put his heart on the line before she left for college.

She'd followed her head instead of her heart.

Merri gave herself a mental shake. How foolish she'd been.

Suddenly, they were back in Dodge. The sleigh moved slowly, gliding down the deserted street. The rain had stopped, but the bitter cold persisted.

Yet not even the cold could edge out the warm hope welling up inside her. She'd fight for Dodge. She'd fight for Matt and Rosie.

No matter what she had to do.

She searched Main Street for a sign that the nightmare might be over, but found none.

The shuttered windows and doors were still there. The aura of desertion and neglect loomed heavy over the small town.

Merri turned to Matt, studying the lines and angles of his face. His jaw had taken on the determined set she knew so well. Perhaps he'd made a decision, too. Perhaps he was ready to fight for Dodge.

Sadness flickered through her at the thought of all the years they'd been at odds, when they might have been friends.

Or more.

She flashed back on everything they'd experienced tonight. The touches. The looks. The attraction that had been rekindled, crashing through her system like an out-of-control train.

Had Matt felt what she'd felt?

Was the desire she read in his features accurate, or was she imagining an attraction where there was none?

As the sleigh slowed to a stop, Merri realized she was ready to tuck away forever her goal of being a surgeon, her hope of one day leaving Dodge.

She was ready for a new dream.

A dream that had been flirting at the edge of her reality for years. One she hadn't been willing to accept…until now.

Maybe dreams and hopes shifted, like the ebb and flow of the tide. Perhaps they adjusted to life and the way things changed, the people you met.

Perhaps they were fluid, intangible things you never quite captured.

And maybe, just maybe, the answer to Merri's hopes and dreams had been waiting for her in Dodge all along.

CHAPTER EIGHT

"THIS IS AS FAR AS WE GO," Tewanda said. "Best of luck to you both."

Matt studied their surroundings. Nothing had changed. "You're going to dump us out here?"

Tewanda pointed up at the street sign. "Exactly where I found you."

"But what—"

The angel held up a hand to stop Matt before he could say another word. "Remember that whole interfering thing I told you about?"

Matt nodded.

"This is where I stop. You'll have to trust yourself."

Matt climbed out of the sleigh, then reached for Merri, lifting her down onto the wet sidewalk.

She searched his face, the touch of panic in her eyes unmistakable.

Matt knew then exactly what he had to do, what he had to say.

"I'll find a way to make whatever you want to do work. You deserve to be happy."

Merri took a backward step, blatant surprise on her face. "You'd do that?"

He reached for her hands. "When I gave you that brochure I did it to get rid of you, but now I want you to do what you were meant to do. We can find another doctor to run the clinic if you want."

Merri drew in a deep breath, her features serious. "What if I was meant to stay here in Dodge?"

Confusion tumbled through him. "But the hospital. The oncology practice." He frowned.

Merri smiled, lighting up her face. "What if I want a life—a real life—here in Dodge?" She pulled him closer. "What if I want more, Matt?"

"Like what?"

"Like you." Her smile widened. "And Rosie."

Matt shook his head in disbelief, stunned at the implication of Merri's words. He shot a glance at Tewanda, hoping for a sign of what to do, but the angel and her sleigh were gone, vanished into thin air.

Matt swallowed, suddenly understanding why it had been his guardian angel who had come calling tonight.

This was his deciding moment. The decision for which Tewanda had prepared him with every scene she'd showed him tonight.

What was the right decision for him? For Rosie? For Merri? He could no longer deny the feelings he'd carried for Merri his whole life.

But years ago, she'd walked away, and, until

tonight, he'd been sure she wanted to walk away again. If he put his heart on the line now, what guarantee did he have she wouldn't change her mind again?

Merri began to frown, worry marring her features.

Trust yourself.

The thought came to him as if Tewanda had whispered in his ear.

Trust your heart.

There it was again. A voice so sharp and clear he felt sure Merri must hear it, but based on the anxious expression on her face, she'd heard nothing at all.

Every shred of indecision left Matt's body, left his brain, and he knew unequivocally what he needed to do. What he wanted to do. What he'd wanted to do for longer than he cared to admit.

Have you ever wanted something so badly you could taste it?

Merri's own words bounced through his brain.

Yes, he had…and he did.

Matt pulled Merri into his arms and lowered his mouth to hers, pressing her lips apart, exploring tentatively, tangling his tongue with hers, tasting, teasing, savoring. He pulled her body to his, pressing his palm against the small of her back, amazed by how perfectly the soft curves of her body fit his hard planes, just as they had years ago.

Did he love her?

A happy laugh burst from his lips.

"What?" Merry matched his laugh with her own, warming Matt from head to toe.

And in that moment, he looked into the depths of her gaze and knew he did love her.

He always had.

A light snow began to fall, instantly coating the sidewalk, sparkling like countless diamonds beneath the Christmas lights hanging from every shop window and the ornaments strung overhead.

Last-minute shoppers bustled along the sidewalk, and everything was just as it had been the moment before Tewanda had whisked Merri and Matt away.

Matt took in the sight, open-mouthed with wonder and relief.

"Do you see it?" Merri asked, emotion almost choking her. "Everything's as it was. It's as if we never left this spot. We're back at the exact moment we left."

The sign for Parker's Diner lit the sky, as did the holiday decorations in the window of Belinda's Boudoir.

"Pinch me," Matt said, laughing. "Here." He held out his hand and Merri lightly squeezed it, hope dancing in her eyes.

"Ouch."

Matt's laughter mixed with Merri's as he reached into his pocket, finding the folded edge of Rosie's letter.

Merri mirrored the move, plucking the slick hospital brochure from the pocket of her pullover.

Matt grasped the edge of the brochure, stilling

Merri's hand. "Are you sure you could be happy staying here, Merri? In Dodge? With me?"

She smiled then, a wide, luminous smile. "Yes," she answered, her voice full of confidence and hope.

Matt slid the brochure from her fingers, ripping the slick paper into tiny pieces and tossing every scrap into a nearby trashcan.

He swept Merri into his arms, swinging her in a circle, closing his mouth over hers even before he lowered her back to the ground.

A horn beeped, startling them both. Merri jumped back a foot and Matt turned in search of the noise, smiling as he spotted a familiar truck slowing to a stop by the curb.

"Jack." Merri breathed the word, genuine happiness in her tone.

"Hey," Jack called out from his lowered window, "I thought you—" he tipped his head toward Merri "—went home, and I thought you—" he arched an eyebrow in Matt's direction "—went for a walk."

He narrowed his gaze. "Did you two have this planned all along?"

The teasing tone of Jack's voice and his wink didn't go unnoticed.

Merri's bright smile and the sound of her laughter ringing through the night sky made everything they'd been through worthwhile.

Every horrible vision. Every fright. Every warning.

Tewanda had known just what she needed to do to bring them to this spot, and she'd done it.

Nicely done, Matt thought. Nicely done.

"Listen," Jack yelled, raising his voice to be heard above the church bells that had begun to peal. "Something's up at the clinic. I need to get you two over there."

The clinic.

Matt had forgotten the surprise the town had planned for Merri's Christmas Eve as a sign of their appreciation for all she'd done. Truth was, he'd been so focused on running the good doctor out of town that he'd shoved any thought of the party out of his mind.

Merri's happy expression morphed into one of concern. She pushed away from Matt and raced toward Jack's truck before Matt could say a word. He decided to say nothing. Why not let her enjoy the full surprise once she saw what…and who…was waiting for her?

He followed close on her heels, coming to a stop when he spotted the Santa standing at the corner of the block.

"Hang on a sec," Matt called out to Jack and Merri, closing the distance between the truck and the stand.

When he skidded to a stop, he could see this Santa was *not* Tewanda. The wrinkles around the man's eyes suggested he was old enough for his beard to be the real deal, and his rich laugh rumbled through his entire body, shaking a belly that was far more solid than the pillow Tewanda had used.

"Have you seen Tewanda?" Matt asked.

Santa frowned. "Tewanda?"

"The other Santa. She was here earlier."

"No one's been here all season except me." Santa patted his chest. "This here's a one-man operation."

Son of a gun.

"So you were here tonight?"

The man nodded. "All night long."

Matt called out a thank-you as he turned back toward Jack's truck.

"Merry Christmas," Santa cried out.

"Merry Christmas," Matt answered, this time believing the words he spoke.

BRIGHT LIGHT SPILLED from the clinic window and music blared from inside the building as Jack pulled the truck to a stop.

Yet the clinic really was the clinic. Everything appeared to be as Merri had left it.

She breathed a sigh of relief and climbed out of the truck, moving quickly toward the front door. Countless people milled about inside, and if Merri didn't know better, she'd think someone was throwing a party. But who?

And why?

As if on cue, the front door snapped open and Melody stepped outside, sporting a Santa cap identical to the one Tewanda had worn all night.

"Melody?"

Merri's sister rushed forward and pulled Merri into a hug. "Isn't it fabulous? Now, we're going to have to do something about this paint job, and where on earth did you get those dreadful chairs in the waiting room? But oh, this is going to be wonderful."

Merri blinked.

Was she still in some sort of suspended reality?

"Didn't you call me from Europe a bit earlier?"

Melody grinned, tapping herself on the temple. "Pretty smart, huh? Those blocked numbers are great. I can tell you where I want you to think I am and you'd believe me."

Merri stared at her sister as if she were looking at an apparition. She'd never been happier to see her and touch her, making sure she was real.

"You look wonderful." She reached up to stroke her sister's cheek.

Melody narrowed her gaze. "And you're positively radiant." She looked over Merri's shoulder, eyes widening when she spotted Matt. "You two finally kiss and make up?"

Merri laughed. "You have no idea."

But Melody had already launched into motion, slipping her arm through Merri's and steering her inside.

"The residents of Dodge, myself included, have decided that this year *you* are our Christmas project."

"Me?" Merri's voice squeaked.

"You." Melody gave a dramatic nod. "For all that

you've done for everyone else over the years, this year, Dodge is giving back."

"Hear, hear." Cheers rang out as Merri crossed the threshold.

Before her stood what had to be half of Dodge's residents, including the full Moose Lodge membership. Relief welled inside her at the sight of Bert and Sally Parker, arm in arm, glasses raised in a toast.

She frantically scanned the room until she spotted Belinda Murphy, who grinned and shot Merri a wink.

Hot tears slid down Merri's cheeks and she did nothing to wipe them away, so filled with joy and relief at the sight of her loved ones—alive and well— she couldn't move.

"Hey, why are you crying?" Rosie appeared at Merri's side, concern on her young face.

Merri hiccuped on a sob and pulled the young girl into her arms. "You're all right," she murmured, not caring that her tears were spilling into Rosie's hair. "You're all right."

A pair of strong arms wrapped around them both, Matt's love and relief tangible at the sight of his beloved Rosie, safe and sound in Dodge.

When they broke apart, Merri cupped Rosie's chin in her hands. "Haven't you ever heard of someone crying because she's happy?"

Rosie scrunched up her features and shook her head. "But we haven't even told you the big news yet—" she peered at Melody "—have we?"

Melody shook her head. "Earl?" She glanced around the room, one arm raised and waving. "Earl?"

Earl Norton appeared from deep in the crowd, holding up a large board covered with diagrams and drawings, scraps of material and photographs of expensive medical equipment.

"Earl." Matt's voice rang heavy with relief.

"How'd that checkup go, Matt?" Earl asked.

Matt clasped a hand on Earl's shoulder. "Better than you could have ever imagined."

"Well—" Earl beamed at Merri "—that's because our Doc here is something else."

"Yes." Matt nodded, wrapping his arm around Merri's waist. "That she is."

"Now, there's a picture," Melody said, surprise and delight dancing in her tone as she studied Matt and Merri together.

Katie looked from Matt and Merri to where Jack stood, holding a tired Connor in his arms. Merri watched her lift a questioning eyebrow, answered only by Jack's shrug.

She laughed to herself, deciding her friends wouldn't believe the night she and Matt had experienced even if they told them about it.

Let them think they'd rekindled their attraction after a Christmas Eve argument at Jack and Katie's. She and Matt would always know the truth about an angel named Tewanda, and they'd be forever grateful.

"Doctor Meredith Downey." Earl stood at attention, extending the display toward Merri. "With gratitude for all you do every day for the town of Dodge, we, the citizens, have arranged for a medical clinic extreme makeover."

Merri blinked, studying the designs and sketches. "I don't understand."

Katie crossed the room with a slumbering Elizabeth bundled into her arms. "I can't believe we were able to keep this a surprise from you. When Melody phoned me tonight, I thought I might blow the entire plan, but luckily for me, you left before you overheard anything." She laughed and shook her head. "Your sister orchestrated this entire thing. Can you believe it?"

"What *is* this thing?" Merri asked, trying to make sense of the display Earl held.

"New furniture. New paint. New window treatments. New equipment." Katie spoke the last word with a soft smile, having listened to Merri's pie-in-the-sky dreams of equipment purchases for years.

"Equipment?" Merri asked.

"The works." Melody snapped open a sheet of paper and read from a list. "X-ray equipment. Lab equipment. An EKG machine." She flashed a bright grin. "You name it, you got it." She tipped her head from side to side. "Or at least, you will get it. It's all on order." She tapped the list. "Everything you've ever mentioned."

"Melody arranged for everything," Earl explained.

The news hit Merri so hard she staggered, and fresh tears of joy blurred her vision.

"I was thinking we'd start with curtains." Melody pranced to the front of the clinic, reaching for the yellowed blinds. "I'm very good with color, so you leave that all to me. By the time you sign off on everything we've ordered, I'll have this place sparkling like new."

"How did you know?" Merri asked.

Melody spun on her heel, dramatic as always, fisting her hands on her hips. "I do have ears. You'd be surprised to know I actually use them. Besides—" she closed the space between her and Merri and gave Merri's hands a squeeze "—I can't think of any investment I'd rather make."

Melody hugged herself and sighed. "You wouldn't believe how good it feels to be home again."

Merri laughed, unable to contain her joy and amazement, all the while thinking of her own immeasurable relief at being home, in the Dodge of her heart. "You have no idea."

Matt anchored his arm around Merri's shoulder, and Melody nodded her head in approval.

A bell on the Christmas tree suddenly shook, sending a loud jingle through the room.

Rosie's eyebrows snapped together. "Wow. Just like that old movie Mom used to watch, isn't it, Dad?"

Merri saw Matt smile, his expression at ease, not a trace of pain in his eyes. "You're right, honey."

"Every time a bell rings," Rosie explained, "an angel gets his wings."

"Or *her* wings," Merri murmured beneath her breath.

Matt looked at her, his eyes wide. "Do you think?"

Merry nodded, filled with a lightness she hadn't believed humanly possible, thinking again about Matt's question.

Are you sure you could be happy staying here, Merri? In Dodge? With me?

She pressed her palm to Matt's cheek and uttered her single-word answer again. "Yes."

Matt smiled, resting his forehead against hers.

In that instant, she knew she loved him more than anything else in the world. She started to laugh.

"What?" Matt's dark eyebrows drew together, joy shimmering in his eyes.

Merri squeezed his hand. "I'll tell you later."

And she would.

After all, their future promised plenty of time… together…in Dodge.

HQN™

We *are* romance™

**A wickedly funny tale about one woman's
best-laid plans....
From *USA TODAY* Bestselling Author**

Jennifer Crusie

Kate Svenson may be a dynamite
businesswoman, but after three
failed engagements, she's decided
she needs a business plan to help
her find Mr. Right. The Cabins resort
is rife with rich and ambitious
bachelors. But they're dropping like
flies, and after fishing Kate's latest
reject out of the swimming pool,
Jake Templeton's convinced that Kate
is nothing but trouble, especially
for him. A man who's sworn off
ambition and a woman poised atop
the corporate ladder don't have
much in common. But with the
unpredictability of the heart, anything
can happen....

Manhunting

A timeless tale from the first name in romantic comedy—
Jennifer Crusie!

www.HQNBooks.com

PHJC290

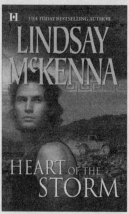

REQUEST YOUR FREE BOOKS!

2 FREE NOVELS PLUS 2
FREE GIFTS!

HARLEQUIN ROMANCE®

From the Heart, For the Heart

YES! Please send me 2 FREE Harlequin Romance® novels and my 2 FREE gifts. After receiving them, if I don't wish to receive any more books, I can return the shipping statement marked "cancel." If I don't cancel, I will receive 4 brand-new novels every month and be billed just $3.57 per book in the U.S., or $4.05 per book in Canada, plus 25¢ shipping and handling per book and applicable taxes, if any*. That's a savings of over 15% off the cover price! I understand that accepting the 2 free books and gifts places me under no obligation to buy anything. I can always return a shipment and cancel at any time. Even if I never buy another book from Harlequin, the two free books and gifts are mine to keep forever.

114 HDN EEV7   314 HDN EEWK

Name	(PLEASE PRINT)	
Address		Apt.
City	State/Prov.	Zip/Postal Code

Signature (if under 18, a parent or guardian must sign)

Mail to the **Harlequin Reader Service®**:
IN U.S.A.: P.O. Box 1867, Buffalo, NY 14240-1867
IN CANADA: P.O. Box 609, Fort Erie, Ontario L2A 5X3

Not valid to current Harlequin Romance subscribers.

Want to try two free books from another line?
Call 1-800-873-8635 or visit www.morefreebooks.com.

* Terms and prices subject to change without notice. NY residents add applicable sales tax. Canadian residents will be charged applicable provincial taxes and GST. This offer is limited to one order per household. All orders subject to approval. Credit or debit balances in a customer's account(s) may be offset by any other outstanding balance owed by or to the customer. Please allow 4 to 6 weeks for delivery.

Your Privacy: Harlequin is committed to protecting your privacy. Our Privacy Policy is available online at www.eHarlequin.com or upon request from the Reader Service. From time to time we make our lists of customers available to reputable firms who may have a product or service of interest to you. If you would prefer we not share your name and address, please check here. ☐

HR07

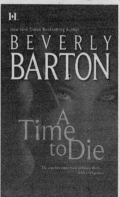

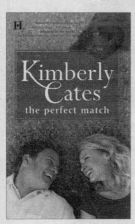

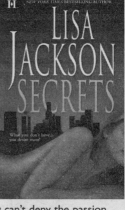

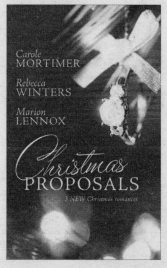